The Doctor's Truth

ADORA CROOKS

* * *

Sign up to get newsletter alerts (plus you get a free MMF romance).

Join the club ➡ https://adoracrooksbooks.com/gift

AUTHOR'S NOTE

Hello dear reader!

Thank you for picking up this book! I hope you enjoy it.

To get the full effect of "The Doctor's Truth", you may want to read the Book 1 first, "The Bully's Dare."

Truth & Dare Duet:

#1 The Bully's Dare

#2 The Doctor's Truth

You can find a full list of content warnings on my website at adoracrooksbooks.com/the-doctors-truth.

Happy reading!

xoxo,

Adora

PART I

CHRISTMAS: WINTER, 2018

1

KENZI

When I was thirteen, my mother sat me down and taught me a very important lesson. "Men," she said, "are only good for two things. Money and sex."

And she should know—she'd been married and divorced three times by that point. She's since doubled the number.

"What about love?" I'd asked, still pimply-faced and doe-eyed.

"Love yourself, darling," she told me as she refilled her goldfish-bowl-size glass of merlot. "Only you can do that."

I take her advice to heart. As I grew up, *loving myself* took on a very physical meaning.

With the stress of my job as a publicist for a pop rock band and no viable men on the horizon, I found only one thing helped me get through the hard times.

Reliable, trustworthy Burtie.

Burtie—named after my first crush, Burt Reynolds—is a pink, long vibrator. He twists. He has ridges. He makes my toes curl in a way no man ever can.

He's also the reason why I'm late to my gate at Heathrow Airport.

The security guard taps my bag. "Is this yours, miss?"

"Yes, it is."

"I'm going to have to take a look inside."

I fidget. I'm bundled up, sweating uncomfortably under two sweaters, a jacket, and a huge backpack. I wish I'd thought to bring a hair tie, because long, static strands of black hair keep getting stuck to my mouth and covering my eyes.

"Okay…I mean, I think I know what the issue is if you just want me to take it out…"

When I reach for my bag, however, he pulls it closer to him and gives me a glare. "Miss, please step back," he says. The security guard has a crew cut and a bulldog's frown, so I take him seriously.

"Okay," I try, "but…"

He unzips my backpack and pushes his gloved hand inside of it. He nudges around a moment, and the bag starts *humming*.

Oh boy. Here we go…

His eyebrow arches. He pulls out Burtie, who vibrates helplessly in the guard's hand.

"I can explain this," I start, when I feel a small human nudge against my legs.

"Mum! We've gotta go!"

Otto, my twelve-year-old, is a bundle of nerves and anxiety on a normal day, but today, his type A personality is really bursting out of its skin. He wears a bulky helmet, and he takes a break from adjusting the strap under his chin to tug on my pants.

Quickly, I cover his eyes with my hand. "Look," I reason with the security guard, "it's not like I was going to *use* it on the plane, but little man here likes to go through the luggage, so—"

"Just take out the batteries," he says, clearly eager to move on to any *non*-sex-obsessed single mom.

And, really, I'm *not* addicted to sex. I can count the

number of times I've gotten laid in the past decade on one hand.

So is it a crime to need a little...*help*...every now and then?

I shove Burtie deep in my bag, pop out the batteries, and zip up my bag so we can book it to the gate.

2

KENZI

It takes an eight-hour flight, a three-hour drive, and a thirty-minute ferry ride to get to Hannsett Island.

I'm feeling the thick fog of jet lag in my skull, but I grip the steering wheel of my rental car, a white PT Cruiser, and knuckle through it. Otto, who slept most of the flight, is now bouncing around excitedly, face pressed against the glass.

"Mum! Look at all the snow! It's like a gingerbread town!"

"Yeah, baby," I murmur. "Just like a gingerbread town."

The last time I was here, over a decade ago, it was a different picture. Summer. Hot sun, crystal-white beaches, kids playing volleyball in the sand.

It's winter now. December 17, to be exact. And Hannsett Island is a ghost town. The tourists, like geese, flew elsewhere for the winter, leaving nothing but locals with parkas and shovels behind. The sun dips low in the sky now, bleeding out a red winter sunset, and the lights flicker on along Main Street. Streetlamps are tethered with holly and Christmas lights. There are a couple of signs of life—a lantern flickering outside of a tavern that calls itself "The

Anchor" and, bizarrely, an ice cream shop—but most of the storefronts look locked down for the winter.

The road is slick, snow drifting softly, and I drive slowly, not putting too much faith in my Cruiser's capabilities.

As we climb the small incline up the island, the Lighthouse Medical Center comes into view. It's a large, multi-building medical center, connected to an old red lighthouse by the edge of the cliff, which gives it its name.

Hannsett Island has two main draws: the sparkling beaches in the summer and Lighthouse Medical, which is known as one of the most prominent medical centers in the Northeast. And, unsurprisingly, one of the most expensive and hardest to get into. The waiting list is a year out.

I know. I've checked. And I don't have a year to spare.

"Are we almost there?" Otto whines. "I'm tired."

"I know, me too, honey. We just have one more errand to run, and then we'll be done for the night, okay?"

"Okay," he grumbles.

I don't blame him for wanting to go to sleep. I want to sleep, too. Hell, I want to do anything *except* for what I'm about to do. It's risky, it's insane, and borderline illegal.

But I've got nothing left to lose.

I find the parking lot at the back of the center and park the car. Otto and I climb out, and he follows me inside. It's freezing outside, and we're met with a gush of hot air as soon as the sliding doors open for us. A statue sits in the lobby—a man holding up the universe. *A guiding light through the dark* reads the inscription, and I really hope it's true.

I head to the front desk and pull on my nicest smile. "Hi!"

The receptionist is probably twenty minutes from clocking out, but she pulls a polite smile for me all the same. "How can I help you?"

"My name is Kenzi Stratton. I'm here to see Mr. Leonard King."

The edge of her mouth slides downward into a frown.

"I'm sorry…he's packing up for the day. Did you have an appointment?"

"Not exactly, but it's really important that I see him."

Her eyes fall to Otto, who is laying his helmet-head on the counter, looking tired. I shift my body between them to get her attention. *Look at me, don't look at my kid.* "I'm with the *Dr. Mazie Show,*" I lie. "Maybe you've heard of it?"

"Oh!" Her eyes light up suddenly, excited. "Yes, I *love* that show. This must be about Jason's appearance?"

"Sure is."

She presses her lips together, thinking about it, though she's clearly made up her mind already. "His office is on the top floor, to the left. If you go now, you might still be able to catch him."

"Thank you."

I quickly grab Otto's hand and lead him to the elevator. He lets me drag him along, and we pile into the elevator.

I press the button and wait. In the metallic walls, I can half see my reflection. My thick black hair looks knotted, and I push my hands over my shirt and pants to remove any wrinkles. I wore a blazer underneath the bulky sweaters I left in the car, and I'm hoping it hides the massive sweat stains that are growing around my pits.

"How do I look?" I ask Otto.

"Like twenty bucks," he assures me.

"Don't you mean a million?"

"No. I mean twenty."

The elevator doors swing open. The hallways are white, nondescript, and I follow the receptionist's instructions and hang a left. There's a lot of empty conference rooms on this floor, the walls layered with glass, and luxury suite hospital rooms. I come to a stop at a door marked *Dr. Leonard King, CEO.*

The shutters hang down around his glass walls, but I can still see a light glowing from inside. There are a couple of chairs in the hallway, and I guide Otto to sit down in one.

"Can you sit here for ten minutes? I'll be right in that room if you need me."

"Okay…and then we can go to bed?"

"And then we can go to bed."

He has a ketchup stain on his button-up shirt, and I lick my thumb and wipe the stain. He makes a face that says *Mum, stop messing with me.*

"You're my bacon," I tell him.

"You're mine," he replies.

No way but forward. I go to the door, take a deep breath. *You can do this.*

No way but forward. I knock on the door and hear a low "Come in."

So I turn the handle and enter.

There's dark carpet on the floors and a beautiful view of the lighthouse outside the large floor-to-ceiling windows.

At a stained-oak desk sits Leonard King himself. He's gotten older since I last saw him—the salt-and-pepper look graduated to a full-on gray beard and white-tipped sideburns.

Still handsome, though. The kind of wrinkled face they only make in Hollywood. Piercing blue eyes, just like his son. Just like his *grandson.*

He has a pair of reading glasses on, and he's examining papers on his desk. When I step inside, he looks up at me from underneath thick eyebrows and narrows his eyes.

"Hi…Mr. King?"

"How can I help you?" Not unfriendly, but curt. To the point. A man who doesn't have time for small talk.

I force myself forward and extend my hand. "Kenzi Stratton. It's been…thirteen years now?"

He takes my hand. Shakes it. "I'm sorry. I meet a lot of patients."

"It's okay. I don't expect you to remember me…last time we met, I was eighteen and pregnant, and you were trying to buy off my baby."

His smile falters. He releases my hand and immediately straightens up in his seat. The color falls from his face, but, to his credit, he keeps his composure, his mouth a thin line. "That's not quite how I remember it."

"No problem—I'll refresh your memory." I drop my purse down on his desk and invite myself into the plush chair across from him. He doesn't move a muscle—I'm not sure he's even breathing, honestly. "August 2005. A precocious, geeky teenager spends the summer on glorious Hannsett Island. Meets a charming, cocky boy—that's your son, Jason King—and decides to lose her virginity. Three positive pregnancy tests later, she comes to you looking for help. You tell her—this scared, eighteen-year-old girl—that it would be better if the pregnancy didn't exist and that you'll help her *take care of it*. You bribe her. Threaten her. And then she and her mother vanish in the wind. Are you following me so far?"

His jaw is so tight, and there's a vein crawling up the side of his forehead, protruding. "What do you want?"

"I want you to take a peek out your window."

He leans over and parts the shutters between his fingers. "What am I looking at?"

"The boy in the chair? That's my son…your grandchild. Otto Stratton. Twelve years old and the best kid in the world."

Those blue eyes turn to me. "If you want money…"

Anger lashes through me, rising up like bile, and it takes everything within me to contain it. "I don't *want* your money. We've been doing just fine on our own." I take in a small sip of breath. Controlled. "Otto is sick. He has been for a while now."

Mr. King steeples his fingers together. "I'm sorry to hear that."

"No. You're not. Trust me, I wouldn't be here if I had any other options." I'm sweating. I'm shaking. But I can't stop now. Not when I'm so close to what I want. "I want you to admit him. Here. He deserves the best care."

Mr. King leans back in his chair. He takes his time, now that our seesawing power play has swung his way momentarily. "And if I say no?" he asks.

"Then I tell my story to all of Jason's new friends and fans." Now my trump card, I pull out my phone and turn it to face Mr. King. I click the thumbnail, and the video plays.

3

———

THE VIDEO

Title: The Dr. Mazie Show, Season 10, Episode 9. Air Date: September 19, 2018.

Episode Description: DR. MAZIE shares the uplifting tale of SUSAN CHRISSY, a mother of five adopted children and a heart transplant recipient. They are joined by Susan's doctor, DR. JASON KING of the Lighthouse Medical Center, to discuss the surgery and importance of post-operation health.

DR. MAZIE

--It's remarkable, it really is remarkable, what you were able to do for Susan.

DR. JASON KING

Yeah, well, we're fortunate enough at Lighthouse Medical to have access to cutting-edge equipment and some of the best doctors in the state.

· · ·

DR. MAZIE

You included. You were named one of the top surgeons in the Northeast in Harper's Medical, alongside a few brilliant surgeons who are twice your age. How does that feel?

DR. JASON KING

Lucky. I feel really grateful.

DR. MAZIE

But that's not the only list...hold on, I think we have a picture here...you also ranked #1 in Pelican Weekly's top hottest doctors.

DR. JASON KING

(Laughing) Oh God.

DR. MAZIE

Curious minds want to know more about the great Dr. Jason King. What do you do when you're not healing wonderful people like our Susan?

DR. JASON KING

Oh, uh, recently? Working, mostly. I just took a break, kinda--

DR. MAZIE

A break! Did you do anything fun?

. . .

DR. JASON KING

Oh—I guess it depends on your version of fun. I just did a tour with Doctors Without Borders to in, uh, Sudan—

DR. MAZIE

Amazing. Well, I think I speak for everyone when I say I want to see more of you. Next time, on the Dr. Mazie Show!

4

KENZI

I leave my number with Leonard King and tell him to call me when he's made a decision. But from the pale look on his face, I'm feeling pretty good about it.

We're in. We have to be in. Otto doesn't have any other options.

And Mr. King doesn't want his legacy, his hospital's reputation, and his son's name smeared across television on the *Dr. Mazie Show*, in front of millions of viewers.

Otto is exactly where I left him, sitting in his chair, kicking his legs back and forth. I give his shoulder a squeeze, and he pops up.

"*Now* can we go?" he asks.

"Yes. Now we can go."

We head to the elevator and ride it downstairs. I numbed myself for my meeting with Mr. King, but now I'm starting to feel it—the panic rising in my throat, like bile.

My shirt is constricting, my lungs tight. I take in small, short sips of breath and unbutton the collar on my shirt.

"Mum?" Otto asks. "Are you okay?"

"Fine, baby. I'm just tired."

The elevator dings and lets us out. I'm a horse with blind-

15

ers, gaze straight ahead for the door, and all I can think about is escaping this hospital, escaping this *island*, so much so that I almost miss it when I hear—

"Kenzi?"

I turn to the voice, but I don't recognize the man that stands before me. There's something familiar about him, a shadow of memory hiding behind him, and I have to squint. "Um…"

He exhales on a laugh. "The summer of Blink-182. Catching fireflies. Dock boy."

My heart nearly stops in my chest.

"Donovan—"

I rush to him and throw my arms around him. It's been thirteen years. *Thirteen years*. And yet when I'm about to have a panic attack, stuck at a crossroads, there is Donovan.

Always there when I need him.

I didn't know I needed him until I have my arms around him, and he has his arms around me, and we're holding each other with a tightness that feels too familiar.

"Hey, stranger," Donovan murmurs as we pull apart. "How long has it been?"

"About ten lifetimes," I respond.

Donovan's real hair color, it turns out, is cherrywood brown. The kind of brown that fluctuates between auburn or blond depending on the light. His curls are coiffed, and he's arranged a perfectly faded stubble that accentuates his jawline and outlines his lips.

Gone is the dyed black hair. The lip ring. The skintight pants and eyeliner.

He wears a lab coat now. A *lab coat*. The boy has left, and a professional, well-groomed man stands in front of me now.

"What the hell are you doing here?" he asks. Even his voice is deeper now. It has grit. It's hard not to get lost in his startlingly intense dark eyes.

"Uh—Donovan, this is Otto. My son." I step to the side to introduce Otto, slipping my hand to my boy's back.

I try to discern Donovan's reaction. To his credit, he doesn't bat an eye. Instead, he smiles at Otto. When he smiles...oh boy. He has dimples in his cheeks and crinkles lining the edges of his eyes. There's something about that—signs of a life well lived, maybe—that makes my heart beat a little faster.

"Nice to meet you, Otto," he says. "I'm Dr. Donovan, an old friend of your mom's."

A bit more than friends. One night, thirteen summers ago, Donovan, Jason, and I tangled limbs and lips in the belly of an abandoned boat. With so much time and distance, that part of my life has felt like a distant fantasy.

Until now. With Donovan standing beside me, it suddenly feels very, very real.

"Hi," Otto says, though I can tell he's gone shy.

"I like your helmet," Donovan says, breaking the ice.

"Kevin won't leave me alone," Otto replies by way of explanation.

Donovan knits his eyebrows. "Kevin, huh?"

"That's what we call his sickness," I break in, translating. "Started as a therapeutic technique...give it a name and it's not as scary, right? But no one seems to be able to diagnose him, so. We might as well call it *something*."

"I've never met a Kevin I liked," Donovan says.

"Kevin McCallister," Otto prompts.

"A brat," Donovan argues.

"Kevin Bacon," I add.

"Overrated."

"Kevin...um...and Hobbs."

"That's *Calvin*," Donovan says. "Now, a Calvin I can get behind. But I tell you what." Donovan crouches down so he's level with Otto, arms hanging loosely on his thighs. "If you've got a Kevin problem…you've come to the right place. Because we know how to take care of Kevins here."

Otto smiles and leans against my legs. "Cool," he says.

"So you're a doctor now?" I prompt.

Donovan stands. "Yep. I've been working at Lighthouse Medical since med school."

"Congratulations. That's huge."

He scratches the side of his neck, as though the compliment is rash-inducing. "It's what I love. One of the best hospitals in the state. I wouldn't work anywhere else."

I have so much I want to ask him. So many questions. But everything gets balled up in my throat when I look into his eyes.

"I've got to tell Jason you're here," Donovan says. "He's going to lose it."

"Jason?" My anxiety spikes. "Jason King?"

He snorts a laugh. "Don't do that."

"Do what?"

Donovan flutters his eyelashes and fans himself as he puts on a falsetto. "Oh, *Jason!*"

"I don't sound like that!"

I smack his shoulder. He laughs at me.

Funny how quickly we fall into these old roles.

"What—are you two friends now?"

"We're more than friends." My eyebrows hike up my forehead. Donovan must hear how that sounds because his face starts to redden. "Not…like that. Get your head out of the gutter." He clears his throat. "We're roommates. Ever since his divorce."

"He's divorced?"

"Feeling a little vulture-y, are we?"

"It's not…like that," I protest.

"Uh-huh. You can ask him any questions yourself. He's on his way to surgery, but I might be able to grab him if he hasn't gone in yet—"

"No! I mean…we're tired. It's been a long day. Maybe later?"

"Come over for dinner tomorrow."

"Great!" I smile widely to hide the fear pounding in my chest. "Can't wait."

And then I turn to book it to the door, but—

"Are you going to give me your number, or am I going to have to track you down?"

"Right! Sorry."

He takes out his phone. I enter my number in quickly so he doesn't notice my hands are trembling. When I give it back to him, he leans in. His lips brush my cheek. I feel the stubble on his beard and catch a whiff of his cologne—peppermint and leather. "It's really good to see you. We'll catch up later. The three of us."

The three of us. I don't know why, but something about the way he says that…it makes my heartbeat flutter in a way that has nothing to do with the anxiety.

I take Otto by the hand, and we exit Lighthouse Medical, bursting into the blistering cold.

* * *

"Mummy, who was that?" Otto asks once we're in the car.

"Just an old friend."

He yawns. "I liked him."

I wring my hands over the steering wheel.

"Yeah, baby. Me too."

5

JASON

*E*very king needs his castle.

This King has something even better: an Operating Room.

It's my domain. I know every inch of it.

It's technically called an Operation Theatre, which makes sense to me because the second I step inside, I feel like I'm on stage. There's the bright glare of the surgical lights. High-definition monitors zoomed in on each small movement of my hands. My surgical team waiting in the wings, rapt and wide-eyed, diligently handing me the tools I need to complete the job.

Today is my specialty—live organ transplant. Mr. Isaac, forty-two, needs a new heart. His two grown kids are waiting for him in the other room.

I'm Jason King, top surgeon at Hannsett Medical Center.

This surgery *will* go off without a hitch. I repeat the words in my head. Over and over until I believe them with every atom in my body.

My patient is laid out on the table in front of me. The anesthesiologist counts him down and puts him to sleep. I can hear the steady beat of his heart monitor. The heat of my breath beats back against my face from inside my mask.

"Status," I request.

"Patient is fully sedated, Dr. King."

"Tunes."

"Yes, Dr. King."

One of the techs hits the button on my iPhone, and immediately my playlist starts going. I lift my hand.

"Scalpel."

The cold metal slides into my gloved fingers.

I'm Jason King, top surgeon at Hannsett Medical Center.

I'm Jason King.

I'm—

"Hey, monolithic moron. Don't fuck this up."

The familiar voice cuts through the still ambiance I've created, rippling across my OR. I lift my eyes from the table only long enough to confirm what I already know: Adam Donovan is behind the thick glass of the viewing area. The doctor has his thumb on the microphone that connects his room to mine.

"You hear a humming?" I ask one of my techs. "I think there's a fly in the OR—"

"That's my patient on your table, King," Donovan warns.

"I've performed 300 successful surgeries in about as many days. I think I've got this under control."

"To the tune of Bestie Boys? Jesus. You're going to make my patient code on the table just from your music choices—"

"Nurse Kapoor, will you cut the chatter?"

She presses a button and cuts the feed.

* * *

The surgery is flawless.

My blood is cold in my veins as I snap off my gloves and wash my hands. I've been hyper-focused on every tiny movement of my fingers, and now I'm finally starting to feel the hit of adrenaline rush through me.

The post-surgery fall out is always a bitch.

I find myself washing my hands much longer than necessary, zoning in and out of focus. Out of the corner of my eye, a figure steps in beside me.

"You missed a spot," Donovan says.

I finally turn off the sink and dry off my hands.

"Here to apologize?" I ask.

His dark eyes meet mine. "You did good. But you don't need me to tell you that."

I shrug. "It is the nice thing to do."

I exit the OR. Donovan falls in step alongside me.

Donovan is gruff. Thorny around the edges. About as cuddly as a hedgehog. But he's different. As the son of the CEO and the top surgeon, everyone at the hospital treats me like a God. Except for Donovan. We've known each other since we were teenagers. He teases hard and I tease back. It's how we've always operated, and there's comfort in that.

"Thanks to you, Isaac's heart will live to beat another day," Donovan says, which is as much of a *good job* as I'll get from him.

"Ditch the old heart. Bring in a new one. If only it were that easy for all of us."

I try not to sound bitter, but I can't help it.

Donovan reads between the lines. "Have you heard from Nadine?"

The mention of her still feels like a thorn in the back of my neck. I roll my shoulders back. "No. I'm trying to just… move forward. Eyes on the future. Leave the past behind. You know?"

Now, Donovan breathes a light laugh. "I have a feeling that's going to be harder than you think."

"Why do you say that?"

"Guess who's in town?"

"Cher. Bono. Oh! The naked cowboy?"

He narrows his eyes at me. "Stop guessing. Kenzi Stratton."

Kenzi. Her name sends a whispering shiver up my arms. I stop in my tracks, my shoes squeaking against the polished hallway.

"Wow. It's been—what. Ten years?"

"Thirteen." Donovan's gaze doesn't leave mine. "I told her we might meet up later. If you're interested."

"Absolutely. I'm interested. Let's do it. Right now."

Donovan's eyes sweep over me. "You need a shower first. And a shave. You look like a bear."

I pick at my black beard. I have let it get overgrown. "Protect our forests."

His shoulders square off. "Not the kind of bear I was talking about."

I growl, low and feral.

Donovan lifts his hands. "I'm walking away."

"Only you can prevent wildfires, Donovan!"

His retreating figure flicks me the bird.

GROUP TEXT

GROUP TEXT: Donovan, Jason, Kenzi

Donovan: Hey. Starting this off. You're welcome.

Kenzi: :)

Kenzi: Wow. Can't believe the gang is back together

Jason: Back in business baby

Jason: Dinner tomorrow night??

Jason: That's a request but also a demand ;)

Jason: You in?

Jason: Hello?

KENZI

There's an intruder in the beach house.

This is the first thought that enters my mind as soon as my eyes fly open.

I can hear the intruder clanging around downstairs.

I'm in bed, Otto beside me—all of his limbs flailing in every direction. For such a short kid, he somehow manages to take up three-quarters of a queen-size bed.

My jet lag has me feeling like I drank a bottle of wine on an empty stomach. But the fear that grips my heart at the knowledge that *someone is in our house* wakes me up pretty fucking fast.

I ease out of bed and, gently, put my feet on the ground. Our luggage is stuffed in the corner of the room—both of us too tired to unpack last night. The floor is carpeted, at least, so my feet don't make a sound as I shuffle to the bedroom door and crack it open.

A definite *clang* from downstairs. Sounds like it's coming from the kitchen?

"Mum?" Otto groans. "Is it time to get up already?"

"Go back to bed," I tell him.

I strain to listen. It sounds like two voices downstairs—a man and a woman. A chill runs through me.

"Otto, go to the bathroom and lock the door. Don't come out until I tell you."

His blue eyes flash. "Is something wrong?"

"*Now*, Otto."

Fun mom is over. Stern mom has arrived.

He gets up and goes into the bathroom. I wait until I hear the door lock. Then, I unplug the bedside lamp, hold it by the neck, and wind the cord around my opposite fist.

I'm going to handle this my own damn self.

Quietly, I creep down the stairs, brandishing my lamp. I see the man first. He's a young guy—in his twenties, maybe—standing in the foyer. And he's struggling with…a tree?

"Hey!" I snap at him, the way you might yell loudly at a bear to seem bigger than you are.

The guy swerves, sees me, and shouts, tumbling backward, the fir nearly falling on top of him. I find myself matching his scream, jumping away.

"What is this, an episode of *Cops*?" My mother steps in from the kitchen. She's wearing a ruby-red fur-lined coat and holding a mug of coffee, casually stirring creamer into it as if her being here is the most natural thing in the world. She narrows her eyes at my lamp. "For the love of God, Aileen Wuornos, put that down."

I lower the lamp, reluctantly, too stunned to speak.

"Where's my Otto?" Pearl asks, glancing around.

"Grandma!"

Otto—like his mom—shares the same inability to follow the rules. He's at the top of the stairs, peeking, but now he comes barreling down. I want to chastise him (*I told you to stay in the bathroom!*), but my energy reserves are depleted, and my weak heart melts when he runs into his grandma's arms for a big hug.

"Oh, my snug-a-bug—I've missed you, darling." She puts

her mug on the ground and crouches to hug him tightly. As she pets the back of his head, she half whispers to me (as though he can't hear her), "I thought we talked about the *grandma* title? What's wrong with G-ma Pearl?"

"G-ma makes you sound like you're in a gang."

Her eyes flicker over me, mouth curled downward disapprovingly. "Apparently, not far from the truth."

I throw up my hands. "I'm making coffee."

* * *

After the initial shock of nearly beating my mother to death with a lamp, we settle down and catch up.

Pearl has been living on the Upper West Side in Manhattan, in an apartment she got divorced-into. That's how we say it these days—divorced-into, instead of married-into. It's how I'm staying on Hannsett, after all; after her divorce to Four, aka Terry, she claimed as part of her settlement his beach house. She's been renting it for years, but winters are rough, and I needed a place to stay, so —voilà.

The guy with the Christmas tree, by the way? Totally lived. Plus, made off with a large tip. Apparently, Pearl hired him to help her lug the tree across the ferry and into our house. It's a four-foot fir, and we tucked it into the living room by the television. The top is a bit bent from crashing down, but hey. That's Christmas.

Pearl picked up an assortment of baked goods on the way over, and Otto chomps down on half a cinnamon roll in front of the television as Pearl and I sit at the coffee table, warming our hands on the coffee mugs.

She's as glamorous as ever—underneath the coat, she's wearing a Christmas-green dress with fringe around the hem and thick, black stockings and gloves. Meanwhile, I still haven't brushed my hair or my teeth, and I'm in an oversized sleep shirt and boys boxers. How I came out of her womb, I'll never understand.

"What did you think of the deliveryman?" Pearl asks conspiratorially and then wiggles her eyebrows. "I gave him my number."

I blow on my coffee. "A little young for you, isn't he? Does he own a yacht?"

"At my age, I'm not looking for *yachts*. I'm looking for biceps. Someone who can carry my groceries and rub my feet."

I'm not going to lie, *access to foot rubs* is actually the best argument I've heard for marriage in a long time. I can't remember the last time my little piggies did anything other than scream at me.

"Question number two," I add, "how did you know I was here?"

She shrugs. "I'm your mother. It's my job to know every-thing about you."

I roll my eyes. "Okay."

"For example." She taps my phone and slides it across the table. "I know that you're avoiding dinner with two men who would like very much to see you."

I snatch my phone. "Do. Not. Read my texts."

She lets out a labored sigh. "It was an accident! Your phone has been off the hook—you're very popular. I wanted to make sure it wasn't any sort of emergency, that's all."

"Uh-huh." I don't buy it, but what can I do? I'm not about to babysit my mother—not when I have an *actual* child who needs my attention.

My attention drifts. Otto laughs at something on the tele-vision and sucks icing from his fingers.

"You should go have dinner with them," she presses. "You used to be such good friends, the three of you."

"Yeah. When we were teenagers."

"So you'll have a lot to catch up on! When was the last time you had a little fun? Just you?"

Forever ago.

"Can't," I say. "We have too much to do. I have to stock the fridge. Unpack. Make dinner. And, apparently, now I have to find something to decorate the tree with."

"What are you making?"

"Salmon and broccoli."

"Otto, darling," my mother calls out, "what would you like for dinner tonight? Salmon and broccoli or pizza?"

Otto jumps up and down like an excited squirrel. "Pizza, pizza, pizza!"

Pearl shrugs. "The boy has spoken. Go have fun. We're having a pizza night."

* * *

GROUP TEXT: Donovan, Jason, Kenzi
   Kenzi: Okay. I'm in. Where?
   Jason: Our place. I'll drop a pin.

KENZI

To tell him or not to tell him?

That is the question.

In the summer of 2005, I met two boys: Jason King and Adam Donovan. One, a cocky, king-of-the-world jock. The other, a loner with a bleeding heart. I fell in love with both of them, in my own way. An innocent love—something not meant to last, maybe, but something meant to burn hot and bright for a summer so that when I'm ninety and on my death bed, I can smile to myself and think, *Well, at least I'll always have the summer of 2005.*

We became glued at the hip. We called ourselves "the Three Muskrats," after an incident with a furry beast at the back of a boat. And that summer, I lost my virginity with Jason buried inside me and Donovan petting my hair, coaxing me to previously unknown heights of pleasure with his words. It's a moment I'll cherish forever—and one I'll never forget.

It was also the night I got pregnant with Otto.

I don't regret anything that happened that night. I *do* regret the way I handled it. Eighteen, naïve, and scared out of my mind, I'd gone to Jason's father for help. Leonard King was (and still is) the most powerful man on Hannsett Island, plus the richest. I wasn't thinking about any of that at the time, though. I was just thinking, *Jason's dad is a doctor. He'll know what to do.*

But bullies don't fall far from the tree. Mr. King proceeded to harass me and tried to bribe me into getting an abortion. So I did the only thing I could think of to do.

I ran. Far. All the way to England.

I've stayed hidden for over a decade, but now that I'm back at Hannsett, I have some decisions to make.

I can't avoid Jason forever. So I'm going to go to dinner. I'm going to do this the way I do everything these days: logically, weighing the pros and cons. It's been forever ago since we saw each other. I have no idea what kind of man he is now. I have to see it for myself. Assess the situation. And then decide how—and when—to tell him that he has a son.

A sick son. A son who needs his help.

And, all the while, try to do so while keeping my heart in check.

Because the real, honest truth is that seeing Donovan yesterday opened up a floodgate of emotions I didn't know I still had inside of me.

Nostalgia. Affection. And—yes—*desire.* The desire for someone living, pulsing between my legs, instead of my go-to silicone friends.

Which is probably why I spend way too long getting ready.

Otto and I packed minimally for our trip over. Depending on how my meeting with Mr. King went, we could either be staying for a few days or a few months. I change my clothes three times before I leave the house.

First option: a navy pantsuit, to show that I've grown up and I'm a professional.

Second option: a purple dress with black thigh-highs to show I'm still as fun as I ever was.

Seeing Donovan yesterday was a stark reminder of just how long it had been. He's changed so much. Have I changed?

I check a lot of the same boxes: black Irish with thick, dark hair, green eyes, a small nose, and a round face. My eyebrows are a little too intense, but I've always liked that about them. I've lost some of my baby face and replaced it with single-mom-face—ever prevalent dark edges underneath my eyes, worry marks at my forehead.

Not quite the devil-may-care, precocious teenager they once knew. I can't help but hope they like this grown-up version of Kenzi, too.

I go with my third and final option: the best of both worlds, a fitted pair of black pants with a tie around the middle, a loose button-up, and a faux leather jacket for warmth.

I tie my hair back into a ponytail, apply my makeup, and reapply deodorant because my pits are sweating.

It's *just* the muskrats, I try to tell myself. So why is my heart jumping rope in my chest?

"I'm heading out," I announce as I descend the staircase, tossing my purse over my shoulder.

I don't get a response, so I glance around. "Pearl? Otto?"

She's left a note on the round kitchen table: *Went out for pizza. Don't call! Xoxo.*

I can't help but smile. I leave, locking the door quietly behind me.

The cold is bone-freezing and chaps my lips. I hug my jacket tighter and slip into the rental car.

Donovan lives on the northern end of the island, and I have to wind down Main Street to get to him. From one end of the island to the other takes less than fifteen minutes, and that's only because I'm obeying the under-twenty-miles-an-hour speed limit. His house stands alone on top of a sand dune, overlooking the beach.

The sunset looks beautiful, streaking golden-amber hues across the sky and ocean.

I get out of the car and take a second to admire it, even as the cold nips at me.

You don't get views like this in London.

There's a stone footpath that leads to Donovan's house, a modern structure built with a sharp triangle slant and wooden slats across the sides. Tufts of dune grass sprout up from the sand. I'm halfway up the path when the door flings open.

A man steps out and lifts his arms wide. "Kenzi fucking Stratton!" he bellows.

He cuts the distance between us with his long-legged leaps and then swoops me up in a bone-crushing bear hug. He smells like chlorine, body spray, and minty aftershave. I close my eyes and inhale. He smells like Jason.

It hits me like a fucking curveball to the chest and knocks all the breath out of me. Probably doesn't help that his hugs are boa-constrictor tight.

"Hey, big guy." I gasp for air and pat his shoulder, like I'm tapping out at a wrestling match.

He grabs my shoulders and yanks me back with no apparent awareness of his own strength so he can look at me —really look at me. The biggest, cheesiest grin plasters across his face, and his blue eyes sparkle.

"Christ, you're a sight for sore eyes," he says. "You look great."

Jason is an eye-contact kind of guy. Not a lot of those left —men who aren't afraid to look a woman straight in the eyes when he speaks.

He makes it look natural. I'd forgotten how good it feels to be *seen*—everyone I'd worked with had their eyes on their phones or their computers and only looked up when you said, "Hey, take a look at this."

Something else I wasn't prepared for, though I don't

know why—those are Otto's eyes staring at me. It knocks me off my center of gravity.

I squeeze his arms to ground myself. "You're not so bad-looking yourself," I tease.

"Come on in—Donovan! Look what I found!"

Jason ushers me in, and I hold up a bottle of wine. "Here. Couldn't come empty-handed."

Jason takes it and reads the label. "Check you out, classing this joint up. I love it. You wanna crack this baby open?"

"Yeah, go ahead."

I unwrap my scarf from my neck and shimmy out of my jacket. Jason takes those as well (a gentleman, who'd have thought?), and as he hangs them up, I survey the place.

It's…shockingly nice.

I don't know what I was expecting. A frat house? Something about two boys living together screams empty beer bottles, strange stains, and movie posters tacked into the walls.

This is a far cry.

White paint, a wooden designer coffee table, an entire wall of exposed brick. A shelf devoted to a record player and a wall of records. Post-modern art on the walls and an ivy plant in the corner.

Donovan always was a bit of an old soul.

I smell sizzling onions and garlic. Donovan is cooking, but he spares a second to glance up at me and gives me a nod. "Hey."

We've already had our heartfelt hellos, apparently—I'm old hat now. I take a seat on one of the barstools and lean onto my elbows. "That smells delicious. What're you making?"

"Stir-fry. Hope you're hungry."

"I am *now*."

9

KENZI

I grill Donovan a little while he finishes cooking: How does he like working at Lighthouse Medical? Loves it. Is he dating anyone? No. How's his father? Passed away a few years ago—he's handling it fine, thanks for asking. Is he still keeping up on *Dr. Who*? He's behind a couple seasons, but has a lot of opinions about Matt Smith.

It's so funny, watching him talk. Here and there, I see the boy I grew up with. But he's also matured so much. His voice has gone deep, gravelly. No more dyed black hair; he rocks his chestnut waves now. Even his fashion sense has changed; his baggy pants have tightened up, and he's ditched the hoodie for a maroon button-up. He's all grown up now—a professional doctor, just like he always said he would be.

Then there's Jason. Physically, he looks so much like he did when we were young. Even his face retains its boyish-ness, his mischievous crooked grin intact. He can wear anything—so he does—just a simple cotton shirt and jeans, but he wears the clothes like he's doing them a favor. When he leans back in his chair and his shirt kisses his skin, it's hard to miss the definition in his chest, the bulge of his biceps. The only thing that really ages him is the black beard that climbs his jaw.

He's different, though. His energy is softer, less chaotic. I remember the jock that pounded back beers in one shot. He drinks O'Douls now—nonalcoholic—and when I ask him about it, he says it's because he's almost always on call.

Have I changed that much?

I lost twenty pounds in 2015. Got a new job. Got a promotion in 2016. Gained back fifteen pounds in 2017. I let my hair grow long these days—dark waves that tumble down my shoulders. My fashion, I guess, is a little more British than when I left: wool sweaters and fitted trousers.

What do they see when they look at me? The young girl they knew way back then? Or do I look as old as I feel—thirty-one going on eighty?

We sit down at their table to eat. Donovan, as it turns out, makes a banging stir-fry. They want to know more about me, so I regale them with the tale of nearly beheading Santa's helper with a lamp.

"Pearl's here?" Donovan asks.

"Apparently. I don't know how long she's staying."

"That's nice, though. Having your mom here."

I squint at him. "Didn't realize you were so sweet on Pearl."

He shrugs. "I like your family."

"Are you having a secret affair with my mother? Is that what's going on?"

"Oh, yeah. Pearl and I are eloping after the holidays."

His eyes meet mine, and there's a little smirk at the edge of his mouth. This is the Donovan I remember. The sands of time were kind to Donovan: he grew up hot, no other way to say it. But underneath all that, he's still a dark soul, snarky to the core. My black-hearted boy.

"What about you?" Jason asks.

"What about me?" I counter.

"Fill us in. All the sordid details." Jason wraps his hand around his glass and settles into his chair, as though he's preparing for a long, epic tale. "For starters, you have a kid now."

"I have a kid now," I repeat. "Otto."

"What else?"

"Well…I lived in London for a couple years. Then Bristol, which is like…England's version of Long Island, I guess. I sort of fell into a job doing PR work for a music group there…the Polaroid Boys…"

"Hold up," Jason interrupts, "You worked for the *Polaroid Boys?*"

Donovan lifts a palm. "Am I supposed to know who this is?"

"You know them—hold on…" Jason starts flipping through his phone.

I groan, "Please don't…"

But it's too late. He finds their one-hit wonder—a high-octane pop bop—and starts to play it.

Donovan shakes his head. "Still doesn't ring a bell."

"Dude! That's so cool!" Jason looks at me, and the wide grin almost makes it worth it.

I shrug. "Sort of. They're teenagers, so it was more like…glorified babysitting. I quit my job to come here. Sold most of my belongings. So. There's that."

"But you did it," Donovan presses.

"Did what?"

"You loved music growing up. And you got a job in music. That says something."

"You're tenacious," Jason agrees. "And they *are* a big deal. You should be proud of it."

I'm not going to lie—I'm not accustomed to having hype men. The people I hung out with at work were mostly disaffected. Then there were the moms at the park, who always treated me like a black sheep—too young, too American. I had a roommate, for a while, when money got tight, but our conversations barely went beyond rent and who took the trash out last.

It's strange to have not one, but *two* guys willing to sing my praises. I feel my face go hot under the attention, and I instinctively duck out of it, dropping my head to slide my hair behind my ear.

"Enough about me," I say. "Someone else talk."

Donovan upends the bottle of red into his glass, but there's only a swallow left. "We need more wine for this conversation."

"Stay put. I'm on it." Jason pats Donovan on the shoulder and rises instead. He points to me. "You need a refill, too?"

I lift my glass. "Yes. Thank you, kind sir."

He bows dramatically in front of me as he takes my glass and steps away to the kitchen.

We're alone now. Mostly. I turn to Donovan and wiggle my eyebrows.

He narrows his eyes at me. "What's that look?"

I shrug innocently. "It's just...cute."

"What is?"

"The two of you. Being so cozy."

He scoffs. "Cute isn't the word I'd use." He sips from his glass gingerly.

"What word would you use?" I prod.

He looks off, contemplates, and then settles on, "*Temporary.*"

DONOVAN

It's strange how not-strange this is. The three of us. *Together again.*

We've eased into the potion of the night where everything is warm, and mellow, and dangerously comfortable. I have an Otis Redding record going, wine is flowing, and Kenzi is here.

Life couldn't be better.

Jason comes back with a second bottle, serves the both of us, but I make the decision to take this bottle a little slower.

Truthfully? I was a little nervous about her coming over. A small, nagging part of me worried that she wouldn't like the ways I've changed.

A stupid concern. We've slotted back into old roles as though no time has passed at all.

Kenzi points her fork between me and Jason. "So how exactly did this happen? The two of you living together."

"I rescued him," I say. "Like a shelter animal."

Jason chuckles lightly. "Yeah—I mean, sort of. So I got married."

Kenzi gasps. "That's right! Mazel Tov."

"Well, don't get too excited," I add. "He also got divorced. Basically in the same day."

Jason scratches the back of his neck briefly. "I mean—we lasted almost a year. That's not nothing."

"I'm sorry. How long ago?" Kenzi asks.

"Six months. So, uh—anyway. She kept the house. I didn't feel like moving back in with my parents—"

I motion. "And he refused to ask for help. So, being the stubborn bastard that he is, he slept in the hospital for—what? A week?—before I dragged him home with me. It was too sad."

Kenzi listens, rapt. She glances around. "Do you have a guest room?"

I nod toward an outline in the wall and point to the living room across from us. "I've got a built-in murphy bed. Those are his digs."

"No shit?" Kenzi says. "I mean, I know it's old-school, but I kind of dig it."

"I *am* old-school," I remind her.

Jason cracks a grin. "You were born to be a grandpa."

"I guess we all grew up, huh?" Kenzi adds, a little wistfully.

"No," Jason protests, his Peter-Pan syndrome suddenly in full effect. "No growing up. We're going to play a game."

Now Kenzi's eyes light up. "What game?"

"Truth or dare," Jason says. "Obviously."

"Obviously."

* * *

Round one goes to Kenzi. "Truth," she says.

"Most embarrassing moment in recent history," I prompt.

She doesn't have to think long. Her pale complexion already starts to go pink with the memory, but she laughs good-naturedly. "Okay—this one is ridiculous. At the airport getting here, I got stopped by security because I had a vibrator in my backpack."

"You just…keep it handy?" Jason asks.

She balks. "I had a legitimate reason!"

I lift a palm. "You don't need a reason. It's absolutely natural to have a sexual relationship with your body. Not to mention, it's healthy. Orgasms release serotonin."

Kenzi motions to me. "Donovan gets me."

Jason shakes his head. "I didn't say it was *wrong*. It's just…funny."

Kenzi scoffs. "Don't sit there and act like you don't jerk off."

Jason shrugs casually. "I don't."

I roll my eyes. "Here we go…"

Kenzi's mouth drops open. "What…? Like, you don't *often*? Or you don't *ever*?"

"Ever," Jason says, and I do my best not to let it get to me that we're having a conversation about masturbation as casually as we'd talk about the weather.

Kenzi squints at Jason as though he's grown a second head. Kenzi, to her credit, never leaves a stone unturned, no matter how strange the topic. "Okay," she says, clearly trying to understand. "Is it like…a self-control thing?"

Jason shifts to his elbow, leaning in. "Let me ask you a question first. Why do *you* masturbate?"

Kenzi's throat reddens a little, but she's too stubborn to let something like *shame* get in the way of her query. "It's my only *me* time," she says. "Look—I became a single mom really young. And I love every second of it. But my entire life is devoted to being a mom. It's…the only thing I get to do that's *for me*."

"Self-care," I clarify, and she nods.

"*Yes*, exactly."

Jason swallows—I can tell because that Adam's apple bobs underneath his beard. "Okay," he says, "I get that. But like, *for me*, what turns me on is connecting with someone. Looking a person in the eye. Making *them* feel good. So when I'm flying solo…it just doesn't really do it for me."

Kenzi looks soft and hazy as she stares at Jason, and she rests her head in her palm. "Must be hard," she wonders out loud, but I can't tell if she intends for the pun or not.

A grin ghosts on Jason's mouth. "I live," he says.

"Can we get back to the game?" I ask.

* * *

"Truth," Jason says.

"What's the most annoying thing about living with Donovan?" Kenzi asks.

I roll my eyes. "Now you're asking for a fight."

Jason squints at me as though he's thinking. "I don't know. He's a pretty good roommate. Well, except…"

"Lay it on me."

"You vanish down these…video rabbit holes." He turns to Kenzi, waving his fork dramatically like a conductor. "He'll come home, sit on the couch, and scroll through YouTube or whatever for hours. It's like a constant stream of mindlessness."

I scoff. "It's called *decompressing*. And you're one to talk."

"What's that mean?"

I turn to Kenzi. "You want to talk annoying noises—he listens to recordings of himself."

"Fuck you, it's meditation."

"Wow. Sounds like that meditation is really working for you."

"Hold on, settle down." Kenzi lifts her palms, lowering the temperature in the room. "Jason, explain."

Jason thins his lips, but then he straightens up in his chair —going into performance mode. "Okay. So you know how you have negative thoughts in your head, right? Like…there's

42

always that voice that tells you that you're doing something wrong or you'll never amount to something. So I combat that by recording myself saying the opposite of those negative thoughts. It's positive affirmations."

I pretend to vomit, and Jason casts me a dirty look. Kenzi, unfortunately, looks fascinated.

"What does your recording say?" she asks.

He shrugs, for the first time, a little bashful. *"You're enough."*

* * *

We go a couple more rounds (I get dared to balance a spoon on my nose, and it takes nearly ten tries; Jason confesses to listening to—and enjoying—the latest Taylor Swift CD).

"Truth or dare?" Jason asks.

"Truth," Kenzi replies.

"What happened with Otto's father?"

Kenzi hesitates a second. She glances down at her plate, then says, "Uh…he was just this guy I met. In college. Didn't want anything to do with it. So."

"That's rough," Jason says, his voice full of compassion.

Kenzi "hmms" and tries on a smile.

As she speaks, however, I notice that she absently toys with her earring, rubbing it between her thumb and forefinger.

It's her tell. The way I always knew whenever she was lying when we were kids. She'd play with her ears, an unconscious little gesture.

I decide not to call her out on it, however. Instead, I swallow back unspoken words with a sip of wine.

"My turn," Kenzi says, quick to change the mood. "Truth or dare, Jason?"

"Truth."

"Since you went for a hard-hitter, I'm going right back. Why did you divorce your wife?"

Jason presses his lips together. "You, uh...know those toys they make for kids...the ones that they make so kids learn their shapes?"

"Sure."

"It was like we were trying to put the circle shape in the square hole, and no matter how much we kept trying, it just wouldn't...fit."

I lean over and stage-whisper in Kenzi's ear, "He has a huge cock."

Kenzi laughs, and Jason stabs his fork in my direction. "Hey. Perverts. I'm talking about something real here."

"Okay." Kenzi flattens her forearms on the table, going into full reporter mode. "Follow up question. Why did you *marry* her in the first place?"

"She was interested in what I had to say. She laughed at my stupid jokes. I thought that meant she loved me."

Kenzi clicks her tongue and shakes her head. "Typical Jason King. Someone shows you the slightest bit of attention and you assume they're madly in love with you."

"I've only been wrong once." There is that arrogant smirk.

"And look how much it's humbled you."

Kenzi is being a pain in his ass, and Jason is here for the challenge.

They're practically eye-fucking each other across the table.

I stab a piece of broccoli. Jason's eyes catch on mine.

"Truth or dare, D?" he asks.

"Dare," I say, because our truths are getting thorny, and no way am I walking into that minefield.

"Okay. I dare you to eat the rest of dinner without using your fork."

If he wants to embarrass me, he's going to have to try

harder. I'm not about to lick the plate like a dog. I set my fork down on the table. "I was done anyway."

"Awww, Mr. Grumpy," Kenzi coos. She picks a piece of broccoli off my plate between her fingers and holds it up to my face. "I'll help. Open."

I oblige. She pops the broccoli in my mouth.

Jason frowns. "You know…*you* can still use a fork, Kenzi."

"Yeah, but this is more fun." She has some sauce on her thumb, so she holds it to my lips. "Suck."

I take her thumb in my mouth and swirl my tongue around the tip of it. This should not be as erotic as it is. But when she's playful and coy like this, I would do anything for her.

Including lick every inch of her clean with my tongue.

She looks pleased with herself. Jason looks annoyed. And I'm trying to keep my cock from tenting in my pants.

"Dessert?" I ask.

11

KENZI

Donovan excuses himself, and for a minute, Jason and I are alone.

The record finishes, and static pops through the empty air. The stylus jumps up, automatically resuming its place.

I move over to the record player and crouch down in front of it so I can thumb through the stack of records fitted neatly underneath. "Alright," I say, "let's see what you boys have in store for me…"

"Better not touch that," Jason warns. "Donovan goes ballistic."

"I'll take my chances."

I find Bonnie Raitt hidden among the stack. I slip her out of her sleeve and carefully switch out the records. I hit Play and immediately start to sway to the song.

I brush a succulent—succulent? It's green and has long, pointed arms that stretch out. I could never keep a plant alive long enough to know what they were called.

"Need a dancing partner?" I feel Jason before I see him; his body comes up against mine, and he takes my hand. He coaxes a spin from me, but I spin away from him instead of toward him and then take off on my own.

"I can keep rhythm on my own."

The edge of his mouth curves upward. "I don't doubt that you can."

I lift my arms above my head, lazily swaying. "You seem better," I comment.

He scrunches his eyebrows. "Better?"

"Calmer. What's your secret?"

"You're going to laugh."

"Maybe."

"Yoga and meditation."

I roll my eyes. "Do they teach you that when you sign up for Doctors Without Borders?"

Jason draws up one of his half-grins. "You watched my Dr. Mazie episode."

Ugh. Caught red-handed. I shrug it off. "I might have... seen bits and pieces."

"The whole thing is so insane," Jason says. "I never wanted to be on TV, and now they're talking about giving me my own segment. The episode kinda blew up, I guess."

I blink at that. "Like...you'd have your own show?"

He shrugs. "Sort of. I went in for a photoshoot like a week ago—totally bizarre experience. They had me put on my surgeon gown and operate on a dummy to take promo pictures." The way he says it, it's like it's *nothing*. Dr. Mazie has millions of viewers. It's a very big deal, yet Jason looks shy about it.

"So you're going for it, huh?" I ask.

Jason shrugs. "My dad says it's good PR for Lighthouse Medical. So. Probably."

Inside me, I feel my knot of guilt loosen a little. Jason has changed—yes. But he's still his father's lapdog. I don't trust Leonard King for a second, and if Jason is still eating out of the palm of his hand...well. Maybe I made the right choice to keep him out of Otto's life, after all.

I turn around so I can face Jason, leaning my back against

the wall. "You don't drink. You don't jerk off. You meditate. You do yoga. I have to ask…are you a good guy now, Jason King?"

His ice-blue eyes look up at me from under a bed of black hair. "I always was. You just didn't look hard enough."

"Mmm, I *distinctly* remember a couple severely asshole-y moments from our childhood."

He lets out a low, half-hearted chuckle. "Okay. Maybe."

"So what changed you?"

He shrugs. "You did."

I blink. "*Me?*"

"That summer was the first time I let myself be vulnerable. Open. Found out I liked it. Figured it was time to change some things."

"What…just in case we run into each other some ten years later?"

A grin sneaks up his mouth. "Yeah. Something like that."

I notice how close he is now. My fingers twitch with the urge to touch his chest and feel the muscles there. Or kiss his mouth and feel the tickle of his beard. His blue eyes drop to my lips briefly before returning to meet my gaze, and I wonder—is he thinking the same thing?

Feeling dangerously close to making a bad mistake, I push off the wall and take a couple of steps away, distancing myself. I turn my back to him and glance around the house aimlessly. "God, this is a beautiful house," I say. I do actually mean that.

"Yeah, Donovan renovated it himself. He did great." Silence lingers between us for a second. "It's really close to the beach," Jason continues after a moment, just to fill the vacuum. "You've can walk there from here."

I swivel around to face him again. "Can I see it?"

He blinks. "Huh?"

"The beach," I clarify. "I haven't been yet."

"It's freezing," Jason counters.

"Yeah, but it's still the beach," I protest.

Finally, a grin draws over Jason's mouth.

"What'd I miss?" Donovan asks as he rejoins us in the living room.

"Polar bear party!" Jason shouts, which I guess is the last word on that.

12

JASON

I don't care who you are—

There's nothing more beautiful than the beach at night.

The sand looks almost white. The sea is a deep, dark blue that tickles the bay. We don't need flashlights, not when the moon is this full and the sky this bright with stars.

I leave my shoes behind and sink my toes into the sand. It's cold, but there's a little daytime warmth underneath it still when you really bury in. I like the chilly breeze coming off the water—it's sharp and clean.

"Last one to the water is a muskrat!" Kenzi shouts and takes off running. I dash after her, kicking up sand under my toes. She touches the water first, and I get to it next. It's like liquid ice, licking my toes.

Kenzi gasps. "Oh my God, it's *freezing!*"

But neither of us move away.

Behind us, Donovan finally catches up, strolling leisurely. He has wine, after all. Precious cargo.

"Truth or dare, D?" I ask him.

"Dare."

"I dare you to howl," Kenzi says. "As loud as you can."

Donovan lets out a loud animal noise. There's no one on the beach—who cares? Kenzi joins in. So do I.

Pack of animals. It feels good. Exhaling vowels, letting the salt air back in.

When I look back at Kenzi, she's smiling. The moonlight eclipses her face and highlights her dark hair.

She's got one hell of a smile. Big, kissable lips.

"Penny for your thoughts?" I ask her.

She watches the water. "This is the first time since getting here that I've felt like I'm home."

"You are home. There's been a Kenzi-shaped imprint in the sand ever since you left."

My dumb joke makes her bite her lip.

I've gotta get my eyes off of her mouth.

"Your toes numb?"

She laughs. "Yeah, kind of. But I don't want to move yet."

"Me neither."

I could watch her like this. All night.

She shifts from foot to foot, drawing her toes through the water and back again. And then she loses balance. Kenzi lets out a quick yelp and stretches out her arms. I grab her quickly, hooking my arm around her middle to keep her from hitting the cold water.

"Shit...thanks," she laughs. Her body heat feels nice against mine. I want to unzip my jacket and let her inside. "Sorry. I'm clumsy."

"You're perfect." The words just fall out of me. But I mean them.

Her eyes meet mine. Those sweet emeralds. Curious, inviting.

I can't help it—I find myself leaning in. I nuzzle against her, my warmth seeking hers. I feel her breath on my cheek when her lips part. My mouth finds hers in the dark. I don't plan it, I don't even think about it—it just feels natural, kissing her like this. The ocean sea licks our ankles and her small body snuggles tighter against mine.

Our kiss is slow, unhurried. She tastes like ChapStick, soft and feminine, and I want to savor this. This moment exactly as it is.

When the kiss breaks, she lets out a small laugh. She tucks herself in, drawing away almost shyly. "Should we...go inside?"

"Absolutely." Even in the dead of winter, a single kiss from her has me warm all over.

I glance back at Donovan. If he noticed our kiss, he doesn't say anything. He stands there, straight as an egret, eyes on the ocean. Sipping from his wineglass.

We walk away from the lapping shoreline. "We're heading inside," I tell him.

"I'll be right there," he replies. His breath crystalizes in the night.

I chase Kenzi inside. The sand grows cold under my bare feet, and we do our best to kick it off on the mat in front of the screen doors.

We slip inside, and I pull the glass door closed behind us. Immediately, Kenzi hugs herself and shivers. "God, the winters get brutal here," she says.

I slip my hands over her sides and rub over the soft curves of her body. "I'll warm you up."

She grins up at me. "You're handsy."

"Do you want me to stop?"

"I should say yes," she says.

"Probably," I tell her.

"Probably."

For a moment, we just stare at each other. Shivering.

"Fuck it," Kenzi says. She grabs my shirt and pulls me in.

We're kissing again. God. I love kissing her. This time she opens up more to me, letting me inside her mouth. I taste her tongue, and she moans, a sound that vibrates through me and makes me diamond-hard.

We stumble through the house, and I lose my footing. We fall on the couch together, and she takes the breath out of me when her body collapses on top of mine.

Kenzi cackles, and the sound warms the entire house.

13

DONOVAN

I stay outside a little longer, wrestling with my demons.

Seeing them kiss like that…it woke something up in me I thought was dead.

I want nothing more than to get in the middle of them.

But there's something inside of me, aching. Something I've kept bottled up for over a decade. Because the truth—the real, capital T Truth of it all—is that I've only ever loved one person in my entire ugly existence.

Kenzi Stratton.

And if her lips touch mine…

I'm afraid my truth will come spilling out.

I steel off my nerves, finish my wine, and tell myself to hold it together. But when I go inside, my resolve immediately cracks.

It's fireplace warm in here, and they're laughing on the couch, tangled in each other.

I close the glass door behind me, and I hate that it catches their attention.

Jason breaks away from their kiss. When he grins at me, it's a dopey grin.

"Hey, man," he says. "You sticking around?"

They're both watching me now. Lust in their eyes. Lips swollen from kissing. They want me to come play with them. They're puppies rolling around in puppy love. They know I'm the stern hand that'll take them both to their knees.

And, fuck, I want it. But—

"I'm going to bed." I try to sound calm, not at all like I'm throbbing in my pants. "You two have fun."

But then Kenzi locks her wide eyes on me. "Please?"

Fuck. Why did she have to say *please*?

14

———

KENZI

For the longest time, Donovan just stands there. There's a storm cloud in his dark eyes. A debate going on within himself.

But my body is humming, and I *want* this, so badly, but…

I know it's crazy, but somehow, it won't feel right without Donovan there, too.

It's the *three* of us. It's always been the three of us.

Then he comes over and sits down on the ottoman across from us. He takes the bottle of red off the table and fills up his glass.

"One more glass," he says.

My legs are tangled up in Jason's, and I reposition myself so I'm sitting up, half in his lap. "Truth or dare, Jason," I say.

He pushes some of my hair back from my face. "Truth."

I glance between the two of them. "Have you guys had another threesome?"

Donovan nearly chokes on his wine.

"No," Jason says. "You're it."

"Okay…have you *thought* about having another?"

"I'd be down," Jason says. Maybe too quickly?

"It would depend," Donovan replies, cagey, his eyes on his glass.

"On what?"

Those dark eyes meet mine now. "On whether or not you were the third."

I grin. "Aw. You guys know how to make a woman feel special. So I'm your golden goose?"

"We had something special. Some chemistry you can't make up." Jason lifts his hand. "Hold on—why am I talking past tense? We *have* something special. Still."

Since he's opened that can of worms, I find myself nodding in agreement. "It all feels…so familiar. I feel like just yesterday, you were showing me around your boat."

Donovan and Jason exchange a look, as though they're telepathically passing information.

I narrow my eyes at them, trying to read their expressions. "What?"

"Show her," Jason tells Donovan.

Donovan shakes his head. "We're definitely not drunk enough for that."

"Show me what?"

"No. Another night."

"Donovan," I whine. "Please?"

Donovan lets out a huge sigh. "Fuck," he mutters, almost to himself.

* * *

We're not exactly in any state to drive, but apparently, where we're going is in walking distance.

The night is bitterly cold, but the red wine and Donovan's dinner have both warmed my stomach and my blood.

Of course, it also helps when, halfway through our walk down the empty road, Jason slings his arm around my shoulders and pulls me into his body heat. He starts singing nineties songs, loudly, badly, and I do my best to join in.

Okay, maybe I'm a *little* tipsy.

Donovan walks us to the Hannsett Island Marina. Which...talk about memories. We walk through the parking lot and down the gravel pathway.

It looks strange in the dark. Eerie, almost. It hasn't changed at all since I left. There's the restaurant to our left—different name but same building. The pool we used to hang out in. The laundry room we used to get high in. There is a row of boats lined up along the pier. They look bright in the moonlight, like swans on the water, lazily bobbing.

"It hasn't changed, has it?" I ask.

"What'd you expect?" Donovan asks. "Flying cars?"

Valid. Valid point.

There's no one here at night. There probably hasn't been anyone here all winter. The marina takes a particularly steep dive after tourist season. Which...it's pretty obvious why.

It's fucking cold. Not exactly "boating weather."

"Where are you taking us?" I finally ask, because I have to tuck my fingers into my sleeves to keep them warm.

"Almost there," Donovan says.

I don't know where I expect him to bring us—the dock master's office? His old trailer behind the pool? Do they still *have* the trailer—?

He guides us down the second pier, and we walk to the very end of it. The cold has frosted over the standing pier lights. The last ship bobs lightly in the water. It's modest compared to the yachts and expensive fishing boats. It's a quaint sailboat, all open wood, and well taken care of. The sail cover is white, tight, and clean. The steering wheel is covered as well, and it looks pretty battened down for the winter.

"Here we are," Donovan says, coming to a stop beside the boat.

I blink at it. He's standing next to it like he's proud. "Did you…buy this?"

But there's that amused *Mona Lisa* smile. He says, "Check the name."

I do. On the back in precise, black lettering, it says, *DOCK BUOY*.

And then I see it. I *recognize* this boat. I gape.

"You did it. You fixed it up."

"It took some doing, but…yeah."

Something twists in my chest. This was the boat we hung out in as kids. The boat I lost my virginity in. And like all of us, it's grown up. I'm…*touched*. "Why didn't you tell me?"

Donovan sticks his hands in his pockets. Shrugs. "I would've. If you'd come back."

"I'm sorry…I didn't know…"

"Don't," he interrupts quickly. "It's not for you. It's for me. That summer meant a lot to me. It's just…a reminder. Of a time I was young and dumb and really, really happy."

Maybe it's the alcohol. Maybe it's the salt in the night air. There's a lump in my throat. Thick emotion. "I think…I need that."

"Need what?"

"A reminder."

Donovan and Jason exchange a look. Can they talk telepathically? The jury is out. Whatever the look meant, they seem to come to some kind of agreed decision, because Donovan touches the railing and asks, "You want to see the inside?"

* * *

Donovan goes first, and then he takes my hand to help me over the railing.

He had a padlock on the cabin door, and it takes him a minute to punch in the combo and open it up.

I have to duck so as not to bump my head on the cabin door coming down.

"I winterized it, so it's pretty much out of commission until the summer," Donovan says as he descends the short staircase. "But you can get the idea."

"I'll just have to come back so I can see it in action," I say. If I'm being honest, I don't see myself coming back to Hannsett Island anytime soon if I can help it.

Then again…the chance to see these two again might be worth the trip.

Donovan disappears into the darkness to flick on the lights from the switchboard and—

He's certainly cleaned the place up. Cherrywood walls. Dark navy cushions. A polished wood table, short shelves with mason jars, bottom shelves for the booze. An old-fashioned oil lantern hangs in the center, which I bet looks beautiful when it's lit.

The tour is short, but Donovan gives it: the stovetop to the left compromises the "kitchen," and then there's a pull-out navigating table. The cushions that surround the table serve as the sitting area. The mast sinks through the center of the sailboat, and behind it sits the v-berth, where he fits storage. Then in the rear of the boat is the bathroom or "head," which adjoins the main cabin.

The main cabin is almost entirely mattress. There's a narrow strip of walking room between the bed and the wall, so we walk along it in a row—Donovan, me, and Jason.

Donovan opens a small closet and pulls out a space heater. He plugs it in on the floor. "It'll take a minute, but then it warms up fast."

"It's amazing," I tell Donovan. There's a small oval window above the bed, and I can see the water through it.

I stumble backward, and Jason catches me. "Whoa there, Trouble," he says.

"Sorry…"

Am I? When I turn to face him, it's only blue eyes I see.

Donovan stands again, and I can feel him behind me, too. There's no room in this cabin…but maybe that's what I like about it.

There's a shift. I don't know what it is—maybe there are memories in the wood of this ship, creeping back into our veins. I can hear my breath—and theirs. The energy between us fizzles.

My heart hammers in my chest. I'm swaying—or maybe that's the boat?

"Is this okay?" Jason asks, his fingertips brushing my cheek, coaxing me closer. I can feel the warmth of his breath on my face.

"Yes," I breathe.

He kisses me. It's gentle and deep. Donovan's hands take my hips, and I lean back into him, encouraging. His lips tickle my throat. The scruff from his jaw feels rough on my skin.

This feels both incredibly familiar and incredibly different. Same guys, same situation…but they're men now. Not boys. I feel it in Donovan's stubble. Jason's muscled chest. The boldness of each deliberate movement.

They were fumbling, exploring touches before. Now, they're confident. Hungry.

For me.

It's enough to make a woman's head spin.

I grab Jason's shirt. "I think we're all…wearing too many clothes."

He grabs his shirt from the back and rips it over his head. "Better?"

I run my fingers like water down his chest, the ripples of his abdomen. "Much."

Fair is fair—I pull my shirt off, tossing it to the side. The fabric flutters around me as I shuck it gracelessly. My bra comes next, freeing my breasts, and I let it fall to the floor.

The chill makes my nipples harden. I reach behind, and my fingertips find Donovan. I'm blind with him behind me, but miraculously, I feel my way around. First: warm skin, his drum-tight stomach. And down, I find his belt. It's clumsy work, but the leather yields to my fingertips and pops open. I press my palms to his abdomen and run them underneath his pants. I feel the heat of his skin, the sloping V of his abdomen, the small, wiry curls. His erection is insistent, and it brushes against me, but I don't touch him there. Not yet. I'm teasing him—and myself.

His breath shudders against the back of my neck, and his teeth graze the skin there. I feel his arm wind around my chest, and his hand grips my throat. A gentle reminder that he's in charge. Jason's lips tease, but Donovan's mouth claims, and I gasp, dully aware that the suction of his mouth is going to leave a purpling bruise tomorrow.

My back arches and twists, unintentionally pushing my chest forward. Jason helps himself to my breasts. He sucks one nipple into his mouth, and then the next, as he undoes my pants. His lips—and my pants—drop lower as this moun-tain of a man sinks to his knees in front of me.

"God, you're gorgeous," Jason murmurs. He nuzzles against my thigh. His breath between my legs makes me buzz. "You smell delicious, too." He gives me a kiss at the top of my thigh. His bright blue eyes meet my gaze. "Can I lick you?"

Sweet boy. I smile and push my fingers through his jet-black hair. "I'll hate you if you don't."

He kisses my sex and I clench. One sweet kiss, then another, and then I feel it…the warm wetness of his tongue, mapping me out.

I moan and arch into his mouth. A hand snakes around my middle—Donovan's. His leather bracelet is rough against my pelvis when his hand slips between my legs. His fingers work me, holding my lips apart so Jason can get deeper. Everything feels so much more intense now, lighting bolts of pleasure rocket through me with every lash of his tongue. I whisper and my knees buckle. Donovan is holding me up, though, his hand tightening at my throat, and I'm completely at their mercy.

"Do you like the way his tongue feels on your pussy?" Donovan asks in a low growl.

"Yes…" Even I'm appalled by the desperation in my voice. "Feels…so good…"

Jason is licking me like a man starved. His tongue swirls my nub and dives deep inside of me. He's buried his face between my legs, and the sharp slope of his nose bumps against my sensitive clit.

"Don't let her cum yet." Donovan's voice is husky at my ear.

My thighs tremble when Jason pulls away. I whine. "No…why…?"

Donovan chuckles. "You haven't earned it."

I bite my lip. "Well, you know what they say…" I twist around and cup the sizeable bulge in Donovan's pants. I squeeze, just enough to hear him sigh. "Once a spoiled brat… always a spoiled brat."

"Get on the bed," Donovan demands. And—has he always been this bossy? I don't think so. But I like it…

I scoot onto the bed. I'm completely naked now, and all theirs.

Jason gets to his feet, unfurling like a long plant. But before he can completely, Donovan takes the back of his head and draws him closer. "I want a taste."

Then he sucks Jason's bottom lip. His tongue reaches out next, swiping inside Jason's mouth. Jason is lust-drunk and needy, and he's practically swaying on his long limbs, a small moan falling from him as Donovan drinks in every trace of my arousal.

When he pulls back from Jason, Jason looks dazed, and I have to squeeze my thighs together to keep myself from soaking the duvet.

"Fuck," Jason says with a laugh. "I need you. Both of you."

Jason climbs into bed with me—no, more like flops into it. We roll into each other, skin finding skin. His laughter is contagious, and before long I'm giggling against him.

"This is new," I say and place my hand on him. He's surprised me with a tattoo. A dove swooping across his rib cage. "I like it."

He grins. "Good, because it's not going anywhere."

I kiss him. He tastes like me—and like Donovan. It's intoxicating.

"I need you inside of me," I whisper against his mouth.

"Yeah…"

We roll around, but this time I pin him underneath me, straddling him. I kiss his lips once more before shifting around so I'm sitting in his lap.

Here, I can reach down and take him in my hand. He's so hard, and huge. Bigger than I remember. How did I lose my virginity to *this*?

"Hold on," Donovan says. He vanishes into the bathroom for only a moment, and when he comes back, he has a condom between his fingers.

He unwraps it for me. What a gentleman.

"Thanks." I take it and shift back, Jason's thickness against my pelvis. I roll the condom over him and give him a couple of strokes to secure him. He moans in response.

I take him between my legs and ease Jason's cock inside of me. He fills me. Stretches me. A delicious, beautiful ache. As I slide down it, I fix my eyes on Donovan.

He's watching me. Watching *us*. His hand reaches inside of his open pants, and he strokes himself.

I reach out and tug at his pants. He finally kicks them off and gets into bed with us.

Donovan is naked now, except for the chain around his neck with two rings, and the leather cuff he keeps wrapped around his wrist. There's something about that I find unbearably sexy. Something about the way the cuff bobs up and down as he strokes his impressive length makes me throb. I fuck myself on Jason's thick cock, head dropping with a moan. His hand settles on my hip, but he's not guiding me. It rests there, encouraging, as he lets me take him at my own pace.

"Let me," I tell Donovan.

His eyes narrow. "Let you what?"

"Suck you. Please." My mouth is dry for the want of it.

His jaw slackens. Then he positions himself in front of me and slips his hand to the back of my head, cradling it. "Come here…"

I like the way his fingers feel in my hair. He holds the long strands back as I bend to kiss the head of him. I have to get on my hands to keep Jason inside of me, all while pleasuring Donovan, too. He's a beautiful man—thick, hard—and the tip of him glistens, leaking with want. I take him in my mouth, tasting the heat of him, the salt of him, and I trace my tongue deliberately over his veins. He throbs in my mouth, and I can hear him moan—or is that Jason?

We're tangled together, all three of us. Pleasure ebbing and flowing in waves.

I love this—crushed between them. The conduit of their desire. The two strong, strapping men are sighing, twitching, moaning my name.

And God, it feels good.

I'm not sure how much more of this I can take. I'm humping Jason like an animal, grinding him deep inside of me as I make sloppy work of Donovan, licking, sucking, swirling. The heat between all three of us is building to a peak.

Donovan's grip tightens in my hair. He reaches his hand between my legs. I'm sopping wet; I can feel my slickness against his fingers, and he finds my clit and begins flicking it mercilessly. His voice is a thick, low growl when he murmurs in my ear, "Cum with me."

I can't stop it. A loud whine escapes me, and everything in me gets tight, so tight, until—

I explode around Jason. My orgasm throbs through me, hard, with pleasure so intense I grip the blanket as I ride it out.

Donovan fills my mouth, the sweet salt of him, and I find myself dizzy as I suck, and pulse, and drink. My entire body feels like a heartbeat; even my skin feels like it's throbbing.

When he starts to soften in my mouth, he slips his hand on my jaw and removes himself from me. Then he kisses me, heatedly. I'm putty in their hands, putty in his mouth.

I can feel my clit still jumping against Donovan's fingers. He's not slowing down. "Ready for round two?"

"Two?" I echo, my voice hazy.

"That was mine," Donovan says in my ear. "Now you have to cum again. For Jason."

My thighs won't stop trembling. Jason's grip tightens on my legs, and he takes a handful of my hair. He lifts his hips to fuck me now, taking me the way he wants it. I'm still half in the throes, and every thrust from him makes me see stars. I can feel his breath on my back, a steady beat.

I'm so sensitive, and Donovan's ministrations feel so good, they hurt. My breath catches in my throat, and I reach up and grip Donovan's shoulders so tightly, I'm sure my nails leave marks.

I cry out when I orgasm a second time. Jason moans loudly as his own release twitches inside of me.

I have to grip Donovan's wrist to get his touches to cease.

"Please," I beg. I'm so sensitive, everything in me pulsing, pounding.

"You did good," Donovan murmurs in my ear—or is it Jason?

I'm swooning. Blissed-out. In my body and out of my mind. They kiss me all over, touch me and hold me, and I wrap myself up in their sweat and their smell as the three of us collapse together.

15

KENZI

I don't remember falling asleep.

But when I wake up, I'm completely disoriented.

My brain peels back days: it's anticipating gray London skies, the nasty buzz of my alarm clock, and the *chick-chick* of the crappy radiator in our flat.

Instead, I hear the quiet lapping of water against the hull of the boat. The low groan as the rubber bumper grinds against the dock. Donovan's soft snores in my ear.

I wouldn't believe last night happened, except I'm wedged between two furnace-hot men. Both naked. Both cradling me. Donovan behind, his arm tucked around my middle. Jason has his arm around me as well, his hand resting at my hip.

Is this real? It feels like a fantasy, a fever dream I made up.

As though to test my surroundings, I reach over and gently rest my hand on Jason's face. I slip my fingers through his dark hair, drawing it back. He's real. Very real.

His eyelids flutter, and those dazzling blues land on me. Slowly, a smile crawls across his face.

"Morning, Trouble," he murmurs.

"Morning," I whisper.

"How'd you sleep?"

"Like the dead."

"Me too." We linger in this, the soft warmth of the morning, and his thumb rubs lazy patterns across my hip. "Last night was amazing," he adds.

"Yeah. It was."

There's so much sincerity in this moment that I make the decision, all at once. I'm going to tell him. Whatever Jason was, whoever his family is—it doesn't matter.

This man, who looks at me with so much adoration even in the harsh morning light…he's a *good guy*. He deserves to know the truth.

I bite my bottom lip. "There's…something we should talk about."

He knits his eyebrows. "What's that?"

"Uh…"

The words almost come out. Almost. But I'm interrupted by the low buzz of someone's phone going off.

"Is that me?" I ask, and Jason shrugs, so I launch myself over him. I bend over the side of the bed. There's a sea of clothes scattered on the floor, and I hunt around until I find the culprit—my phone, hiding in my jacket pocket. I glance at the caller ID, and immediately my heart leaps into my throat.

It's Mr. King.

I fumble out of bed (and get a couple of groans from Jason as I climb over him and knee him in the stomach on accident). I yank my pants on my hips and pull my phone to my ear, rushing out of the bedroom and closing the door behind me. There's not a lot of privacy on a boat, and leaving the bedroom suddenly feels like a bad idea because I'm shirtless and *freezing*. My nipples are painful knots on my chest. I ignore it to put my phone to my ear and clear my throat.

"Kenzi Stratton," I say, trying to sound casual, but my teeth are chattering.

"Otto has an appointment at noon," Mr. King says—no bullshit, getting straight to the point. "Don't be late."

I release a breath I hadn't realized I was holding. I'm so relieved, I have to sit down before I fall down, and I flop onto the bench hard.

He's going to treat my son. Otto is going to get the help he needs.

"That's…great. That's really great to hear."

"And Kenzi…?"

"Yes?"

"I do have one stipulation."

Yesterday, I was fire and brimstone. Today, I'm not above begging. "Sure. Anything."

Mr. King's voice goes forceful. "If you tell Jason about Otto's paternity, I'll blacklist you and your son from the hospital immediately."

Cue icicles forming in my chest. What *can* I say to that?

As much as I want to tell Jason…that's not why I'm here.

I'm here for my son. For Otto. And I'm willing to do *anything* to get him the treatment he needs.

"Understood," I say, as serious as a drill sergeant.

"Good," Mr. King says, then adds, "See you at noon."

With that, he hangs up.

My heart is ricocheting in my chest. Forget coffee—I feel like I've been injected with straight adrenaline. I'm wide-awake and ready to go into action.

When I reenter the bedroom, Jason asks, "Everything okay?"

I sit on the side of the bed and tug my shirt over my head. "Yeah. I just have to go."

He slips his hand to my leg. "You have to stay."

"I have to go."

DONOVAN

Kenzi takes off in the morning. Jason and I throw on clothes and walk her back to her car. It all happens in such a rush, I don't have time to digest last night.

And maybe that's a good thing.

I have about enough time to wash my mouth and change my clothes before I have to go to work.

"Carpool?" Jason asks, so I oblige.

I fill up a thermos of coffee. We take my car.

I turn on my car and, immediately, we're blasted with scream-o. I dial my music down to a low, demonic rumble.

"How can you still hear anything?" Jason asks.

"What?" I reply.

"I said, *how can you still hear—?*"

I arch my eyebrows at Jason.

"Oh. I get it."

"At least you're pretty," I tell him.

The radiator rattles as it tries hard to complete with the thirty degree weather outside. I have to blast the vents open to clear the frost haze from the window.

I keep the music on so he doesn't try to talk to me. It's too early in the morning, I haven't had coffee yet, and I'm certain we both smell like sex.

I feel hungover. Not drunk hungover—emotionally hungover. Like last night was a bizarre dream. Like I didn't spend all night with Kenzi moaning in my ear and Jason swearing in my bed.

It seems too insane to be real.

We split at the hospital, and I work off the feeling. A couple of hours in, one of the nurses lets me know that Otto Stratton is waiting for me in Room 122. I go in—in doctor mode now—and greet the family. Kenzi has brushed up; she's washed her face, combed her hair, and thrown on some clean clothes. She also avoids eye contact, which I think has something to do with the fact that Pearl is watching her like a hawk. Pearl isn't an idiot, and probably has suspicions about what her daughter was up to all night.

I turn my attention to the one person I can control: my patient. Otto has warmed up a little to me today. He's a sweet kid, and smart, capable of talking me through all of his symptoms. His accent is funny—some American-English hybrid—but I like it. *Strange* is my language.

I do have a hard time ignoring the fact that there's something naggingly familiar about Otto. But I push it aside for now.

We go through the standard checkup before I order a round of blood tests and an MRI so we can get to work.

Then I leave them to it. I spend most of my day in the critical care wing, visiting with patients, going over labs, training my residents. I have to coax one of my residents down when she nearly stabs a patient through trying to draw blood.

White-coat life isn't always glamorous.

Jason has surgery at two, and *golden child* isn't answering my texts, so I have to hunt for him.

I find him in an empty, dark exam room, slumped forward in the chair, lips parted. "Resting" his eyes.

We both were up all night fucking. We're both exhausted. I get it. But that doesn't mean that I have to put up with it.

I flick on the light and kick him in the shin. It wakes him with a start.

"You have surgery soon," I tell him and toss the file into his lap. "Drink some coffee."

"No can do," he says as he starts to thumb through the file. "Stimulants make my hands shake."

"Yeah, well, I'm pretty sure falling asleep on the operating table is bad for the patient, too."

He glances up at me and flashes me a grin. "Just getting a little REM, baby. I'm bright-eyed and bushy-tailed now."

Things I hate about Jason King: he's right. He does look bright-eyed and bushy-tailed. Brighter than me, if I'm being honest, and I'm already on my third cup of coffee of the day.

Jason King is not made for hospitals. He wants to be saving the world like Indiana fucking Jones. He'd be happy joining the Peace Corps or Doctors Without Borders and jetting off to some third-world country. He's said as much—multiple times.

But when your father owns an incredibly lucrative medical center, you don't have much of a choice in the matter. It's his legacy to work here until his father retires, at which point, he'll fill the old man's shoes.

Circle of life and nepotism. Some of us are born with golden spoons. That's just the way the world works, and I've lived with that chip my whole life.

Doesn't mean I have to stand for his laziness, while the world just falls into his lap.

He looks at me in a way I can tell that there's something brewing behind those blue eyes. Finally, he says, "So...last night was pretty wild, huh?"

My belt buzzes. Thank God. I'm not ready to have this conversation with him.

I lift the pager. "I've got to take this."

"Sure," he says, "we can talk later."

Or never, I think. *We can talk never.*

17

———

KENZI

here's a scene in Nathaniel Hawthorne's *The Scarlett Letter* when one of the characters comments that, even if the woman were to cover up the letter *A* that displays her sin for the world to see, she would still be marked by the shame within her heart.

I can relate, suddenly. I crept in the house as quietly as I could when I got home, but my stealth was no match for Pearl's hound-dog nose. I've spent all morning dodging her questions about last night, and when Donovan enters in his lab coat, I physically have to look away. I can *feel* her watching me, gauging my reaction.

"He's such a good doctor," Pearl muses when he exits. "Such good *bedside* manner. Don't you think, darling?"

"Does anyone need anything?" I ask suddenly. I need an excuse to get out from under her prying eyes.

Otto sits on the table, and he shrugs. "I'm a little hungry," he says.

"Yeah?" I perk up like a dog with a tennis ball. "I think I saw a vending machine down the hall. Will that tide you over?"

He nods. "Packet of crisps?"

"Copy that," I say. I swivel around in my chair and get to my feet.

"Wait." My mother starts fishing around in her purse. I realize she's picking out coins.

"Pearl. You're aware that I'm a grown-up, right?" She blinks at me, big eyes, confused. I wave my wallet at her. "I've got this."

"Are you sure...?" She sounds suspicious, as if my money isn't mine, as if I don't have a salary that would let me afford a meager snack.

"I'll be right back," I tell her. And I exit the room before she takes any more air out of my confidence.

The vending machine is all the way down the hall. It's pretty quiet on this floor, and I make it to the machine undisturbed. There, lo and behold, are salt and vinegar chips, dangling from the ring at the very bottom.

Except when I take out my wallet, something stops me. A piece of tape over the credit card reader and a message in ugly marker: CASH ONLY.

"Son of a..."

I don't have cash. I never carry cash. This is the twenty-first century...*who uses cash?*

Pearl does. And she's going to roll her eyes, and the next hour will be full of *I told you so*s if I go back and beg her for quarters now.

On the other hand...

I bite my lip.

The chips are, really, *very* close to the bottom. Nearly hanging off, really. I'd practically be doing gravity a service if I released it.

I glance behind me. The hallway is empty. The coast is clear.

I crouch down, knees on the polished floor, and lift the flap to reach my arm deep into the machine. There's a wide enough opening that I can slip my hand into it. I have to shift in my spot and twist a bit, but I'm almost there…

My fingertips brush the ruffled edges of the chip bag.

But I can't reach enough to actually pull it down. *Damn.*

I hear footsteps down the hall. Startled, I yank my arm back—

But it won't budge.

I twist, squirm, but, somehow, I've got myself trapped. A snack thief locked in a bear trap of her own demise. I put my good hand against the glass and try to tug my arm out, but it's somehow lodged itself in the contraption that's meant to release the candy.

This is how I die. Utter humiliation in the middle of a hospital. Like a kid with her hand *literally* stuck in the cookie jar.

"You need a hand, pretty lady?"

That voice. I could crawl away with shame…if I wasn't stuck.

"I *have* a hand," I groan. "That's the problem."

Jason crouches down beside me so he's in my line of vision. I have to say…seeing him in a lab coat? It's a damn good look on him.

"Hi," he says, and his smile is so charming, I could die.

"Hi, back at you."

"What exactly is going on here?"

I sigh. "I was…trying to get Otto a bag of chips. And it didn't take my credit card, so…"

"You don't carry change?"

"Who carries change anymore!"

"Okay…" he says gently, like he's trying to coax out a lion. "Can you move it?"

"Uh…" I twist my arm a little and wince. "Sort of?"

"You mind if I…?" He points to the machine.

I lift my working arm and drop it. "By all means."

He scoots forward, lifts the flap, and reaches his arm up

in it. We're incredibly close like this, our legs practically scissoring, his knee nudging my groin. I can smell his cologne—like earth and man. I feel his fingers slide up my arm until he reaches the contraption that's caught me in its teeth. Gently, I feel him prying it with his thumb. "This might pinch…"

It does pinch, and I gasp when, for a minute, the teeth bite tighter into my skin. But then they release. Quickly, before the candy-monster changes its mind, I yank my arm back. It slips from the jaws of the vending machine. I cradle it.

"Thank you," I tell him. "That was…dumb."

"I'd like to say determined. Are you okay?"

"I think…"

He glances at my arm. "Can you wiggle your fingers?"

I extend my arm and play piano in the air. I nod.

"Good." He leans in and kisses the backs of my fingers. "Can you feel that?"

"Yes…"

He takes my index finger and slips the digit into his mouth. He sucks it and lightly rolls his tongue over the edge of it. In a flash, I suddenly have the memory of him swirling his tongue over my needy little clit. His eyes meet mine, as though he can tell what I'm thinking, and he grins. "Can you feel that?" he asks again.

"Yeah…" I say. I'm already breathless. I can feel it in the tips of my fingers. The hard pebbles of my nipples. The clench of my cunt.

"Good news…I think you're going to live."

"My hero."

"You better be glad I found you here and not Donovan."

"Oh, yeah. He would've left me. Teach me a lesson."

"Would you have learned?"

"Me? Learning a lesson? Seems unlikely."

He snorts a laugh. "That's why I don't try. You're a grown-ass woman. You can make your own mistakes."

"You're a good person, Jason."

"So are you."

Something about that makes me shy. I shrug my chin into my chest. "I wouldn't be so sure."

"No, I guess not. You're a bad girl. A naughty girl."

I scoff on a laugh. "You have me pegged."

Our eyes meet. "What are you doing for the holidays?" he asks.

"Um…"

I know what I *want* to be doing. But I also know what I should be doing—avoiding Jason at all costs.

"Retract that question," he says stubbornly. "I know what you're doing. There's a Christmas Eve ferry ride they do every year. They put on a band. Serve hot chocolate. The whole thing. Departs at seven thirty. Otto will love it."

"I'll think about it."

He squints at me. "You do this a lot, don't you?"

"Do what?"

"Pretend like you're going to commit to something and then bail at the last second."

"I do not!"

But even as I protest, I feel my face flush. I *am* notorious for backing out of any and all plans.

He holds out his hand and extends his pinky. "Promise you'll come."

I snort a laugh. "What are we, twelve?"

"Muskrat swear that you and Otto will be on the ferry Christmas Eve."

I hook my pinky in his. "We'll be there."

"Wasn't so hard, was it?"

I crinkle my nose at him.

JASON

I let Kenzi leave with her vending machine loot and her promise that I'll see her later.

I'll hold her to it. She's ignited something in me and, now that she's back in my life, I have no intention of letting her wiggle out of it again.

I find Donovan in the lab. He's sitting back in one of the chairs, staring at a wall of MRI scans tacked up side by side.

He doesn't seem to notice when I walk in. Donovan is picking at his bottom lip, something he does when he's thinking really hard. I don't think he has any idea how distracting it is.

"Is that Otto?" I ask, closing the door behind me.

"Mmhm."

I pull up the chair beside him. I dig the toes of my shoes into the floor and roll the chair back and forth aimlessly as I take a look at the brain scans. Blue-and-black images of a little boy's brain tacked up to the wall.

"What are we looking at?" I ask.

"Nothing," Donovan says. There's frustration in his tone. "His scans are clear."

"Good news for Otto."

"Maybe. It still doesn't explain the seizures."

I lace my fingers in my lap. "So what's your diagnosis?"

He lapses into thought for a minute. "He could be faking the seizures."

I feel my mouth turn downward. "Seriously? That's a little cynical, even for you."

Donovan shrugs. "Single mom. Busy mom. Kid wants attention. It's a great way to get it. He might not even be aware he's doing it."

I press my lips together. "I guess."

"I'm going to run a couple more tests. See if we can induce it with stress."

"Sure." I nudge my chair back and forth on the wheels. "I convinced Kenzi and Otto to come to the Christmas ferry ride. You should join us. You can…observe Otto. See how he handles it."

Donovan glances at me. "I'm not going to babysit Otto so you can fuck."

My mouth drops open. "That's not what I said!"

He rolls his eyes.

19

KENZI

The ferry ride can't come soon enough.

We leave the medical center with no answers but promises of results to come.

Otto and Pearl and I spend the day together: we shop around some of the open stores on Main Street. So many of these stores haven't changed—the ice cream shop has the same sign of a narwhal with an ice cream cone for a horn. We pass Hanson's General Store, where Donovan and I once shoplifted candy from, on a dare, and then both felt so bad about it we left two dollars in the tip jar. We go into a tourist shop with postcards and T-shirts, and beach equipment in the back, and Otto helps me pick out a couple of ornaments for the tree.

I'm trying to be present, but my thoughts keep drifting to last night. It feels like some kind of fever dream. Every now and then, I remember the deliciously full feeling of Jason inside of me or the low rumble of Donovan's growls, and suddenly I'm squeezing my thighs, trying to ignore the throb.

I also pick up tickets for the Christmas Eve ferry ride.

* * *

December twenty-forth is bitterly cold. It's going to be freezing on the ferry, so I pull on a dark dress and thick stockings that I roll up my thighs.

While I'm changing, my eyes land on my backpack. Burtie is in there. It's been days since my last mind-blowing release around Jason's cock and Donovan's fingers. I'm wound up, and I'm tempted to relieve some of this pressure, but—

"Mum! I broke a button on my jumper!"

A mother's job is never done.

Miraculously, the three of us somehow get dressed, get in the car, and make it to the ferry before it departs.

I'll admit, Jason wasn't wrong: it actually is pretty magical.

The cold wind that whips off the ocean feels like beestings on my cheeks, but it's worth it to watch the ferry lit up like this. The siding is draped in strings of pine and holly with large red bows wrapped on every pole. Christmas lights sparkle around the sides and around the enclosed deck. There are two levels to the ferry, and there's a stage jutting out from the second level where a band is set up but not yet playing. They have holiday music going over the speakers in the meantime. There's a small cart up front, too, and it looks like they're handing out hot drinks.

We hand over our tickets at the gate and then climb the ramp to board. Everyone is dressed in thick, puffy winter coats with scarves wrapped around red faces.

The first thing I do is look for Leonard King. If he's here, I want to avoid him at all costs, even if that means abandoning ship. Luckily, I don't see him anywhere—maybe this is too "pedestrian" for him. Whatever the reason, I'm grateful not to be in his crosshairs.

The ferry lets out a couple of bursts from the horn, and the engine churns as the workers toss thick ropes onto the deck.

I wrap my fingers around the cold railing as the ferry pulls away from Hannsett Island.

"Hey, stranger."

I glance over to see Jason standing beside me. He has both hands on the railing, but he looms over me in a thick dark wool jacket. His smile is crooked and uncharacteristically shy.

"Hey," I say back.

His eyes flicker to Otto. He crouches down then to get on level with the kid. "You must be the man of the hour." Jason grins.

And I swear—my heart collapses in my chest in that moment. I don't know what I expect—will Jason look into those blue eyes and immediately recognize his own? Will Otto see himself in that strong jaw? Will they connect on some incomprehensible level, that somehow they'll just see each other and *know*?

I lose the ability to inhale. Meanwhile, Jason lifts his palm. "Up top."

Otto politely gives Jason a high five. Jason drops his hand down. "Down low."

Otto moves to give Jason a low five, but Jason retracts his hand too quickly with a grin. "Aww, too slow."

Otto crinkles his nose. "That's not very nice."

Jason blinks. "What? No...I mean, it's a joke. It's fun. Don't kids do that anymore?"

Otto looks up at Pearl. "Can we get hot chocolate?"

"Of course," Pearl says and slips her hand to Otto's back, guiding him toward the drink station.

"You're my bacon," Otto tells me.

"You're mine." I squeeze his hand, and he leaves with Pearl.

Jason unfurls, getting back to his feet, and he rubs his hands together as though to warm them. "Tough audience," he says.

"Yeah," I say, "he's too old for his own good."

I don't know why, but I'm relieved. Jason is awkward with kids. He and Otto don't immediately click. This isn't one of those heartwarming feelings you get after watching man-returns-from-war-to-hug-his-dog videos. It's just…two people. Existing.

I can breathe again.

Jason resumes his spot beside me, elbows on the railing, one foot kicked up against the side.

"What's the bacon thing?" he asks.

"Oh—well. When he was little, I asked him what he loved most in the world. And he told me, *bacon*. So it's been a running joke, I guess. Instead of saying the dreaded *L* word—"

"*Love?*" Jason asks dubiously. "That word?"

"Right, that—instead of that, I tell him that he's my bacon, and he tells me I'm his."

"Or you could just say *I love you*."

"Wouldn't feel the same."

"I get it," Jason says. "It's cute."

I shrug. "It's us."

"How are you?" he asks me. He sounds like he genuinely wants to know, too.

"Freezing."

"I can think of one way to warm you up…"

His body is close now. He leans in, and I can feel the heat of his breath on my cheek.

I shift away. "People are going to see."

"And?"

"And…you just got a divorce. Isn't your family all about… propriety? Appearances? It might look bad."

"Maybe I'm tired of being good." He puts a finger underneath my chin, tilts my head up, and closes his mouth over mine. It's hard not to melt against his lips.

But I break away. I put my hand on his chest, forcing distance between us.

"Jason...look. The other night was fun. Really...amazing. I needed that. But."

"*But,*" he repeats.

"But...I have a lot on my plate now. With everything that's going on with Otto...I don't really have room for another man in my life."

"I respect that. So what about an arrangement?"

I squint at him. "What kind of arrangement?"

He shrugs. "I just think about those poor vibrators you have at home. All those batteries you must run through."

I scoff and roll my eyes. "Wow. Call PETA."

"I was thinking...how about the next time you want to cum, you buzz me instead?"

My eyebrows nearly fly off my forehead. The way he says it...so *casually.* Like he's offering to carry my groceries for me. "Oh yeah?"

Those ice-blue eyes meet mine, and he doesn't drop eye contact. "Any time of day. You need me, I'll be there. And I'll make your thighs shake."

I bite my bottom lip. "I think I might need...a test drive..."

He glances around, and then he slips his hand into mine. He tugs me off the railing. "Follow me."

"I have to stay here, Otto—"

"Is with Grandma." He steadily pulls me forward. "We won't be gone long. I promise."

I should know better. I'm an adult now. I can't afford to be sneaking around with Jason goddamn King.

So why do I follow him around the side of the ferry, to the back, and through a green door marked "Staff"?

Immediately, we're greeted with the loud grinding of the engine. It's a beast—a copper metal thing that churns and hisses in the middle of the room. The wall is covered with levers and gages measuring…who knows?

Next to the instruments are large posters retelling the history of the ferry, with old black-and-white photos of it from way back when.

"Are we supposed to be in here?" I ask. I have to get close to him to raise my voice over the sound of the engine. The smell is rough, like fumes.

Jason crinkles his eyebrows at me. "Whoa. Trouble. Are you a rule follower now?"

"I'm a mom. A mom who doesn't want to spent her night in the brig."

"Relax. They give tours here all the time. No one cares." His fingers link with mine again—his black gloves are soft, and he guides me further inside. We move around the copper monster, and Jason tucks me into a room that is barely the size of a phone booth—it looks like some sort of operations room, maybe, with a desk full of switches and levers. When he closes his lips over mine again, this time I find myself leaning in. I search his mouth with my tongue, tasting his heat, and I can feel the vibrations of his moans.

"I've been thinking about you all day," he murmurs against my mouth, and his words send a tingling straight between my legs.

"What have you been thinking about?"

"Kissing you. Touching you." He bites the tip of his gloved finger and retracts his hand from the fabric. Then he pockets the glove, and I feel his bare hand draw up my thigh. It slides over my legging, then under my dress, until he touches the soft skin there.

His eyes hook me in. "Tell me if you want me to stop."

"Is this a prank? Am I going to end up walking home without my panties?"

A grin coasts his lips. "That would be sweet justice, wouldn't it?"

"Or karma."

"You have trouble trusting people, don't you?"

"You have no idea."

"Close your eyes."

I do. I hear him rustle, and then I feel the softness of his scarf wrap around my eyes. He knots it tightly at the back of my head.

I do a bad job at biting back a smile. I feel his breath at my ear, and then I hear him murmur, "This is part one of a ten-part series called…How I Learned to Let Go and Enjoy Life. A meditation session by Jason King."

I chuckle. "You're such an idiot."

But then he leaves me, and suddenly I feel his breath ghosting my legs. I sit back, leaning into the small covered stool here. His fingertips climb my thighs first, inching up the fabric of my dress, and then I feel his soft kisses on my skin.

My sex clenches with anticipation as his hot breath beats against my thighs. His fingers wrap around my panties and push them to the side. I feel him nuzzle, and then there's that burn of his coarse beard against my sensitive skin. His tongue meets my slit, licking me with slow, languid strokes, as though he's really savoring every bit of my taste.

I nearly hit the wall. I reach back and balance one hand against the desk, the other hand gripping his hair. My legs are wrapped around his shoulders, and I'm helpless here, helpless to do anything except spread my legs further and grind wantonly against each lash of his tongue. He crushes his face between my legs, and I feel a moan leave his lips and vibrate through me. His tongue curls inside of me, his strong nose nestled against my sensitive nub, and I thank God for that obnoxiously loud engine now because there's no way I can stop the loud whimpers that fall from my lips. I'm gasping and panting, my heels digging into his back as he licks me deeply, drinking me in. The scratch of his beard mixed with the softness of his tongue sends strange pleasure-pain signals bouncing around in my brain, and before I know it, I'm tugging his hair at the roots.

"Oh God…" I gasp as I feel that low pinch in my sex. He lets out a low growl of encouragement and doesn't slow down—I don't know *how* he's breathing, but I don't care. All I can think about is reaching that pinnacle under his tongue.

I bite my lip until I taste copper to keep myself from screaming. My orgasm explodes from me, and Jason is relentless, coaxing throb after throb from me with the unending circular movements of his tongue. He licks, and sucks, and nibbles my sensitive skin until I'm trembling and can barely keep myself upright.

Slowly, he pulls away from between my legs and readjusts my panties. I feel him push the scarf up my face, away from my eyes. "Look at me," he demands, and those blues are so bright, so intense, that I can barely catch my breath. His lips are red and wet, and he licks them as he scans my face. "Fuck," he says, "I love the way you're looking at me right now."

"How am I looking at you?" I ask.

"Adoringly." He pets his thumb over my cheek. "I want to make you cum a million times."

I can't help but grin at that. "You'll have to carry me out of here."

"I'm okay with that."

His lips brush against mine, and I reach down to unhook his belt. He stops me, though, his hand on my wrist, and shakes my head. "No, Trouble. That's not what this is."

"What is this?"

"I needed to taste you again, and I couldn't wait another second."

I rest my forehead against his. I feel swoony and

unearthed—maybe it's the powerful orgasm or the boat rocking underneath us, but I can't get my bearings.

"You're going to be bad for me," I inform him.

He grins. "I hope so."

DONOVAN

I've lost Jason. One second, he's next to me; the next, he's gone. He's like a dog—short attention span, throw a Frisbee and it's see-you-later.

I don't much feel like mingling, so I snag a cup of hot cider and find a bench to sit on. I can see Hannsett Island from here, the twinkling Christmastime town it is this time of year. The Lighthouse Medical Center is the brightest spot on the island, a castle on a cliff.

I know a lot of people resent the small towns they grew up in. Not me. Hannsett Island holds some of the worst and best years of my life inside of it. I might be a Scrooge who scowls at the capitalist trap of holiday tradition, but I like routine. I like predictability. I like knowing that, every year, the Hannsett Island Ferry is going to look like Rudolph barfed all over it, and Mrs. Prichard is going to make the same watered-down cider, and Jeff Goins is going to belt carols like his life depends on it just so he can remind everyone later about that time twenty years ago when he *almost* got into Juilliard.

My parents passed on—my mom when I was a teen, my

dad almost five years ago—but Hannsett Island, in its own way, adopted me. It takes care of me, and I take care of it.

I sip the cider. Sure enough, it's watery, and it burns the roof of my mouth, but I'll probably grab another before the night is over just so Mrs. Prichard can waggle her eyebrows and go, *Can't get enough, can you?*

Another loner orbits nearby. Otto has broken away from the festivities. He's leaning against the railing, pressed up on the fake garlands and red ribbon. His bulky helmet slides forward a little as he gets on his toes and peers over the edge to watch the water churn below.

"That's how the mermaids get you," I say, because I'm an asshole, but he's also leaning pretty far.

Otto startles, as though he was doing something wrong, but when he sees me, he gives a shy smile. "I was just looking."

"Wanna keep me company?"

"Okay." He sits down beside me. He tucks his hands in his lap, looking small.

"You like the water?" I ask.

He nods. "Yeah. I love swimming."

"You'd like this place in the summer."

"That's what Mum said." He rocks in place. "My last birthday, we had it at the community swimming pool. It was really fun. I can hold my breath longer than any of my friends."

"Aquaman, over here."

He beams. Fuck, he's a sweet kid.

"When's your birthday?" I pry, because I have a nagging that won't leave. My Miss Clavel senses are tingling, and they have been ever since I first ran into Kenzi and Otto at the medical center.

"May 12th," Otto says.

It doesn't take me long to do the math.

A May birth means he was conceived August or

September, probably. And if we roll it back to August, thirteen years ago…

Kenzi isn't in college, like she said she was. She's on the floor of a tattered sailboat, losing her virginity with her two best friends in the same room.

That jet-black hair. Those ice-blue eyes. It all makes sense now. Why Kenzi left in a rush. Why she never came back. Why she lied over the dinner table about Otto's father.

He's a mini- Jason King.

My brain is going into overdrive to process this information. But Otto is a kid—just a kid—and so I try to reel myself back in and have a conversation with him. "May 12th," I muse. "Let's see…that makes you a Taurus."

Otto's eyes get wide. "What's a Taurus?"

"It's the star sign you were born under. Everyone has one. Taurus is a good one. It's a bull. It means you're strong. Your emotions are powerful."

Otto seems to think about this. "Are you a Taurus?"

"No. I'm a Virgo."

"What's a Virgo?"

"A pain in the butt." I nudge his attention toward the drink cart, where Pearl is glancing around, clearly looking for him. "I think your grandma has another hot chocolate with your name on it."

He gets up but stops after taking a couple of steps. He turns and asks, "Are you going to still be here?"

My chest cinches. I nod. "I'm not going anywhere."

"Okay." Satisfied with that answer, he takes off toward Pearl.

Cute kid.

Good kid.

Fucked-up kid if he's got any of Jason in him.

Speak of the devil…

Jason and Kenzi reemerge from…*wherever* they were hiding, walking up the deck. Jason, who can't lie to save his life, looks not like the cat that ate the canary, but more like the canary that ate the cat.

"How're we hanging?" Jason asks, tossing himself beside me and throwing his arm over the back of the bench and, consequently, around me.

Jason has a habit of taking up enough space for three humans.

"This is a family event," I inform him, "and your breath smells like pussy."

As quickly as he settled, he retreats—Jason pushes off of the bench and starts toward the bathrooms. "I'll be right back."

"Good idea. Wash your beard."

Kenzi takes his spot. Now it's the two of us. The carolers finish their mournful rendition of "Ave Maria," and everyone claps because it's over. Now, the band—the *real* band, some guys from Brooklyn that they had to pay the LIRR fare for, probably—starts up. It's a brass band, and they launch into a jazzy version of "Santa Baby," immediately livening up the audience.

"Are you having fun?" Kenzi asks.

"Living the Christmas spirit," I respond acerbically.

Her eyes are distracted, glancing around worriedly. "Have you seen Otto?"

"Yeah. He's with Pearl." The dim twinkle lights that hang from the ship give Kenzi's skin a soft glow. She rakes her fingers through her thick raven hair, taming it a bit.

I hug my arms over my chest. "About Otto. Anything you want to talk about?"

She blinks at me. "What do you mean?"

I purse my lips. "Jason is crap at math. I'm not. You want to change your story about his father?" She squints at me. I expound. "At dinner. You played with your earring. It's always been your tell."

"Jesus." She exhales the word. "You have the memory of

an elephant." She rolls her hands over her thighs uncomfortably as she looks everywhere except at me. She's looking for an exit.

"I get it," I say, because I have to say something to keep her here. "Eighteen. Pregnant. I'd run, too. Does he know?"

She looks back at me, and I see it now—the fear in her eyes is raw. Palpable. "You can't say anything," she says, her voice a rushed whisper. "Please. It's complicated, you wouldn't understand—"

"*Wouldn't I?*"

Her lips seal at that. The look in her eyes, it's that of a cornered animal.

"Please, Donovan," she repeats. The urgency in her voice is sharp, metallic. It's that feeling of having a razor pressed to your skin—not deep enough to draw blood, just enough to make a dent the flesh. The chilling anticipation of pain.

She thinks I have her heart in my hand. She has no idea that the opposite is true.

"I won't tell him."

Her eyes brighten a little bit. Or maybe it's the Christmas lights twinkling in her irises.

"But..." I add, "as...lovely as the other night was, I think we should stay just friends while you're here."

The light in her dims. But her smile remains intact. "Of course. Whatever you need."

"That's what I need."

She extends a hand. "Friends?"

"Friends."

We shake on it.

"Also. Whatever is going on with you and Jason..."

"It's stupid," she says quickly. "Insane. With...*you know.* Otto. It makes no sense. I know I need to step away."

"Don't," I tell her. "I haven't seen him this happy since Nadine. I think he needs this as much as you do."

"Right." She's looking off to the water again. That ten-mile stare.

"Anyway," I add, "maybe Jason and his big dick will convince you to stay."

She laughs at that. It's a beautiful sound. "Asshole."

"Slut," I retort.

She rests her head on my shoulder, and the both of us look out into the limitless inky black of the ocean, the smattering of stars.

"I missed you," she says, so quietly I almost don't hear it.

My heart kicks. "Missed you, too."

A flurry of movement lands in Kenzi's lap. "Mum!" Otto grabs at her arm, tugging her. "I got to steer the ship!"

Kenzi gasps audibly. "What? That's so cool!"

I can't lie—seeing her in mom mode makes a smile tug at my lips.

Pearl and her fur coat step beside Kenzi and lean over. "It has Fireball in it," Pearl whispers fugitively as she extends a paper cup.

"Pearl, seriously?" Kenzi complains.

"Whoa!" Jason dramatically bursts into the scene—he splays his arms out suddenly, as though he's catching himself from falling, and his whole body sways as if we've hit an iceberg. "Do you guys feel that?"

"Feel what?" Otto asks, entranced.

"The music in your bones!" Jason grins—a dopey fucking grin—and starts snapping his fingers to the beat. "C'mon! Let's dance."

A grin splits across Otto's mouth. Jason—the ball of cheese he is—has gotten everyone excited now. He gets Otto dancing, and Pearl, and takes Kenzi's hand and gets her to her feet as well.

I cross my arms and dig my hands into my armpits. But it's no use. Between the four of them, they manage to drag me off the bench and pull me into their dance circle.

KENZI

My head feels like a lead balloon.

Somewhere between the Fireball cider and an all-night dance party on the ferry, I contracted a hangover. To my credit, I'm a lightweight these days, and it doesn't take much to push me over the edge.

My mouth is dry, and my head hurts. Merry Christmas to me.

I pull myself out of bed, rinse out my mouth, draw the comb through my hair a couple of times, and then mom up. I pull on a pair of Christmas pajamas that are plastered with Rudolph's face—the same pajamas I've worn every Christmas for the past five years in a row.

I exit my bedroom to go wake Otto up, but he's already out of bed. I hear the echo of Christmas music from downstairs, and the smell of coffee is absolutely heavenly.

I go downstairs, and for a second, the sight makes my heart swell.

A hastily dressed Christmas tree with presents for Otto stuffed underneath. Otto in his (matching) reindeer pajamas. Pearl in the kitchen, swearing as she uses an oven mitt to fan the smoke away from burnt pancakes.

It's not much...but it's *ours*. And I wouldn't want Christmas any other way.

"Mum!" Otto shouts when he sees me, then shoots me a glare, thoroughly offended. "You slept through 'Little Drummer Boy'!"

My favorite yearly tradition with Otto—we make a holiday playlist. At first, I made them on my own as a way to unwind from the Christmas stress. But eventually, Otto's peeking over my shoulder turned into "what are you doing?" and "can I help?" and soon enough, we were picking out songs together.

Now, every year, we build the Christmas playlist. Together. And from the sound of it, we're on Dave Matthews' "Christmas Song," which means we're on track four, and yes, I have missed quite a bit.

I slip my fingers through his hair. "Think we can do a replay? Just this once?"

He sighs, as though the effort to rewind is exhausting, as though he's ever known a *real* rewind button, where you had to wait for the cassette tape to spool up. "I guess," he mutters and slumps off his chair to go to my computer, which is connected to the Bluetooth speaker.

I go into the adjoining kitchen and greet my mother with "Merry Christmas."

"Merry yourself. Coffee?" she asks.

"Please."

She pours me a cup, and Otto tugs my leg.

"Mum! Do you want your present?"

I can't help myself—I sit in the kitchen chair and scoop him into my lap. "You are my present."

His hair smells like cookies and little boy.

He wiggles out of my arms. "Gross!"

I make an *ugh* noise. I don't love this age where he won't hug his mother as long as he used to.

But he only takes a couple of steps before he looks back at

me, squints, and then appeases me. He leaps up and wraps his arms around me, giving me a good squeeze.

My heart is too full. My boy is too sweet to me.

"Thank you, buddy," I tell him.

"That's your mushy-stuff limit for today, Mum, okay?" he informs me.

I give him an a-okay. "Got it, bud. Boundaries."

He gives me a wary look before going back to the Christmas tree.

But I don't want to give him boundaries. I want to hold him and never, ever let him go.

Pearl slips behind me, and I feel her hand on my shoulder. She's wearing her terry cloth robe, and she smells like peaches and the coffee in her mug. "He'll be okay, darling," she tells me, in a voice low enough that only we can hear.

I reach up and squeeze her hand. "I know. Everything is going to be okay."

And for the first time in years, when I say those words, I actually believe them.

PART II

NEW YEAR'S: WINTER, 2018

2 2

GROUP TEXT

GROUP TEXT: The Muskrats

Kenzi: Okay, boys. Family friendly activities to do in a Hannsett winter?

Donovan: The aquarium

Jason: Aquarium.

Kenzi: Okay. So not the aquarium?

Jason: We'll take you! Field trip!

DONOVAN

Hannsett Aquarium isn't incredibly popular in the winter, but it's still one of our few local diamonds.

The aquarium doubles as a learning center for budding marine biologists, so it has a lot of interesting, hands-on displays about the local flora and fauna. As soon as we get our tickets and head in, Otto makes a beeline to the touch tank.

I follow him. "Pretty cool, huh?" I ask.

"They're like aliens," Otto says, his voice reverent. He shoves his whole arm in the tank, not seeming to notice when the water climbs his sleeve.

"Yeah, I guess they are pretty strange."

"Touch the stingray!" he says. "It's so weird!"

I snap off my cuff so I can reach into the pool. The water is lukewarm, and I graze my fingertips over the stingray's back. Its skin is smooth but rough to the touch, like leather.

"Hey!" Otto says excitedly. "We match!"

"What do you mean?"

Then he sticks his arm at me, his small hand in a fist, forearm upward. He points to his wrist. The skin there is covered in small, angry pricks—scars from where doctors and nurses have broken into his veins again and again and again to get to the bottom of his ailments.

The scars on my wrist? They're a little different. I like to think of it as an *I Survived Adolescence and All I Got Was This Fucking Baggage* souvenir.

Instead, I smile at him and say, "You're right. We do match."

Then I snap the leather cuff back over my wrist. Out of sight, out of mind.

"I want to swim with the sharks," Jason announces suddenly as he and Kenzi finally catch up to us.

"Me too!" Otto says.

"Yeah? Come here, I'll toss you in the tank."

Otto laughs at that and darts away as Jason comes after him.

I fall in step beside Kenzi. She links her arm in mine, and this feels weirdly comfortable. The four of us on a family outing. We walk through a tunnel that's built in the middle of a tank. On either side of us and above us, through the Plexiglas, small sharks and stingrays and multicolored fish jet back and forth.

"I guess the sharks were on the nice list," Kenzi remarks, pointing to a faux Christmas tree installed in the bottom of the tank.

I groan. "I hate the holidays."

Kenzi slips her hand over my chest. My body is unaccustomed to things like *gentle touches*, and instinctively I feel myself recoil.

"What're you doing?"

"Checking to make sure you still have a heart."

"You're wasting your time. I took that out with my appendix. Just another useless organ holding me back."

She knits her eyebrows. "You're joking."

"Yes. I'm joking. I still have my appendix."

"No…" She stops us suddenly and stands in front of me, forcing my gaze to meet hers. "I mean…the Donovan I knew only wore black and was cynical, sure, but he had a big heart."

I press my lips together. "Yeah, well. When you grow up as the island punching bag, you either give up and roll over, or you grow fangs."

She frowns at that, then moves her hands to my face. She pushes my upper lip back, exposing the gums. "Hold still, vampire. Checking your teeth."

"All the better to eat you with, my dear."

KENZI

t least Donovan is smiling again, so that's progress.

It does worry me, the coal black of his eyes. The years have hardened him.

And who could blame him? I remember how terrible the kids were to him growing up. But still, he didn't leave. He stayed here and stuck it out.

I understand the impulse to turn your heart to stone before someone breaks it again.

But, for a minute, we're kids, playing around the aquarium. I'm baring his teeth, he's struggling to get away from me, when we hear, "—Dr. Donovan?"

I take my hands away from his face, and we both turn to see a woman behind us. She's wearing a ripped band shirt and long dangling earrings.

"Hey," Donovan says, and his smile is genuine. Donovan is a man who reserves his affection only for the deserving, so when he takes her in a light hug, I already know that she's a good person. He peels back and turns to me, motioning to her. "Kenzi, this is Maria. She lives on the island."

"I'm a frequent flyer at the hospital," she says. "Dr. Donovan has saved my life more times than I can count."

"You're a good patient," Donovan says.

"Two years in remission," she says.

"And counting."

She motions to a boy who has his nose flat against the glass. "That's my little monster, Diego. He gets mad when he doesn't get to come with me to the hospital." She tightens her hands into little fists, playing the part of a small child. *"Oooh, but I want to see Dr. Donovan!"*

"He doesn't say that," Donovan counters. But he's smiling.

It's nice to see Donovan like this. Caring. Compassionate. Kind.

Maybe he doesn't have a heart of stone, after all.

"Diego!" she calls, and his head snaps toward us. "Come say hi!"

Diego throws his head back and lets out an exaggerated whine before dragging his heels over to the adults.

"My, uh, monster is around here, too—" I don't have to look far; Otto steps in beside me. I slip my hand to Otto's back. "This is Otto."

"Hi," Otto says.

"Cool helmet," Diego responds.

"Thanks."

My little boy sways a little closer to me. He immediately gets shy around other kids—too often, they tease him for his helmet. Diego seems completely unfazed, though; I imagine growing up on an island of sick people must desensitize him to the weird.

"Have you seen the horseshoe crabs yet?" Diego asks, and Otto shakes his head. "They're sick! C'mon!"

Like that, the boys take off. My heart gets tight in my chest. Has Otto...*made a friend?*

Maria rolls her eyes, but she's smiling. "Can't keep them down, right?"

"Wanna walk with us?" I ask—because my son isn't the only one who can make friends.

Maria joins our small group as we follow a few feet behind the boys, letting them run amok while we dissolve into easy conversation. She tells me she's a housekeeper at one of the large hotels on Main Street during the day and a bartender at the Anchor at night. Diego's father cut and run when her cancer diagnosis became too scary, and we bond over the precarious daily routines of single motherhood.

We walk through the entire aquarium, and when we exit, it spits us out on the docks. They have a couple of impressive old ships tied up to the dock for display, and I notice Otto staring longingly at one of the ships.

I'm not the only one who notices. Donovan asks, "You like the ships, huh?"

"Yeah," Otto says, his eyes not moving. "They're pretty cool."

"You know," I tell him, "Dr. Donovan has a boat of his own. If you ask nicely, maybe he'll take you out on it."

Otto looks at Donovan, wide-eyed. "Can I? Please?"

Donovan grins. "Tell you what—when it gets warmer, I'll do you one better. You can steer it."

But Otto looks crestfallen. "I might not be here when it gets warmer."

My heart misses a beat. "What does that mean?" I ask playfully. "You've got a trip planned that I don't know about?"

He scowls at me. "You *know*."

That sends shards of ice through my chest. "No," I say firmly. "I *don't* know what you mean."

"I don't want to talk about it." He escapes the conversation and goes racing after Jason, who is testing the strength of one of the ropes with Diego.

Maria steps in line with me and sighs. "It's not easy, is it?"

"What?"

"Having the hard conversations. Especially as teenagers? *Ugh.* They don't want to talk about anything! When my diagnosis got worse…Diego and I had to have some very serious conversations. We used to talk about it as if I might *go away* one day, you know? Like it was a trip I was taking…and it would be okay."

Something about this grates me—it feels like a nail file on toenails. Molar-clenching. "We don't have those conversations," I say stubbornly.

She shrugs. "Maybe you should. These things…they're out of our control. It might make him feel better to talk about it—"

"I don't think I need a lesson on how to parent my child— I've been doing pretty well for twelve years, thanks." I'm in a bad mood. A burned-your-tongue-before-your-favorite-meal bad mood.

To Maria's credit, she smiles. "Each to his own," she says, and that's the end of that.

She's being nice. She's only trying to help. But my heart feels like one of those lionfish we saw inside—full of spikes. I try to compromise with "Sorry. I'm just a little on edge—"

"Hey," Maria says, and she puts her hand on my arm. "You don't need to apologize to anyone. Okay? It's okay."

She squeezes my arm, and I feel like I can breathe again.

25

JASON

*I*t clicks now. I see Maria and Kenzi hang out together, and I think to myself—

Holy shit, what is the one way to a single mom's heart?

Her son. Obviously.

If there's anything I know anything about, it's Hannsett Island. So it's easy to walk Otto and Diego through the aquarium. And they're cool kids—I remember what it was like at that age, a bundle of energy and excitement.

Otto, I think, is warming up to me. When we're outside, hanging out by the boats, I show him and Diego how to tie a cleat knot with one of the loose lines hanging on the dock. Otto is a smart kid and gets it right on the first try.

"You're a rock star, buddy. Up top."

I hold up my palm. He squints at me.

"Not falling for *that* again."

Okay. So maybe I still have an uphill battle to climb. I sit down beside him. "What's in the backpack? Hit me with a juice box."

He's got a pink-and-purple backpack, and he pulls it into his lap, unzipping it. "I don't have a juice box."

"What do you have?"

"Mineral water." He pulls the bottle out, holding it out to me.

"Mineral water? What are you, ninety?" I take the bottle and chuck it toward the trash can by the aquarium. It bounces off the rim and nearly hits a woman rolling a stroller.

"Fucking asshole!" she snaps at me.

I cover Otto's ears. "Hey! There are kids here!"

She flips me off.

Whatever. I glance down at Otto. "Hey, you want some ice cream?"

"It's winter."

"Yeah. Best time for ice cream." I walk over to where Kenzi, Maria, and Donovan are standing. They look deep in conversation. "Hey, the boys and I are going to get ice cream. Is that cool?"

Maria shrugs. "That's fine with me."

Kenzi lifts her eyebrows. "Ice cream? It's freezing."

"Never too cold for ice cream."

Inside, I'm saying, *Look at how cool I am with your kid. Wouldn't we be a good pair?*

She hesitates, but then she finally says, "Yeah...okay."

I turn back to the boys. "Onward!" I say, pumping my fist in the air, and they get hyped.

* * *

Ahoy! is, amazingly, one of the tourist shops that stays open in the winter.

They've got all kinds of great winter flavors, too—peppermint bark, gingerbread cookie. I go with old faithful, butterscotch in a waffle cone, but Otto gets a kids' scoop of gingerbread in a cup. Diego gets cookies and cream. The three of us go outside, and I clear the dusting of snow off one of the picnic benches so we can sit down without sticking to it.

Funny to think that, over a decade ago, I shared this bench with Kenzi. Now, I'm eating ice cream across from her son.

He's a shy kid, and his eyes avoid me as he stabs at his cup.

"What do you do for fun?" I ask, trying to break the ice. I don't know why, but I have this unconscionable need to get Kenzi's kid to like me.

He shrugs.

"C'mon. I know you've got something you like to do. Do you play sports? Basketball?"

"I love basketball!" Diego says.

"I can't play basketball," Otto says. "My helmet gets in the way."

"Right—how about drawing? Do you draw?"

"I can't draw."

I point my spoon at him. "I'm hearing a lot of *can'ts* from you. What's that about?"

He shrugs again. Pokes at his ice cream.

"You can put a pencil on paper, right?"

"I guess."

"Then you can draw. That's all there is to it. Look—my dad used to tell me, the only thing that separates winners from losers is that winners never quit. You can't let *anything* stop you from doing what you want to do."

He stares at me for a long time. "Do you think so?"

I wag my spoon at him. "I *know* so. You have to write your own path, you know? No one can do that but you."

He seems to think about that for a moment. There's a change in his expression, like he's really taking my words to heart. Then he puts his spoon and cup down. "I have to use the bathroom."

I point to the shop. "Inside, door on the right."

Otto gets up, swings his backpack over his shoulders, and then heads inside.

I won't lie—this kid thing? I wasn't sure how it was going to work. But I'm actually enjoying it. Otto is a cool kid, and I'm feeling good about myself, like maybe I made a small but important difference in this kid's attitude.

It feels really good to help him out.

Diego launches into a conversation—and, damn, the kid can talk—and I listen and nod for a bit as I dive back into my ice cream, freezing my tongue.

My phone buzzes. It's Kenzi:

[text: Kenzi] How's Otto?

I text her back a picture of the ice cream cones.

[text: Me] Chilling.

She sends a thumbs-up emoji.

I finish off my cone and then toss it. Diego finishes an overlong description of the *Transformers* movie.

Otto has been in the bathroom for—what. Five minutes? Ten?

I decide it's time to check in.

I duck inside. The immediate change from cold to hot is smothering. I go to the men's room and knock on the door.

"Hey, buddy. How's it going in there? Going number two? That's cool—you know, sometimes it helps if you hum. Relaxes the muscles—"

The door swings open, and a grown man glares at me.

"Oh. My bad. Is there a little boy in there?"

The line of his mouth thins. "What do I look like?"

He exits, and I glance in. Single stall…no sign of Otto.

When I get nervous, my blood pressure drops. I get scary calm. I can feel it now, my blood turning to ice, that soul-leaving-my-body sensation. I look around the ice cream shop, but there's only one other customer here. There's a girl behind the counter, texting, and I approach with a smile. "Hey. How's it going?"

Her eyes lift, and I see her do "the look"—a prowling scan down my body—and she suddenly loses interest in her phone. "Can I help you?"

"Have you seen a little boy running through here? Yea high, pink backpack?"

She shrugs. "You're a dad, huh?" She bites her lip. "Do you need a babysitter? I can give you my number."

"You've been a lot of help. Thanks."

I move quickly out of the shop and scan the area. Nothing but picnic benches and a dusting of snow on everything.

The weather is brutal, and there's hardly anyone around, but I stop everyone I see and ask if they've seen a boy that fits Otto's description. Finally, a woman lets me know she saw a kid with a backpack walking down Main Street on his own.

How far could he have gotten? I race down the street, looking everywhere. I try not to think about the cars rolling by. Or the slippery ice on the sidewalk. Or the freezing water on the docks across the way. I try not to let my mind run to the worst-case scenario.

Shit. *Fuck.*

Otto is nowhere in sight.

I bite the bullet. I have no other choice. I pick up my phone and call his mom.

"Hey," I say, "so you're not going to like this—"

* * *

We split up to cover more ground.

Maria and Diego cover the aquarium. Kenzi takes her car back to the house, in case Otto has hitched a ride there.

Donovan and I take his car and drive in circles up and down Main Street. We circle the ice cream shop, around the bookstore, up and down.

"What did you say to him?" Donovan asks.

"I don't know! We were just…talking about normal stuff. And then he went to the bathroom and never came back."

"Define *normal stuff.*"

"Like…taking charge. Writing your own destiny."

"Okay. Maybe leave Guru Jason at home. Sounds a little existential for a kid."

"He started it!"

My stomach is in so many knots, I can barely breathe.

Then I see a flash of pink, and my hand clutches the dashboard. "Stop. There. On the ferry. Pull in. Is that him?"

Across the gravel parking lot of the loading dock, I can see a small child sneak aboard. They're taking the lines off the huge pilings, casting off, when Otto ducks underneath the rope keeping passengers from boarding and scrambles up the ramp.

"I see him," Donovan says and immediately turns left in the parking lot.

The ferry blasts its horn, signaling its departure. He barely brings the car to a stop before I open the door and leap out. Donovan is close on my heels.

The ramp has already been pulled up, and the engine is churning.

"It's pulling away," Donovan says. His voice is thin with panic, and I can practically hear his brain working. "I'm going to find a radio."

"Good idea."

Donovan rushes to the ticket seller's booth, and I can hear him demanding that the guy use his radio to contact the ferryman. I don't have a plan, but I don't stop moving forward.

I race to the very edge of the dock. The street falls away into a steep drop, nothing but a worn rope keeping me from the churning, icy water below.

John, a straggly dude who works the ferry on the off-season, comes up and puts his hand on my chest. "Hey—no more passengers right now. Sorry, Mr. King. It's already departed."

"There's a kid on there," I say. "He's all alone."

John looks at me, then looks at the ferry. "Shit—okay. Here's what I'm gonna do. I'll radio Mike and he'll bring him back on the return trip."

"The *return trip?* I can see him—he's *right there.*"

John grimaces. "Like I said, it's already departed. There's nothing I can do—"

"Otto!" I shout his name, and the kid turns. He's clutching his backpack, and when he sees me, his eyes go wide. "Don't worry, buddy!" I tell him. "I'm coming to get you!"

I push past John and swing my legs over the rope barrier. I'm on the very edge of Hannsett Island now, clutching the rope behind me. The ferry is five, six feet away. Below, a drop into freezing cold water, and the low growl of the engine chopping and churning.

"Yo..." John's voice behind me, "Mr. King, you gotta come back over..."

The passengers on board turn at the commotion and stare at me, bug-eyed.

But the ferry moves forward, inching away from the landing platform, and it's now or never.

I take a breath.

"I can do this," I say out loud, and in that second, I believe it.

I jump. I launch myself across the empty air between the dock and the ferry. There's a scream from someone on the ferry. I scramble, reaching, and I manage to grab the railing. The force of hitting the side of the boat knocks the breath from my gut, but I *made it.*

The ferry is slippery, covered in snow and ice, and my shoes can't get any traction. As I try to strengthen my grip, I feel myself slip, and I just barely catch myself, hanging half on the railing, half on the decorative garland that loops around the siding.

It's a struggle to hold on, and the muscles in my arms quiver. A pair of hands grabs me by the jacket. "Are you insane?" the attendant asks as he hoists. Another passenger helps, and between the three of us, I manage to awkwardly scramble over the railing and finally hit the deck.

I'm short of breath, adrenaline screaming through me. But I'm alive. And there's Otto—looking like a gazelle face-to-face with a lion.

I approach him, put my hands on my knees, and catch my breath. "Whew! Nothing like a hit of excitement to wake you up, right, bud?"

"I'm sorry…" Otto says, his voice shaky.

I need to sit down. I plop down beside him, leaning against the wall, and lift my hand. "I'm not mad," I tell him, because he looks like he needs to hear it. "Just…can you please hold my hand?"

He does. I don't let him out of my sight, and I don't let go of his hand as the ferry chugs along.

JASON

I pull some strings and manage to convince the ferryman to get us back to the dock. Donovan is waiting for us. He looks pissed, though I can't tell if he's mad at me, or Otto, or both.

"Kenzi's waiting at the house," he says. We get in the car.

The excitement of the whole thing kept me warm, and I don't realize how cold I am until I'm in front of the car heater. I put my hands on the vents and glance in the back seat. "You warm enough back there?" I ask him.

"I'm fine."

Otto is somber in the back seat. He stares out the window with the eyes of someone ten times his age.

"I know it's rough, buddy," I tell him. "What you're going through…it's a lot for anyone to handle. But running away isn't the answer."

"Yeah," Otto says, his voice small. Out of the corner of my eye, I see Donovan adjust his hands on the steering wheel.

"Do you want to talk about it?" I ask.

He's quiet for a minute. Then, finally, he says, "Sometimes, I feel like it'd be better if I wasn't here. Then everyone wouldn't have to worry about me so much."

"I understand why you'd want to escape. But sometimes it's good to just think about it, you know?" I continue. "Take a moment. Breathe. Have you tried meditation?"

Suddenly, Donovan hits the brakes, and the car gives a lurch forward. I brace myself with a hand on the dash and look at the road, expecting to see an animal. Nothing. It's empty.

But Donovan's jaw is tight, knuckles white on the steering wheel.

"Hey, you okay?" I ask him.

He exhales tightly. "We're not meditating. We're taking a detour."

"Where?"

But he doesn't answer. He just turns the car around.

He pulls us off the main street. We drive the strip of road that follows the coastline for about five minutes until he pulls into a patch of empty dirt on the side of the road.

"Everyone out," Donovan says.

The three of us climb out. I recognize where we are—we're on the other side of the boatyard, which is closed up for the season. The side of the road is covered in browned and frozen-over dune grass, and Donovan leads us down a small path through the elm trees. It takes us out to the edge of a cliff. We're on the north side of Hannsett, nothing out here except a long stretch of water and red and green buoys blinking in the distance.

"What're we doing here?" I ask.

"This is the Screaming Rock," Donovan says matter-of-factly.

"Why do they call it—?"

Donovan moves to the cliff's edge, buckles down, and screams. The sound he makes is a scream I've only heard once before—when I had to do an emergency amputation on a man who'd gotten tangled in a propeller. It's the sound of limb being severed from muscle, of losing something you should never have to lose, and it sends a chill through me.

Then he stands, immediately collected again, and takes a step back.

"You okay?" I ask him.

He gives me a look—like I'm crazy for asking that question, like it's perfectly normal to have that much pain bottled up inside of you. "Your turn," he says to me.

I shake my head and cross my arms. "I think I'm good. I don't have…all of that."

His mouth turns downward. "Your parents are ruthless. You got married and divorced in the same year. And no matter what you do, you'll never make your father proud. But you're right. You're *good*."

Alright. He has a point.

I shuffle to the edge. Below, I can see waves crashing against the rocks, sending up white foam. He's right. No one can hear you out here.

I take in a deep inhale. I think about Donovan's words. I think about my father, most of all. I imagine I'm inhaling every *yes, sir* and *no, sir*. Every word I held back when he uttered bigoted phrases. Every time I repeated his *own* words to other people—people like Donovan.

And then I let it out. I scream. I can hear the sound carry across the water, echoing back at me.

It's a powerful feeling.

The act feels exhausting and invigorating at the same time. I step away and move back beside Donovan.

"Better than meditating?" Donovan asks.

"No comment."

"Your turn, Otto," Donovan says.

Otto stares at the cliff for a second, eyes wide. I sway beside Donovan. Our shoulders brush. "You think we might've scared him?"

But then he lets out a shout of his own. It's a shrill, pitchy noise, but it's a *damn good* scream. He doesn't stop there, either. He takes a rock out of the ground, chucks it at the water, and shouts, "Screw you, Kevin!"

Donovan and I exchange a look, and immediately, I know we're on the same page. We take Otto's lead and reach down, unearthing small rocks from the hardened ground beneath us. We chuck them at the water, and all three of us shout at the top of our lungs:

"Screw you, Kevin!"

Our voices echo and carry. I imagine them skipping like stones across the flat surface of the ocean, traveling who knows where. Far away.

Otto sniffles. When he turns back to us, I can see his cheeks are splotchy red and wet with tears. "I think I'm ready to go back home," he says.

This kid is so brave. So strong. And my heart cracks wide open in my chest for him.

I give his back a rub. "You've got it, buddy."

We pile in the car, and Otto is still quiet. But he seems in a better mood somehow. He doesn't have that faraway look in his eyes.

The screaming took it out of all of us—him especially—because he falls asleep against the window.

It's getting dark outside now, and Donovan has to put on the headlights on the way to Kenzi's. The weather is picking up a little. Small white snowflakes sparkle in the car's beams.

"That was a good idea," I tell Donovan.

"Yeah, well. The Screaming Rock has been good for me over the years."

"So, what. You'd just go out there and scream?"

"Sometimes. Sometimes I'd curse people out. Or things. *Fuck you, MCATs* was a popular refrain for a minute."

I can picture it: teenage Donovan, the kid who smiled as he cleaned other people's yachts and then went home to a trailer behind the marina. Peddling his bike out to the cliff edge at sunset and screaming his heart out.

A thought nags at me. "Did you ever scream my name?"

His eyes flash over me briefly before latching on the road again. "In your dreams, Hotshot."

DONOVAN

*Y*eah, idiot. I screamed your name. More times than I can count.

* * *

I pull the car into Kenzi's driveway.

She's already out front. She's standing in the snow like a statue, in a sweater that isn't thick enough, her arms wrapped around her, hugging her chest. I doubt she's moved from that spot for the past hour.

Jason rouses Otto. "We're here, buddy."

Otto's lips pull into a thin line, like he's about to face a harsh sentencing. The three of us exit, and immediately, Kenzi crouches in front of Otto and takes his face in her hands.

"Are you okay?" she asks, her eyes scanning him for signs of injury.

"I'm fine," he mumbles, shame-faced. "I'm sorry..."

She pulls him against her, hugging him tightly. "You're okay," she murmurs. "That's all that matters."

The fear in her voice is palpable. She kisses the top of his head and then ushers him inside. "Go inside, okay? Grandma's made dinner."

"Love Missus P's cooking," Jason says. Which is when Kenzi turns on him, and he stops dead in his tracks.

"*You*," she hisses. "You lost him!"

She has all the fury of a mountain lion right now, and even Jason recoils. "Technically, it was more of a runaway situation—"

"Never in my life—"

"Mum!" Otto steps in between them suddenly. "He's right. It was me. I tricked him."

"Otto, go inside," Kenzi says, her teeth chattering, from anger, or cold, or both.

She launches into another tirade on Jason, but my attention is on Otto…

Because all of the color has left his face.

I catch him just before he hits the floor. Otto is twitching, seizing in my arms.

"Oh God." Kenzi immediately drops to the ground beside us. "Otto, honey, look at me—"

"It's okay," I reassure her. I gently lower him to the ground and get him on his side. I take off my jacket and quickly fold it under his head. He jerks, spasming, but this will pass soon.

Kenzi, on the other hand, looks like she wants to die. Her bottom lip is quivering, but she keeps it together.

"Start the car," I tell Jason.

As Jason gets the car going, I do a quick check on Otto's vitals. When his body unwinds from its rigid state, I inspect his face and peel down his eyelid.

That's when I notice it. The yellow in his eyes.

KENZI

"Focal segmental glomerulosclerosis."

Donovan spouts off the words like they mean something to me. It's another string of hospital gibberish. Words that sound like a life sentence and feel like weights on my heart.

We're in a glass room, separated from the waiting room, which I guess is designed to give loved ones a little privacy while receiving hard news. I don't feel safe, though. I feel like a goldfish on display.

"What does it mean?" I ask.

At least Donovan's eyes are kind, familiar, and they never leave me. He sits calmly in the chair across from me, and I hug my arms around my chest.

He translates. "It's a rare disease that causes benign cysts to build up in the kidneys and prevents them from working properly."

"So his brain…?"

"Completely normal. The seizures came from the toxic buildup that occurred when the cysts overpowered his kidney function, not from any damage to his brain."

Hospitals, I find, are like intricate games of Whack-A-

Mole. As soon as one problem goes away, another one pops up.

Donovan is incredibly calm and level as he delivers the news. I try to match his energy, but I feel like I have pins stuck in my throat.

The next question I ask is selfish. "What causes it?"

There's a small, quiet part of me that is constantly terrified that I've done this to Otto.

Donovan's brown eyes are gentle. "It's inherited. The reason it's so rare is that *both* sets of parents have to have a recessive abnormal gene."

I blink. "Do I have it, too?"

"Not exactly. You could go your whole life without knowing you have a recessive gene. To you, it's normal, and your body functions as it should. It's just when your genes come in contact with a similar carrier that you have a perfect storm."

I let the information sit with me. "If only one of us had the gene…"

"It's hard to say," Donovan reasons. "Otto might've shown similar signs, but the chances are slimmer."

"So what you're saying is…really bad things happen when Jason and I procreate?"

"And really good things," Donovan reminds me.

The news has me off-kilter. I feel myself sway briefly in my chair, and I grip the armrests for something to ground myself. "What comes now?"

"There is no treatment," Donovan says, "but with medication, we can manage the damage to his kidneys. In Otto's case, I'd want to get him on the transplant list immediately."

"I'll donate," I say quickly.

"We'll test you," Donovan says. "But there's no guarantee you're a match. Finding the right match…it can take years. In the meantime, we should start looking at getting him dialysis a couple times a week."

I'm underwater. My brain is swimming. "Please give me good news."

Donovan reaches out and takes my hand. He squeezes it. "He's young. He's strong. He's got the best team of doctors on his case. Now that we know what it is, we can properly treat it instead of throwing darts at the wall and hoping something sticks. I know it's scary to hear…but this is a step in the right direction for him."

His words should be reassuring. But my skin feels numb. My face feels hot. And my insides are screaming.

It's me and Otto. Against the world.

I pull my hand out of his and tuck it into my lap, folding into myself. Donovan is warm and gentle right now, but his closeness feels like an acid burn on my skin. "I need to see my son."

Donovan nods, understanding. He doesn't try to touch me again. "Let's go."

* * *

Jason is sitting outside Otto's room. Loyal watchdog, guarding.

When he sees us approach, he stands immediately. He has concern etched all over his face. "How is he?" he asks.

I know what he's trying to do—he's worried. He cares. But he's in the wrong place at the wrong time. The anger inside of me is whip hot and wants to lash out at someone, and right now, Jason is the perfect target.

"How *is* he?" I repeat. "You mean, now that he's not lost on a strange island in the middle of winter?"

He cringes. "I know. I'm sorry. I turned my back for one minute. It won't happen again."

"No. It won't." Jason is a full foot taller than me, but I find myself going toe-to-toe with him, all blazing fury. "I don't care if it was one minute or one second. It just proves what I knew all along—every time I *start* to trust you, you do something so goddamn thoughtless or inconsiderate. You haven't changed at all."

"Kenzi." Donovan says my name as a gentle chastisement.

But Jason shakes his head. "It's okay." His mouth draws into a thin line. "You're angry. You have every right to be. But you know I wouldn't let anything happen to Otto."

What I *know* doesn't matter. My feelings are in full force right now. The backs of my eyes are stinging, but I *will not* cry in front of him.

I can't get the thought out of my head:

If I had been with anyone—*anyone*—else, Otto might be healthy right now.

The perfect storm. That's what Jason and I are. That's what we'll always be.

"I don't want you anywhere near me or Otto," I tell him, my voice trembling. "Do you understand?"

Jason doesn't say anything to that. The blue eyes—they just look hurt. And confused.

And they look so much like Otto's that I want to scream.

"Stay away from us," I tell him and go into the hospital room to be with my son.

DONOVAN

*Y*ou know the only thing worse than a breakup between two friends?

A breakup between two friends who weren't even *technically* dating in the first place.

I'm trying to unwind with *Bladerunner* and a bottle of wine. Feeling nostalgic, I guess, I picked up a bottle of nail polish on my way home on a whim. Now, I'm coating my thumbnail in black. You can take the boy off Myspace, but you can't take the Myspace out of the boy. It's relaxing in a soul-calming way. Maybe there is something to this mediation shit Jason keeps talking about.

Meanwhile, Jason is having an existential crisis.

He's stomping around the house. Going from the bathroom to his pull out bed to the bathroom again.

Jason walks around barefoot. Constantly.

I'm pretty sure if it wasn't unsanitary, he'd walk through the hospital barefoot too if he could.

Every time he comes home, the first thing he does is shuck off his shoes and socks, like he's living in some monk's temple.

I, on the other hand, walk around in my boots until I remember they're attached to my feet.

And I guess, in a way, that's an easy way to describe us. Jason leaves his baggage at the door. I carry all the dirt and grime of my life around with me, until my bandages become twisted badges of honor.

"I'm going to do it," Jason says. Through the open bathroom door, I can see his frame hunched over the sink. He's staring himself down in the mirror, an electric shaver in hand.

I can tell this is a big deal for him. You can always tell what's going on with someone by the state of their hair.

He's been holding on to that beard since his divorce with Nadine. I get it. It's the symbolic act of letting go of a ghost.

"Okay," I say.

Those blue eyes flicker from the mirror to meet me. "You're not going to convince me out of it?"

I heave a sigh. "Jason—and I can't stress this enough—I don't care about your facial hair. Do what you want."

He stares back at the mirror. His lips press into a thin, determined line.

"Time to make some changes," he says. Then the buzzing starts.

* * *

Kenzi isn't any better.

I see her at the hospital when she comes in for Otto's visits. Or, sometimes, after my shift I'll go to her place and invite myself to family dinner. Family movie time. She seems grateful for the extra pair of hands, anyway—Kenzi could never admit it, but she could use the help. Pearl isn't exactly one to get her hands wet doing the dishes.

But every time we're alone, she immediately launches into another conversation about Jason. Currently, her favorite thing to do is list all the reasons she despises him, each reason pettier than the last.

I know what she's doing. She's trying to put some distance there. Trying to convince herself out of her feelings for him. And I let her, because it's what she needs. Tonight, the agenda on the table is:

"—and it *genuinely* bothers me that he doesn't jerk off."

"Uh-huh." I scrub caked mac and cheese off a plate. "What about it bothers you?"

She sighs, like it's obvious. "He *needs* other people for his own pleasure. It's codependent."

"Or," I counter, "maybe he just values intimacy over orgasms."

She squints at me, like I've just stabbed her in the back. "Seriously?"

I shrug. "Just a thought. But what do I know. I jerk off every time Brad Pitt has a new movie out. Speaking of." I dry off my hands on a dish towel with a mermaid on it. Then I reach into my saddlebag hanging off the back of a chair and hunt around until I find what I'm looking for. I pull out a small, thin, silver box with a ribbon around it and hold it out to Kenzi. "Here. I couldn't find a good time to give you this. Merry Christmas."

She blinks at the gift like it might grow teeth and bite her. "You didn't have to."

"I'm aware."

She starts to pull on the ribbon, but I quickly interject. "Open it when you're alone. Not here."

She presses her lips together in a smile. "You're the worst. Now I need to get you something."

"Please don't."

"What? Why not?"

"Knowing you it will be something…bizarre."

"Hmm…how about a taxidermized frog? Wearing a top hat and a cane. Like the WB frog, remember?"

It takes everything within me not to smile. "Case in point."

She presses a kiss to my cheek. Her scent lingers, though—an intoxicating hint of peach.

"You're sweet," she says.

"Keep that to yourself."

Out of the corner of my eye, I see Otto's small figure approach. I put a little distance between Kenzi and me, relaxing into the counter instead, and dry my hands on a dish towel.

"Hey, Otto," I say, alerting Kenzi to his presence. "What's up?"

He's already tucked into his pajamas: a cozy-looking long shirt and pant set covered in rocket ships. He hangs on the back of a chair. He rocks back and forth, rocking the furniture with him—in kid language, he's *playing it cool*. "Nothing. I was just seeing if you wanted to watch a show with us."

"What're we watching?"

He bunches his shoulders high around his ears. "Whatever."

"Hmm. Does that mean I get to pick?"

He nods eagerly. I imagine anything I pick will probably be better than the reruns of *Golden Girls* Pearl has put him through.

"Okay," I say. "Knock, knock."

Otto perks up. "Who's there?"

"The Doctor."

"Doctor Who?"

"Exactly. Your education starts now. We start with season one."

KENZI

Three episodes of Dr. Who later, and Donovan and Otto are still swathed in the blue-light flicker of the television.

They've taken over the love seat, Donovan hunched forward, watching intently. Otto is mesmerized, his mouth partly agape. He's tired, though, I can tell because he's half-slouched against Donovan and, toward the end of the episode, his eyes start to droop and he cuddles the quilted blanket tighter around his little body.

I'm curled up in the adjacent lounger. I spend more time watching *them* than I do watching the TV.

When the credits roll, I finally break up the fun. "Alright, buds," I say. "We should probably think about getting ready for bed."

"One more," they whine in unison.

I lift my eyebrows pointedly at Donovan.

Donovan seems to remember he's an adult because he nudges Otto. "Your mom's right—we've got to leave some surprises for tomorrow. C'mon. Let's get to bed."

Otto looks morose about it. He sighs dramatically (I know, I'm the anti-fun mom, everything is the end of the world) and tosses the quilt off himself before melting out of the love seat.

Before he goes up to his room, he stops and turns around to look at Donovan.

"Are you coming back tomorrow?" Otto asks.

Donovan's eyes flicker up to me. "Sure. If it's okay with your mom."

"Of course. But Dr. Donovan can't come back if he doesn't leave." I muss up Otto's hair and press a kiss to the top of his head. He wiggles out of my grasp.

"G'night, Dr. Donovan."

"Sweet dreams."

Otto trudges to his bedroom. I walk Donovan out. He pulls on his coat and then hangs in the doorway, wrapping his scarf around him.

"You know you don't have to come back tomorrow."

"I know I don't *have* to," Donovan says. "I'd like to."

"Are you sure you can't stay?" I ask him. "I can make the couch."

"I'm positive. I have to put the other child to bed."

"Jason. Right."

"He misses you, you know."

"Yeah…well. Maybe he should've thought about that before he let my only child run off on his own."

Donovan is bundled up now, but he doesn't leave right away. Instead, he offers, "Just…throwing this out there. And then I'll leave you alone for the night."

He's got his best-friend voice on. I cross my arms over my chest, bracing. "Alright…"

"Is it *possible* that you're looking for reasons to hate Jason…because hating him is easier than telling him the truth?"

I button my lip. "It's—"

"Complicated. I know." He shrugs, then says, "Think about it."

Then he steps forward and brushes his lips against my cheek. I feel the scrape of his stubble. The warmth of his breath.

"Good night, Kenzi," he says, and his voice is a low murmur, a lion mountain's purr.

"Night," I say.

I lean against the doorway, hugging myself. The cold is sharp, and it slices through my clothes, but I stay outside until his car pulls out of the driveway and vanishes down the road.

I put Otto to bed, which takes no time at all since he's already half-asleep. I quietly close his door behind him and go back downstairs.

The TV has gone into screensaver mode, slowly changing through *you might like* science fiction titles.

I click the remote, and it goes dark. I realize all at once that there's nothing left to do. Normally, I'd use this time to do the dishes, but Donovan has already taken care of those. The dishwasher is humming quietly to itself. The counters are cleaned.

The house is taken care of. Otto is safe and sound. Pearl is asleep. And, for a minute, I'm all alone, with nothing to do.

The concept is foreign. I don't know what to do with this stolen time I have. I'm too wired for bed just yet. I go into the kitchen and uncork the bottle of red Donovan left. There's enough for a glass, so I help myself to it.

That's when I remember—Donovan's gift. It sits on the counter inconspicuously.

After all, Donovan did specify *alone*. The box is about the length of a pencil and neatly wrapped with silver wrapping paper. On the front of the box, he's cut out a square of wrapping paper, folded it, and tapped it into the shape of a note which reads, *For the woman who treasures her alone time.*

A delicious sliver of childlike excitement runs through me.

My nails make quick work of the wrapping. It's a small black box, and when I open it up, what's inside makes me smile.

That bastard. What was I expecting? Jewelry? Something sweet?

No. Donovan gets me what he knows I'll want.

It's a small, silver vibrator.

I pick it out of the velvet-cased box. I've become something of a connoisseur of vibrators—rabbit vibrators, bullet vibrators, butterfly vibrators—and this one seems simple enough. The surface is metallic, smooth, and I know from experience that it'll slide well once it's wet.

The top screws off, so I untwist it and check—yep, he's already installed batteries. Bless him. According to the instructions, it's also waterproof. Doubly blessed.

There's a discreet black button on the top of it, and I turn it on.

Immediately, my nipples go tight underneath my shirt.

Holy cow, the vibrations are powerful. I press it to the tip of my finger, and it makes my whole hand tremble.

Already, I feel my panties grow damp at the prospect of playing with this.

It has been a long time since I've indulged in some me time…

And I do have the night to myself…so what's stopping me?

Fuck it.

I throw out the wrapping and tuck the vibrator into my pocket. I take my glass of wine and go upstairs into my room and into the bathroom.

I lock the door and draw a bath.

I'm my own best boyfriend. *You've had a long day, Kenzi… you deserve a hot bath, a glass of wine, and an earth-shattering orgasm.*

I get out of my clothes, drop them in the hamper, and

adorn a fluffy robe instead as the water goes. I turn Pandora on on my phone, low, to a chill, bluesy station. There's a small side table, and I carry it over to the bathtub, prepping. On the table sits my phone/radio, my glass of red, and my shiny new silver friend.

I let the claw-foot tub fill up until water is trickling into the spillway.

When I step in and ease myself into the tub, the water is almost too hot. I have to slowly lower myself into it, and my skin tingles at the change from the winter-cold to the steamy bath. I let my body adjust, loving the steam on my face, the way the water melts the ache from my shoulder blades and lower back.

I lean my back against the tub, close my eyes, and exhale a deep sigh. My breasts rise slightly out of the water, and so do my knees when I part them. I don't need to warm up, but I tease myself anyway, drawing my fingertips over my pebbled nipples. I dip my hand under the water, over the softness of my belly, the small patch of hair between my legs. When I finally reach my core, I can feel how swollen my nether lips are already.

Water drips from my fingers and onto the side table as I pick up the vibrator. I dip it underneath the water and press it between my thighs, teasing myself a little. The metal slides effortlessly against the slipperiness between my lips.

I close my eyes. My thoughts drift to the ferry ride. Jason's hands on my hips. The curve of his grin. The way he looked at me like I was his entire world.

I click the button, and immediately my toy jumps to life. I gasp as the powerful vibrations rocket through me. I click the button again and find that it has different speeds—slow, medium, and fast.

God bless you, Donovan.

I leave it on the slow speed at first, letting my body get used to it.

Already, it's making my toes curl. I forgot just how wonderfully good this felt.

My legs lock, and I turn it up a speed. I swallow back a moan as pleasure lashes through me.

My cunt is raw and sensitive, and when I slip the vibrator inside me, the sensation is so good, it's almost painful. I jerk and have to bite my lip to keep from crying out.

My fantasies are running wild. In my mind, I'm back in the dark, shadowed dance floor of my favorite club in London. Except Jason is there. We're dancing. Swaying together.

Between the crowd of bodies, I imagine Jason slipping his hand between my legs. I imagine he tells me how much it turns him on to turn me on, as his finger crooks deep inside of me and he fingers me, right there on the dance floor.

I'm soaking the vibrator, and it's hard to get any friction now as it slides inside me. I trace it up my slit, and the rounded tip nuzzles directly against my swollen clit.

Then I test fate and turn it up. High speed.

I can't hold back; I gasp loudly. My cunt clenches, and my nipples ache as hot bursts of pleasure rocket through me. I'm getting tighter, closer, and I close my eyes tightly, back on that dark dance floor, and I see—

Donovan. The smoldering look in Donovan's deep eyes. Donovan, who takes my face in his hands. Who brushes his painted thumb against my bottom lip. Who whispers darkly in my ear, *Cum for me, Kenzi.*

My legs quiver as I brace my heels against the sides of the tub. I'm thrashing, water splashing, as I torture my clit with powerfully delicious vibrations, drowning in the waves of my own pleasure. I'm there, I'm *right there*, and I grind against the edge. My want tastes like metal, and I choke on my breath.

"Kenzi."

"*Donovan...*" I moan.

"Kenzi!"

No—wait—that voice isn't coming from my fantasies. It's coming from *outside*. And it sounds like…

"Jason?"

I quickly turn off the vibrator—or try to; I'm still getting used to it, and it takes a couple of clicks of the button to get it to stop its delicious humming.

My cunt is fluttering on the screaming edge, pulsing weakly, painfully. So close to the mind-blowing orgasm it wanted, I could cry.

But this is…weird.

I get out of the tub and wrap my robe around my wet body. I unlock the bathroom door and glance around, trying to find the source of…

"Kenzi! Over here!"

I snap my gaze to the source of the noise and…*you've got to be kidding me.*

There's Jason. And his stupid smile. In the flesh.

Crouching on a tree branch outside my bedroom window.

Immediately, I fly to the window, unlock it, and shove it open. "What the hell are you doing?" I hiss.

"So, it turns out, this is harder when you're not a teenager," Jason says. The tree is half-white with snow, and he does look a little unsteady, clutching the thick branch with red, cold-bruised fingers.

"Are you *insane*?"

He falls to the side a little, and my heart lurches as his grip on the branch wavers. "Whoa!" Then he grins. "Just kidding."

I nearly shut the window in his face, when he adds, "But really. It is pretty slippery."

"Get inside. Now."

Mom voice. I reach out a hand, and he manages to shimmy over the branch. He grips the window frame and pulls himself the rest of the way, ungracefully half falling, half climbing inside. He's a bull in a china shop, and his tall frame bounces against my dresser, making the whole thing shudder.

"Sorry," he says and then gets to his feet. He shivers dramatically, shoving his hands under his armpits. "It's cold out there, did you notice?"

"You're a child." I'm spitting mad. "An actual child."

His eyes flicker over me. "I hope I didn't...uh. Interrupt anything."

He's staring at my hand, which is when I realize...*dear God*. I'm still holding *it*.

In my rush to save the Jason-cat from the tree, I completely forgot to put away the vibrator.

I go to shove it in my robe pocket, but my thumb accidentally bumps the button. It jumps to life in my hand, and I swear, my face getting hotter as I have to cycle through every *goddamn setting*—which two seconds ago I loved and now I loathe—in order to get the thing to stop again.

"Looks like fun," Jason says, and I hate that he approves of it.

"It's the middle of the night!" I snap as I finally manage to wrestle the vibrator into my pocket. "In winter! You can't just...climb into people's bedrooms! If you'd gotten hurt..."

"Would you have cared?" he asks bluntly.

"Of course I care!"

"You're not answering my calls. Or texts."

"You know, some men would take that as a hint..."

Was that too harsh? Some of the boyish mischief dies from his eyes. He sobers up then, giving a nod. "I know. And if you want me to leave you alone after this...I will. I promise."

My boiling rage lowers to a simmer. When you peel back his reckless and silly antics...it's clear that he's just uncomfortable.

"I want to invite you to our New Year's party."

"What in the hell would make you think I'd want to go to a party with you?"

"Because there's something here. I know there is. And I need you to give me another chance. Just one. Please."

"Oh, go with him, Kenzi!"

I nearly scream. I swivel around to see my mom standing in her own robe, peeking in through my cracked-open bedroom door.

Jason lifts his hand in a half wave. "Hey, Missus P."

"Hello, darling. Did you shave your beard?"

"Yes, ma'am."

"It's a *lovely* look."

"Thanks—"

I throw up my hands. "Oh my God! Let's just invite the whole island to my bedroom!"

Jason pulls his lips together. "Ten p.m. At the Anchor. Totally casual. Locals. Karaoke. You can bring Otto." Those blue eyes drink me in. "Just think about it. All I ask."

"I'll think about it," I say.

But I keep my arms tight around my chest. I'm not budging.

"Okay." That, at least, has brought a little bit of the hopeful spark back to his eyes. He jabs his thumb over his shoulder toward the window. "Well, I'll just see myself out—"

"The *door*, please. Like a human."

Jason slips past me. He gives Pearl's shoulder a pat as he exits. "G'night, Missus P."

"You should go," my mother urges in an urgent whisper as I take the door from her, gently closing it. "I'll watch Otto. It will be perfect—"

"I'll think about it. *Good night*, Pearl."

Finally, I close everyone out.

I exhale. Count to three.

I go back into the bathroom. My wineglass is still there, the bath still drawn.

I'm wound tight. Frustrated. But the mood is killed, and my bath is cold.

I feel rotten. Jason—kind, sweet Jason—is doing everything in his power to get me back. But his father's shadow hangs over me like a cloud. Meanwhile, I nearly humped myself to a mind-blowing orgasm with Donovan on my brain.

This complicates things.

I pull the plug on the tub, letting the bath drain out.

KENZI

’ve made up my mind not to go to the New Year's Party.

Otto and I are spending it together, snuggled up on the couch with bowls of ice cream, waiting for the ball to drop. The news flashes from various spots all around the world, and we watch people celebrate as new anchors get progressively drunker.

Pearl, however, keeps dropping hints. She's wearing a sequined dress and a paper crown with the numbers 2019 across her head and clicking around the house in kitten heels. My mother will always dress up for a party—even if that party takes place entirely in the living room.

"Look at what I found!" she says. She holds up a velvet emerald-green dress.

"Where did you find that?" I ask.

"At the bottom of a suitcase you have yet to unpack," she says triumphantly.

"For the last time—*please* stop going through my things. And thank you."

"It's pretty," Otto says, and I muss his hair.

"Thanks, buddy. Maybe I'll wear it later."

"Or you could wear it tonight," my mother presses. "To a certain party."

"Are we going to a party?" Otto asks.

"No, buddy. It's just us tonight."

"Okay. Cool." He yawns—a big yawn. "Because I'm thinking about bed soon maybe."

My poor boy has been exhausted lately. The dialysis has eradicated the seizures, but it also knocks him out. It's 10:00 p.m. and he can barely keep his eyes open.

I slip my fingers through his hair. "Don't you want to stay up and watch the ball drop, buddy?"

Otto shakes his head, blinking heavily. "Just tell me how it ends…"

The kid is exhausted. I can't blame him.

I'm tired, too. Tired and wired, all at the same time. Even after I read to Otto and tuck him in, I feel on edge. I try brewing a cup of tea, hoping the warmth of it will kick in and lull the frenetic parts of my brain to a tamer state.

No luck.

"Do you think Anderson Cooper is single?" my mother asks as she watches the TV and fans herself with her 2019 crown.

My eyes land on the dress. She's draped it across the chair, and now it's sitting there. Waiting for me.

I tighten my fingers around my mug. I can feel my mother's eyes on me, questioning. I glance at the clock.

It's only eleven. There's still time…

Maybe I can turn these flats into glass slippers yet.

"Screw it," I mutter. I lift the dress from the chair.

"That's my girl!" Pearl smiles.

DONOVAN

"Do you think she'll come?"

Jason hasn't taken his eyes off the door all night.

The Anchor is packed. Regulars. Doctors off shift. Fishers and seasoned boaters. I prefer this crowd over tourist season. They drink stouts, laugh heartily, and have that same sun-leather skin my dad had.

The Anchor is a haven for locals, which is why it's my go-to spot. The walls are a dark, polished oak, decorated festively with mistletoe and pine. They've got booths, round tables, a pool table, and a couple of muted TVs with an eye on the Times Square ball drop. There's also a stage, where they're doing karaoke all night long. So far, it's been a lot of Billy Joel and Jimmy Buffett.

I've been hanging out by the bar, where Maria is bartending. But it's hard to enjoy my discounted cabernet and the fourth rendition of "Piano Man" when Jason keeps pacing, looking for Kenzi.

I haven't seen him this glum in a while. He looks good tonight—he's wearing a button-up that stretches across his biceps, top buttons released enough to show off a sliver of chest underneath. Black pants that rest snug on his hips.

He could have his pick of the litter for his New Year's kiss. He's already gotten lingering stares from every woman at the Anchor.

But he's laser focused, eyes on the door. Waiting for her to walk in.

"She'll come, right?" he says. "I mean, it's New Year's."

"You need a fucking fidget spinner," I tell him. "Settle down."

He slumps against the bar. Looking like a kicked dog.

I sigh. "Enjoy yourself. Sing a song. That will make you feel better."

"I'm not in the mood."

And then the song changes—an instant rapid-fire drum solo—and the light turns back on in Jason's eyes.

"Oh fuck! I love this song!"

Sometimes, he has the attention span of a toddler. Just need to distract him with a shiny set of keys to get him to perk up.

"Up next, Jason King with 'One Week,'" the announcer says.

Jason blinks at me. "Did you put me on the set?"

I shrug, answering without answering. "Knock 'em dead."

His grin lights up his whole face. "Love you, man."

"Love you, too."

I lean back against the bar and watch him take the stage.

It doesn't matter that his heart is hurting. Jason King always comes alive for an audience. He takes the micro-phone, gets into a Michael-Jackson-esque pose, and immedi-ately the Anchor gets noisy with whoops and claps.

I can't help the grin that climbs my face as I watch him light up the crowd.

"Listen to him," I hear a grumble behind me. "Sounds like a bag of cats getting choked to death."

I turn. Nick is at the bar, along with two of his pug-faced cronies. Nick is one of the few locals. He and Jason used to be best friends growing up. Only Jason changed. Nick never did. He's still the same bitter bully he's always been. Only now he works as a waiter at the marina restaurant and shucks clams in the summer—a lifestyle that makes him rougher and constantly smelling like cigarette smoke. Currently, he's hunched over his pint, cackling at Jason's expense.

Jason might be an idiot. But he's *my* idiot.

Only I get to insult him.

"Hey." I flash Nick a razor-sharp smile. "Be like Bambi."

He narrows his eyes at me. "What?"

"If you've got nothing nice to say, shut your mouth?"

"Or what?" His hand tightens around his pint.

Smoothly, I inform him, "I can break your fingers and reset the bones in thirty seconds as though nothing happened. Don't test me."

The color falls from Nick's face. "Whatever," he says. I relish in the scent in his fear as he sulks away.

"Since when did you become the one who threatens violence?"

To my left, Kenzi appears. As if out of nowhere. My heart kicks.

"You showed up." I state the obvious, like an idiot.

She leans against the bar and lifts her eyebrows at me. "I thought beating people up was Jason's schtick."

"Yeah, well. He became a guru."

"And you?"

"The student became the master."

Her eyes following Jason's performance across the stage. "He wasn't lying about the karaoke. Is he…really going to take off his shirt?"

"Yeah. He's a performer."

God, she looks beautiful. The deep green of her dress

brings out the color of her eyes. She pulled her dark hair back in a messy braid, like it was something she whipped together while running out the door. Something about the rawness of her look right now strikes a chord in me.

Maria comes over, and the two women greet each other. "Happy New Year."

"Happy New Year! Where is Diego?"

"With his aunt. What can I get you?"

"A pinot noir, please."

"Put it on my tab," I tell Maria.

"Thanks." Kenzi's gaze turns back to Jason. He's in the grand finale, and he's got half the bar on their feet, singing along with him. His charisma is infectious. Despite herself, a smile reaches her eyes. "God, he's something, isn't he?"

"He is that." I side-eye her. "Are you going to sing one?"

She raises her eyebrows at me. "Me? No way. I still have the worst stage fright."

"Do you still write?"

At that question, she looks at me blankly. "What?"

"Your music."

She blinks and then says, "No one's asked me about that in a while. Uh...no. Not really. I guess other things just... took precedence."

"You should get back into it," I say, and she scoffs, so I press, "It was really good."

"For a teenager."

"For anyone."

There's that smile, a little of Kenzi's old mischief trickling back in. "Hey," she says, "thank you for my present."

"Good, huh?"

She smiles. A secret smile that makes my blood rush.

"Very," she says.

"Good. Now I know what to get for White Elephant next year."

She laughs at that. All at once, it hits me in the chest—

Jason wasn't the only one waiting on pins and needles for her to show up. I'm glad she's here.

"Kenzi!" Jason finishes his set and practically barrels through the crowd to get to her. Her back goes stiff when he approaches, and he comes to a halt in front of her, hair slightly mussed from his performance, big, dopey grin on his mouth. He took off his shirt during the performance, and now it hangs in his hand. His muscles practically glisten with the light sweat. "Fuck, you look good," he says, which is when I realize I wish I'd told her that.

"Thanks," she says. She tucks a stray strand of hair behind her ear. I can tell she's trying to look anywhere but his bare chest.

"Is Otto here?"

"He had a long day. Went to bed early."

"What's the saying? When the mice are asleep or something?" He waves over Maria. "Let me get you a drink."

She taps her glass. "Already got one."

"That's cool. Maria! Shots! Please and thank you."

He's a ball of energy, a Labrador with a tennis ball. I've never seen him trip over his feet to impress a girl before. I rein him in when Maria pours all three of us tequila shots. Already, my liver hurts, but I take it anyway. "C'mon. Let's toast."

"What are we drinking to?" Kenzi asks. "The new year?"

"And the old years," Jason responds.

"The return of the muskrats," I say, and they both agree to that with a "hear, hear" as the three of us clink glasses.

33

JASON

*N*ow that Kenzi is here, the New Year's party is in full swing.

I redress. We drink. We catch up. We laugh.

It feels fucking fantastic to have her here.

I try to convince her to get onstage, but she shies away from it, and Donovan says he'll only go up if they let him sing Blink-182's "Happy Holidays, You Bastard." They will not.

Upon Kenzi's second drink, however, she says she'll "look" at the set list. I see her eyes light up at a song.

"Do it," I say. "Whatever it is. Just do it."

She bites her lip. "Fuck it," she says and then puts her name down.

I've never heard Kenzi sing before. But, as it turns out, she *slays* Fiona Apple's "Criminal." She laughs nervously at first, but by the second bridge, she's closed her eyes and melted into the song. She cradles the microphone like a pop star and shimmies her shoulders to the beat.

It's beautiful to watch her blossom. I'm completely, irrevocably charmed. I howl in support when she ends, and Donovan wolf whistles.

Kenzi returns to the bar, but first she stops in front and bows dramatically. Donovan and I give her a second round of applause.

"Okay—that was ridiculous," Kenzi says. "I'm going to launch myself into the sun now." But she's grinning while she says it.

"Hold on." I put my hand on her shoulder. "Before you do that—I have to get your signature. My friend Kenzi is a *huge* Fiona Apple fan. She's going to be so pissed she stayed home and missed out on seeing you live."

"Shut up," she says, but the compliment just widens her grin. "What time is it?"

Donovan checks his watch. "Ten 'til."

The music changes. It's a slow, intimate number.

Perfect timing. I extend my hand toward Kenzi, palm upward. "May I have this dance?"

She wrinkles her nose. "You are so corny."

"That's not a no."

"It's not." She takes a sip of her wine and then gives it up, putting it on the bar with Donovan.

"Oh yeah, don't mind me," Donovan says. "I'll just…watch the drinks."

Kenzi takes my hand. Her palm feels small and hot in mine.

"Do I make you nervous?" I ask. The bar doesn't have a dance floor, but it does have a small clearing of tables, and I take her there and pull her against me.

"You make me a lot of things," Kenzi non-answers and looks up at me from under her long eyelashes.

I rest a hand at the small of her back and take her hand in mine, leading us in a gentle sway.

"Is this okay?" I ask.

"Yeah," she murmurs.

Close together like this, she feels small. The top of her

head just comes up to my clavicle, and I cradle her against me. The need to protect her is a living, breathing animal beside me—but protect her from *what*, I haven't figured out yet.

All I know is I want to make her feel safe. Always. When I feel her soften and relax against me, my heart tests the limits of my rib cage. I rest my chin lightly on the top of her head. She smells like strawberry shampoo, the kind of cheap stuff that you buy for kids, and I drink in the scent.

"I've changed," I tell her.

"Well, you've *shaved*," she murmurs into my shirt. "That's not exactly a personality trait. It's facial hair."

"No, I mean…I know we've had fun tonight, but I want you to know that I've grown up."

"Hmm. Stubborn, persistent, doesn't know how to take a *no*. I don't know, those all sound pretty familiar to me."

I let out an exhaled half laugh. "Okay. Some things are the same."

We sway together. She nestles in where my shirt splits, and I can feel the heat of her breath against my chest.

"I care about you," I persist. "And Otto. Very much. When you came back to Hannsett, it was like…the light turned on again. Like there'd been a piece of me missing for so long and I had no idea. Now, with you here, it finally feels—"

"Whole," Kenzi finishes my sentence.

"Yeah. Exactly."

We lapse into silence for a minute, just savoring each other's company.

"I don't want tonight to end," Kenzi finally confesses to me.

"It doesn't have to."

She buries her face in my chest. "Just dance with me, please."

I give her hand a squeeze. "You've got it."

We melt into the rhythm together, letting our bodies do the talking. As far as I'm concerned, we're the only two people in the room.

34

DONOVAN

I watch from my post at the bar as Jason and Kenzi get lost in each other's arms. I don't think they even notice when the song switches and the room changes tempo.

The sight of them does something to me. It feels like a fist around my heart, squeezing too hard, too fast. My pulse quickens, but it's something else, too.

Comfort, maybe. It's hard to tell—the sensation is so fucking foreign.

Maria takes a break and folds her elbows onto the bar beside me. Her eyes land on the pair on the dance floor. "Aw. That's sweet."

"What? The two of them?"

"No. The way you *look* at them."

I scrunch my eyebrows and put my wineglass to my lips. "I have no idea what you're talking about."

"You should go. Dance with them."

"Someone has to watch the drinks."

"Mmhm," she hums, clearly dubious. I feel her eyes scan me. "You are always taking care of other people."

"It is my job. Literally."

"If I may ask…when you are done taking care of everyone else, who takes care of you?"

"I'm self-sufficient," I retort. "Like a cat."

She shrugs. "Even cats need a scratch behind the ears every now and then."

"Don't make me cough up a hairball."

She laughs. Then a customer calls her name on the far end of the bar, so she rises from her elbows. "Try to have *some* fun, Dr. Donovan," she chides before she goes. "It won't kill you."

Won't it?

Kenzi and Jason come back to the bar. Kenzi is breathless, her cheeks flushed. "How long do we have?"

"Under a minute."

"Can we go outside?" she asks, her gaze bouncing between the two of us. "I'd love some fresh air."

"Couldn't agree more." I swipe my leather jacket off the back of the barstool and slip into the sleeves.

35

KENZI

There's relief as soon as we step outside—a cold burst of air that feels like a kiss against my skin. The heat and sound of the Anchor were all at once suffocating…

But *this*. This feels nice.

The Anchor is tucked away on the edge of the cliff, within walking distance of the Lighthouse Medical Center. I can see the glow of the building through the pine trees.

I can still hear the clamor of noise inside, but it's muffled now. More importantly, I can hear the sound of the surf. When I glance up, the sky is so inky black, it sucks my breath away. It's covered in stars—a winter spread, the Big Bear hanging low in the sky. He won't climb back up across the hemisphere until summer again.

Will I be here to see him make his trek? The future seems like sand between my fingers, so impossible to grasp…but right now, I'm okay with that.

Everything is changing. The year. My son. *Me*. But it feels manageable…so long as I have these two men beside me.

Maybe I don't know what's coming. But I know that I feel

stronger here. Drinking in the night sky with Jason and Donovan.

Inside, I can hear them start the countdown. A couple of smokers outside pick it up.

"Three...two...one!"

Jason's arms gently slip around my middle. This time, I don't pull away.

Instead, I lean into it. I twist my body around, rise to the tips of my toes, and connect my lips with his.

We enter 2019 with a soft, sweet kiss. He tastes like tequila, and my thumping heartbeat, and *Jason*.

Out of the corner of my eye, a shuffle of movement beside us. Donovan—the lone wolf—kisses no one when the ball drops.

Jason and I apparently have the same thought at the same time—*that won't do.*

"C'mere, buddy—" Jason suddenly grabs Donovan by the front of his shirt and yanks him in for a kiss.

I see the surprise on Donovan's face, and his body goes rigid, but he doesn't pull away either.

When Jason releases him, I slip my hands on either side of his face. "My turn."

"Happy New Year," he says.

"Happy New Year."

It's supposed to be simple. Playful. A small peck on the mouth.

But when my lips meet his...

Fireworks go off in my stomach.

His kiss is warm. He smells like leather. When he exhales, I feel his breath patter against my cheek.

"Hey, check it out," Jason says.

Donovan and I break apart. Fireworks—real fireworks—are exploding over the water. I was so lost in Donovan's kiss, I didn't even notice.

It's impressive, huge sparks of light and color exploding across the sky, the reflection scattering across the dark sea.

But I'm having trouble concentrating. My heart is pitter-pattering in my chest. I'm acutely aware of Donovan's body right behind me. Even over the booming and cheering, I can see the rapid rise and fall of his chest. I can hear the lightness in his breath.

Jason's bare arm brushes against mine. I can feel the light tickle of his arm hair, like there's electric static between us.

No one says anything for a second…we lapse into silence as the fireworks boom. But the arousal is so thick in the air, it practically has its own scent. A sharpness, like red wine.

"Should we go somewhere?" Donovan asks us. "Somewhere private."

The promise in his words makes my heart thud and my cunt clench.

"Yeah…" Jason says. "I'd be into that."

His voice is thick. He wants this, too. Just as badly as I do.

My eyes travel across the horizon. The lighthouse is silhouetted behind bursts of blue and yellow lights. "I bet the view is beautiful up there," I muse.

"Only one way to find out." Jason tilts his head. "C'mon."

"What?" Astounded, because he can't be serious…but his long legs take him fast, and he's already steps ahead of us. Donovan and I follow after him, and I repeat, "Jason, *what?*"

* * *

Donovan and I wait outside while Jason talks with the lighthouse keeper.

He's this grizzled, old man who looks positively dwarfed next to Jason. But he nods as he listens, and then the two shake hands.

"What do you think they're saying?" I ask.

"Twenty minutes at the top for a blowjob?" Donovan guesses, and I elbow him in the side.

Jason comes bounding back to us, all grins. "Check it out." He dangles a pair of rusted keys that look like they might've unlocked a pirate's treasure chest in a past life.

"Jason." I gawk. "How…?"

"Rule number one of being friends with Jason," Donovan says, "never ask *how*."

"I can't help that people like me," Jason said. "Also that I'm beautiful."

"Told you," Donovan says, and I stifle a laugh.

Jason cocks his head. "Told her what?"

"Don't worry about it." I slip my hands over his chest and nuzzle in. His nose feels cold against mine. "Are you going to show us inside or what?"

He grins. "Right this way, m'lady."

He leads us to the lighthouse and opens the rounded door. The walls are blue stone, and when we go inside, it's not much warmer than outside. Probably something to do with the fact that there's no ceiling—just a winding staircase that goes around and around until it gets to the top. There are lanterns on the walls, which gives the place a golden glow, and they illuminate old maps of Hannsett Island and mounted descriptions of the history and inner mechanics of the lighthouse.

"No chance they installed an elevator?" Donovan asks, sizing up the winding staircase.

"Last one to the top is a muskrat," Jason says and launches toward the stairs.

We dash up, my heels clicking, their shoes slapping. The staircase is narrow, old, and I grip the railing and try to avoid the vertigo of all the turns. Finally, we get up to a landing, and Jason uses the key to unlock a door. It takes us outside again, this time onto a small platform. I know I shouldn't, but I lean over the iron railing and look down—we're four, maybe five stories up, but it feels taller since I can see past the snow-coated ground, down the cliff, where the waves churn below.

The railing is so cold, it hurts to touch it, but the thought of plummeting down makes me grip it hard.

"Right behind you," Donovan says, as though he can smell my fear. His hand touches my side, and the solidness of his touch relaxes me enough to keep moving forward.

It's a small climb into the glass cavern of the overlook. Jason takes my hand to help me step up. It feels like being in a fishbowl. Curved windows line the walls, giving a panoramic view of Hannsett Island. I'm sure it looks beautiful in the daytime, but at night it's mostly just dark—save the ever-glowing hum of the medical center, the green and red lights blinking in the water, and the burst and explosion of color that fills the sky every couple of minutes.

In the middle sits the eye of the lighthouse—the giant lantern. For something so old, it looks almost futuristic; it has panels of glass, one layered over the other, like ripples receding from the center. The light itself isn't lit, but there are tiny floodlights that surround it, and crystal shards of light bounce off the lantern, scattering rainbows across the floors and ceiling.

"Looks like you were right," Jason tells me. "It's way cooler up here."

"It really is beautiful," I agree.

For a second, the three of us just stand there, watching the explosion of lights. The reflection of the fireworks lights up their faces—Jason, grinning, as happy as a kid at a candy store. Donovan, quiet, contented.

I want to hold on to this moment forever.

"There is one more thing..." Jason says.

"How can there be more?"

He moves behind the lantern and pulls at a latch on the floor. A hatch opens up, and then Jason vanishes down it.

"Come on!"

I glance at Donovan, but he shrugs, as clueless as I am.

I follow Jason down the staircase and gasp when I see what's underneath. "You've got to be kidding me—"

Down the spiral staircase is a suite. Wooden cabinets, a king-sized bed, velvet red carpet on the floors. A mermaid sculpture hangs above the bed, her red hair wild and untamed. On the bed: plush pillows, a quilt, and a purple stuffed whale. Although the lighthouse itself is old, this room has clearly been renovated sometime in the past five years. It's even warm in here, and I can finally take down my hood.

"Is this for us?" I ask.

"We've got it all night," Jason says, then adds, "If you want it."

There's an octagonal window that's nearly as tall as I am. Outside, a firework sizzles out, dripping like a chandelier, and the reflection cascades across the flat, dark water.

"Is this a big, dramatic ploy to get me to forgive you?" I ask.

"No," Jason says. "This is a big, dramatic ploy to get you to sleep with me."

That sends a shiver through me. His lips connect with my throat. I feel the heat of his mouth, and I melt into his kiss as his arms wind around me so he can simultaneously unbutton my coat. It falls away, and I press my palms flat against the glass in front of me.

A familiar pair of fingers loops through mine, pinning me down. Donovan's leather band kisses my wrist. Excitement whips through me and I squeeze his fingers tighter, keeping him to me.

"I need you," I whisper, my voice raspy with want. "Both of you."

"You've got us," Donovan's voice growls in my other ear, and I shudder.

There are hands, undressing me. Lips, caressing my skin.

I feel a hand on my throat, holding me in place, and it constricts my airflow just a little. I reach up and grab the wrist—I feel the leather band there. My dress puddles down at my feet, and I'm exposed, naked in front of the New Year's fireworks. Fingers roll over my nipples, pinching, and I gasp as each squeeze sends another jolt of lust straight between my legs.

"How badly do you want us?" Jason murmurs—the angel on my left.

I can't answer—my throat is too tight. A hand slips between my thighs, over my panties, and even here I can feel him coaxing my nether lips apart. I know I must be soaking straight through the thin cotton because Donovan (my devil to my right) gives a low, pleased hum. "Ah. *That* badly."

When those bold fingers slip underneath my panties and glide along the sensitive skin there, I sink forward, my body flattening against the cold glass. I moan, pushing my hips forward against the hand, feeling the heat of both their bodies behind me.

They've only barely started touching me, and already, I'm tremblingly close to an orgasm.

Those clever fingers start to rapidly flick my clit, and I cry out. I reach down, grabbing Donovan's arm, stopping him. "Please," I beg. "I don't want to cum…not yet."

His fingers retreat, slipping out of my panties again. I whimper when they leave. My sex is throbbing.

"C'mere—" That's Jason's voice, and he guides me to turn around, pressed against his chest. He lifts me suddenly, and I wrap my legs around his hips. I kiss him deeply, swooning, and he carries me as if I weigh nothing, my rear cradled in his hands. He carries me to the bed and unwinds my limbs from him gently so he can take off my pants.

My boys are undone—Donovan's shirt unbuttoned, hanging loose, and I rip Jason's shirt from him as he unbuckles his belt. He pushes his pants and briefs from his hips, freeing his cock, and my throat goes tight with need. It's rock hard, blushing red and ready for me.

As if he can see the feverish want in my eyes, he grins at me. "You want me inside you, baby?"

"I *need* you inside me," I correct.

"Say please, Trouble."

"Please, Trouble."

He chuckles and covers my mouth with his. His tongue swipes against mine. I feel him nestle between my legs, and then, all at once, he's inside of me.

I moan loudly, feeling cracked open. I hug my legs around his hips, pulling him deeper until he's in me to the hilt. I feel solid warmth at my back, and I relax into Donovan's embrace. He sucks my neck, nibbles my ear. I run my hand up his thigh, settling into his lap. I can feel the hardness of him.

"You're doing good, Kenzi," he whispers to me. They've traded roles now—Donovan, murmuring sweetly into my ear as Jason fucks me hard, deep. Dots of pleasure explode behind my eyelids with every thrust, and I drop my head back against Donovan's shoulder and let out loud, desperate whimpers. Just when I think I can't possibly handle any more, I feel Donovan's hand run down my tummy, the roughness of his bracelet brushing my skin. His fingers climb down my pelvis, between my legs, and he finds that little bundle of nerves, drumming it underneath his fingertips.

I shout. I rip into Jason's back. I'm sure I leave marks. Jason growls against me—the three of us sliding together, one unit—and I feel him losing control—

A bolt of fear slices through me suddenly, like lightning.

Jason. No condom. *Bad things happen when we have sex.*

"Don't cum in me," I beg Jason. "Please."

"I won't," he says breathlessly. "I promise."

And I must trust him—I must really trust him—because I let myself go. I lock my legs around his hips and rut forward, riding him, humping Donovan's hand. Sweat drips down my tits and my hair sticks to my back, but I'm so close to that perfect precipice…

My orgasm nearly blinds me.

I arch into Donovan's fingers and explode around Jason's cock. They caress me and kiss me as I writhe through waves of pleasure.

Here, in our little bubble, I'm free to be selfish. I'm free to want. It's exhilarating.

I spend myself until I have nothing left to give, until I'm whimpering and the flick of Donovan's fingers feels painful. I grip his wrist, and he slows his touch before stilling completely.

"Oh my God…" I murmur, completely blissed-out.

"Fuck, you're beautiful," Jason murmurs and licks sweat from the base of my throat.

I feel the heat of him, the hardness of him. Throbbing inside. But true to his word, he doesn't cum in me.

Instead, he says, "I'm going to pull out, okay?"

"Okay…"

He shifts between us, and when he leaves my body, I feel tremendously empty.

I grab the back of his head and dive my tongue into his mouth. He sighs against me. When I release him, Jason latches onto Donovan, as though he's a scuba diver and we're his only source of oxygen.

He kisses Donovan…and kisses Donovan. They fall together and don't stop kissing. The way they kiss is messy and swoony and makes my cunt clench.

When Jason finally releases Donovan, their lips are plump and they're short of breath.

"If you want to get inside," Donovan says, "you're going to have to get me something."

"Like…a nice watch?"

Donovan gives Jason a look like he's lost his mind. "No. Idiot. Lube."

"*Right*. On it."

Jason gets up and goes into the bathroom. He hunts around for only a moment before he comes out with a jar of Vaseline between his fingers. "Found this in the first aid kit."

"That'll do."

I lie back on the stuffed pillows. I feel boneless, and spent, but my blood hums as I watch Donovan and Jason learn each other.

Jason breaks apart to pull Donovan's pants from him. I can't help it—my lips go dry at the sight of Donovan's naked body. He's sleek, toned, and the rings around his necklace look messy across his chest. Jason seems to admire it, too, because he slides his hand down the front of Donovan's body.

"Fuck, you're beautiful," Jason says. He's genuine, too; I don't think he even notices how often these little notes of affection fall from his lips.

Donovan shifts underneath Jason. "I'm ready."

Jason pops the top of the Vaseline jar and sets it to the side. He scoops a dollop out and slips his hand between Donovan's legs.

"How's that?"

A light laugh from Donovan.

"You don't have to be gentle," he says. "You're not going to hurt me."

"Okay…"

When Jason fits himself inside of Donovan, Donovan moans, and the sound pulls a throb from between my legs.

"God, you feel good," Jason murmurs.

"Less talking," Donovan grunts, his eyebrows knitting, "more of what you're doing with your hips."

Their bodies rock together, moaning, sweating. I have to touch them, so I do; I slip my fingers through Donovan's hair. He leans into my touch, so I run my hand down, slipping it down his chest, his abdomen.

I graze the curly hair between his legs.

"Is this okay?" I ask.

"Very," he pants.

I shift my body and tuck in beside his. I run my fingertips up the length of his cock. He's so hard, but his skin is silky soft. I trace the veins of him and then finally take him fully in my hand. His breath catches at that, and I stroke him, slowly, listening closely to the spots that make him moan and pant a little quicker.

I love peeling this man apart. Discovering the hidden parts of him. And he's unraveling now, under my hand and Jason's thrusts. Donovan braces himself, one hand on Jason's chest, the other on my arm. His grip tightens and he pivots against us, conducting the pace and rhythm of his own pleasure.

"Fuck, don't stop," Donovan hisses between his teeth, eyes closed tightly.

"I won't," Jason says—that same, breathless promise he gave me. Jason's body is a powerful, sculpted tool, and he wields it to pleasure Donovan and me first before hunting for his own release.

I feel Donovan twitch in my hand, and he snarls through a curse as he explodes.

It looks like pearls strung across his sculpted abdomen, and I find myself drawn to it. I bend down and trace my tongue along his taut skin, licking up the sticky mess he left. His muscles twitch and vibrate as I slide my tongue over him, making sure to clear every drop.

But I'm not satisfied. I want more, so I take him in my mouth. Donovan curses, and his hips buck once with surprise. I suck on him, savoring every ridge and vein. He's so sensitive that I don't have to wait long before I get what I want; he's like salt water in my mouth, and I swallow him, all of him.

Even a woman as greedy as me has to stop eventually. I remove him from my mouth with a pop and settle down beside him.

"Fuck," Jason says as he settles onto the opposite side of Donovan. Then he repeats, "*Fuck*. Am I imagining things, or are the three of us *really* good at that?"

"You're not imagining it," Donovan confirms.

"Insanely good," I agree.

"What happened to the fireworks?" Jason asks.

"*What* fireworks?" Donovan counters, and the three of us laugh.

* * *

I'm not conscious of falling asleep. But I open my eyes, and suddenly, it's dawn.

Through the wide window, I can see tendrils of neon pink and orange stretching across the sky.

It's a new year, and already things are looking up.

The three of us are naked, tangled up in bed. Donovan is tucked in the middle, and the whale plushy has somehow made it into Jason's arms.

They're both deep asleep, but I'm suddenly wired.

Our clothes are scattered across the whole room. I don't bother trying to scavenger hunt for my dress, but I do slip on a pair of panties and Jason's jacket. It swallows me, practically dress-size on me anyway.

I climb the steps and quietly open the hatch so I can slip out. The view from the top is magnificent in the morning. I can see the horizon now. As the sun comes up, it illuminates the water, sparkling across the light swells. It's cold up here, bitterly cold, but I don't want to look away, so I linger.

"Mind if I join you?"

I glance over my shoulder. Donovan peeks out from the hatch, his leather jacket over his bare shoulders, pants pulled back around his hips.

I scoot. "I could use the body heat."

He sits down on the floor beside me. He opens up his jacket, and I crawl up against him. For a minute, it's just me, Donovan, and the sunrise.

"I know you wanted to keep things platonic," I tell him. "I'm sorry if tonight complicated things."

Donovan shrugs. "We could never be just friends."

I don't know if the *we* he's referring to is Donovan and me, or Donovan and Jason. I don't ask for clarity.

I feel his dark eyes on me. "How do you feel?"

What a loaded question. On one hand—relief. My chest is a cracked eggshell, yolk spilling out bright and yellow. I feel *right* here.

On the other hand—the secret I'm keeping from Jason feels like a bag of stones tied to my ankles and tossed into the deepest part of the ocean.

"It's complicated," I answer.

Donovan nods, as though he knows every nuance in the word *complicated*. And maybe he does. If there's anyone who understands me, it's him. "At least it's a beautiful view for your existential crises."

I rest my head on his shoulder. "I'm glad you're here."

"I wouldn't be anywhere else."

"Tell me I'm a good person. Please. Even if it's not true. Just…I need to hear it."

He scoffs at that. "I'm not going to tell you that."

"But—"

"If you were an angel," he says, his tone suddenly firm, "I wouldn't like you so damn much." He looks me in the eyes. "Screw good. You, Kenzi, are my favorite person. Because of everything that you are. The good, the bad, and everything in between. You're perfect to me."

I bite my lip. "I don't know what I'd do without you."

"You don't have to."

"Do you promise?"

"I promise."

His breath crystalizes. Words unsaid trail between us like white ghosts in the early morning sky.

"I'm freezing," I say, which is true. I can't feel my toes.

"Christ. Of course." There's an urgency about him all of a sudden.

He gets me up, and we go back downstairs, closing the hatch behind us and sealing in the heat. I let the jacket fall to the floor and climb back into bed. I didn't realize how cold I actually was, but now I can't stop shivering.

Jason, still half-asleep, drops the whale and rolls around to wrap me in his arms instead. "You're ice-cold," he mutters.

"Sorry."

"Don't apologize. Put your feet in my legs."

I nudge my cold feet between his calves. Donovan takes off his clothes and gets into bed behind me and wraps his arms around me, his skin furnace hot. Slowly, I start to thaw.

Maybe this year will be okay, after all.

PART III

THE DINNER: JANUARY, 2019

JASON

When I was sixteen, I won the all-stars swim meet for my high school.

I swam faster, made cleaner strokes, and controlled my breath better than all my peers. On my last lap, however, I hit the wall too hard and banged up my wrist. By that point, I already had the lead, so I was still able to book it to first.

My teammates congratulated me, and so did my coach, and they gave me a trophy the size of my arm. But even dripping wet, panting for breath, I could still feel my father's ice-cold glare from the stands.

"What happened out there?" my father asked me when we got into the car.

"It was a mistake," I told him.

"What do you think happens when I make mistakes in the OR?"

"People die."

"That's right. People die." I remember focusing on the blinking of the turn single light, just zeroing in on it, because as long as I kept my gaze there, I didn't have to look at him. I didn't have to see the disappointment in his face. And if I focused hard enough, I could detach my emotions from my body, flying them high above me like a kite, and save the tears for later.

"Kings can't afford to make mistakes," he told me. "Do better."

I still swim. In case you're curious.

You might think something like that would've turned me off water, but I can't help it. Swimming is in my blood. It's one of the few places where I can completely clear my brain.

Lighthouse Medical has a long pool in the rehab wing. It's heated and keeps the same temperature all year around. At 9:30 every morning, there's a group exercise session for certain patients in physical rehab. So at 8:30 a.m., I steal some time vanishing into the water and do laps.

For a few minutes, the world is gone, and all I can hear is the rushing in my own ears. The raggedness of my own breath as I push myself to my own limits, just because I can.

When I'm in the water, no one needs me. Water doesn't put demands on me. All I have to do is put one arm in front of the other and keep breathing.

I lose track of time. When I come up for air, clutching the side, I'm eye-to-toe with a familiar pair of dress shoes.

I blink water from my eyes. My father crouches on the platform above me, the edges of his white coat brushing against the damp tiles. He's holding out a white towel.

"We need to talk," he says.

"Coming out." I rub my hand over my face and then sink underneath again. I push off the edge and rocket to the stairs.

I make a point not to come up for air until I reach the steps. Even then, I stay under water as long as I can, until it feels like my lungs will burst from the empty pressure.

What could we possibly need to talk about?

Word travels fast in Hannsett. Everyone knows everyone's business. Does he know?

It's been two weeks and three days since New Year's Day (but who's counting?), and still Donovan, Kenzi, and I haven't actually defined what *this* is. Sure, our schedules don't help—Kenzi rarely gets a second to herself, and Donovan and I are nearly always at the hospital. When the three of us do hook up, it's a secret, private thing, something that's ours and no one else's.

I guess I like that aspect about it—having something that's mine. But there's a large part of me that wants to scream about it from the rooftops.

Maybe it'd be okay if my dad found out. Maybe it's better to let this secret out than crush it deep down inside.

At least, those are the words I use to reassure myself to keep my heart from launching out of my chest.

When I exit the pool area, my father is waiting for me. I thank him for the towel and pat myself dry. He's wearing a pale blue button-up and dress slacks underneath his white coat, and I feel exposed in only my swim trunks, but I try to shake the feeling off.

"What's up?" I ask.

"I've been talking with one of the producers on the *Dr. Mazie Show*. They saw the promo images, and they're ready to pull the trigger on this. But there's a couple details we need to discuss first."

"Okay..."

"Come over to the house. Friday. We'll have dinner."

I rub the back of my neck with the towel. "I, uh—have something going on this weekend. With a couple of friends."

"Bring them. It won't take long. You know Clara cooks for a small army."

"Sure."

"Seven. Don't be late."

* * *

I dry off. Put my uniform back on. And walk into the general care unit—to an incredibly irate Donovan.

"All good?" I ask.

He's leaning against the receptionist desk, bitching with one of the nurses. When he sees me, his scowl deepens.

"Ask your friend," he says and then tosses his patient file on the desk. I glance at the name. NICK THATCHER.

Of course he's giving Donovan trouble.

"I've got this," I tell him. I take the file. "Which room?"

Donovan lets out a tight sigh. "This way."

I follow him to the exam room. We go inside, and there's Nick, sitting on the table.

We were tight. For a long time. He's an asshole 90 percent of the time, but when he cares about you, he's about as loyal as they come, and I can respect that in a guy. But we've grown apart since—especially since—my divorce from Nadine.

Which is funny, because she never liked him, either.

The first thing I notice about him is he looks like he hasn't slept. His hair is scraggly, and his eyes look bloodshot. When he sees me, he grins and lifts a palm. "My man!"

"Sup, brother?" I clasp hands with him, keeping it friendly, even as I can feel Donovan's disapproval behind me. "You doing alright?"

"Yeah, healthy as a horse. Just getting my yearly."

"Well, you're in good hands." I pat Donovan on the shoulder. "Donovan's the best doctor in the hospital."

Nick's smile doesn't drop, but his eyes harden. "Nah, man," he says. "He's not touching me."

"What's the problem?" I push.

He snorts on a laugh. "You're kidding me, right?"

"We don't have to do this," Donovan mutters beside me and shifts his weight from one foot to the other.

But I can't let it go. I lift a palm. "Hold up. Donovan is literally the best doctor in this entire hospital."

"Who, dick boy?" Nick says, with a jagged grin, and the words hit my ears strange.

I'd forgotten we used to call Donovan that.

Worse—I'd forgotten I was the one that *coined* the term.

It'd seemed funny and harmless when we were teenagers. It feels like chewing on pebbles now.

Donovan goes red at the old nickname, and I feel anger start to boil in my gut.

I try to keep my voice controlled. "If you don't want the best of the best, that's fine, but you can check yourself in somewhere else."

Nick's gaze flickers between the two of us. "Oh, yeah. It makes sense now. Why you stopped hanging out. Why you left that fox of a wife of yours. You two are too busy sucking each other off now, huh?"

My lips thin. "You're overstepping, Nick."

"*I'm* overstepping?" He sneers. "You think no one saw you two pawing at each other on New Year's? Makes me fucking sick. Does your dad know about it?"

I set my jaw. Donovan lifts his hands. "Alright, I'm out. You two have fun."

Donovan starts to leave, but that must get under Nick's skin, because he hisses, "Sure, just run away, you fucking—"

And then he says that word. My father's favorite *F* word. And my blood goes cold.

My pulse quiets. The hospital vanishes around me. I stop thinking about Donovan, about Nick, about anything. All I can think of is *that word*. I turn to him. "What'd you say?" I ask him.

"I just called your boyfriend a—"

Before he can say it again, my fist meets his mouth.

* * *

Donovan and I cool our heels in the courtyard outside Lighthouse Medical.

Being the kid of the CEO of the hospital has perks. For

example, when security escorts you out, you know that you're not going to lose your job in the morning.

Probably.

The cold is bitter. The grass has iced over, and it crackles under my boots. We sit side by side on the landing, just taking a moment to breathe after everything that went down.

"You didn't have to stand up for me," Donovan finally says. "I'm capable of taking care of myself."

"I know. But it felt good."

Donovan lets out a half laugh. "So much for meditation."

I shrug. In the summer, the courtyard is filled with people —people in wheelchairs sitting under the trees, patients recovering from physical therapy doing loops around the center, and doctors and nurses sipping on coffee between shifts. But in January, no one's outside.

It's just the two of us. And I'm feeling close to Donovan now, so maybe that's why the next words slip out. "Hey. I'm going to dinner at my parents' house on Friday. You want to come?"

Donovan turns to me, eyebrows lifted. "You're inviting me to family dinner?"

"Yeah."

He thinks about it. "What about Kenzi?"

"Yeah, of course. I'm inviting her, too. But I'm asking you first."

Donovan stares at me for a long time, then he turns away. "Yeah. Okay."

"Cool." I keep my voice cool, but my heart is hammering and my nerves are all bundled up in my throat. I'm freezing my balls off, but instead of complaining, I shove my hands into my armpits.

Donovan glances at me, then knocks his hand against my shoulder and stands. "I'm starving. Let's go get something to eat."

37

JASON

I call it "taking the day off."

Ignore the fact that you got escorted out of your place of work twenty-four hours ago.

Ignore the fact that your dad texted you to tell you that you're not allowed back in the hospital until you, and I quote, "grow up."

I'm taking the day off.

I put on a wet suit and go for a long swim on the bayside. I cook. I meditate. I catch up on emails and try to ignore the nagging feeling of dread.

And, about halfway through the day, I decide to pay Kenzi a visit.

She's hard to catch on the phone. Takes her forever to respond to texts, and forget about calling, she won't pick up. So I decide to play it old-school. I show up on her front door and knock.

Lucky me, she opens the door. And, fuck. She looks cute. She's messy-cute, which just so happens to be my favorite kind of cute. She's wearing an oversized green patterned Christmas sweater and a pair of sweatpants. Her dark hair is pulled back in this messy pigtail, small tuffs poking out at odd angles.

When she sees me, her jaw falls. "I thought you were UPS."

"Disappointed?" I ask.

"No…obviously not. Uh, come in."

She opens the door and lets me inside. I shake off my jacket, which has flakes of snow on it, and hang it over the back of one of her kitchen chairs. "Where is everyone?"

"Pearl took Otto for his dialysis," Kenzi says. "And I'm… doing laundry…"

The way she says it, her voice sounds a million miles away. I can see why cleaning up is a task. There's a dauntingly large pile of clothes on the couch.

"You need a hand?"

She bites her bottom lip. "Yeah. Sure."

I scoop up a pile of folded shirts and help her carry it into her bedroom. The house is a bit of a disaster zone, but that's what kids do. They shake everything around. Still, Kenzi seems distracted, and she rapidly tries to pick up a little, kicking toys into corners and cleaning off the counter space. When we get into her room, immediately, she swipes a pile of dirty clothes off the floor and shoves them into the bathroom.

"I'm sorry," she says, "the house isn't always like this."

"I like it how it is," I tell her.

She rolls her eyes and closes the bathroom door. "Aren't you supposed to be at work?"

"I'm taking the day off." If you say it enough times, it must be true. Slowly, I set her folded clothes down on top of her dresser. "Actually, there was something I wanted to run by you…"

"I'm all ears."

"So my parents are having this family dinner thing on Friday. I want you to come."

Her eyebrows hike up her forehead. "What...like...with your family?"

"Exactly like that."

"Will Mr. King be there?"

"He is my dad. So. Yes."

"No, I know. Of course. I just..." She rakes her fingers through her hair, looking distracted again. "I'll have to see. Everything is so busy lately. With Otto doing dialysis, I really don't want to leave him alone for long periods of time..."

"It'll just be dinner. We can bring you back before your pumpkin rots." I sit on the edge of her bed so I can better look up at her. "Unless there's something else on your mind..."

I can't get over the way her lips thin when she concentrates—she always looks angry when she's focused, which should *not* be as charming as it is.

My heart cracks open, and there's nothing I want to do more than scoop her up in my arms and feel the soft warmth of her against me.

Fuck. I'm such a sucker.

Finally, she drops her arms and says, "It just seems...like a *girlfriend* activity."

"I guess."

"And I think things are good as they are right now, you know? Without putting labels on them."

She won't look me in the eyes when she speaks, though. Inwardly, I feel a pinch of fear.

We're in two different places. I want to move forward. And she wants things to stay exactly where they are. Eventually, this is going to be a problem, and the knowledge is enough to make me start to panic.

I try to see things her way. I try to meet her halfway. "You can come as a friend, then. No pressure."

Those vibrant green eyes connect with mine. She hesitates, then steps forward close to me. "Look...I lived alone for a really long time. For years, it was just me and Otto. What you're offering is really sweet, and I want to be open to it. But the truth is, I liked it. I *like* doing things on my own. I want to do my own laundry and open my own doors and…well…"

"And…?"

"And, sometimes, I want to get myself off. On my own."

A slow grin draws up my mouth. "So that's what this is about."

"It's not funny!"

"No. It's not. Sorry. Hey." I cup her face. "We don't have to put labels on it. Okay? No sweat."

"I'm sorry. It was really sweet of you to invite me."

"I'm a sweet guy."

"You're too sweet."

"Not that sweet." To prove my point, I catch her bottom lip between my teeth. She gasps.

That noise shoots a jolt straight to my cock. I get an idea.

I kick off my shoes and climb onto the bed. I slip my fingers through her hair, kiss her, and murmur, "Get in my lap."

"What are you doing?"

"Compromising."

She does, straddling me. I love the feel of her—her gentle weight.

I kiss underneath her ear. Her throat. And I murmur there, "Show me how you do it."

"Do what?"

"Pleasure yourself."

She bites her own lip.

She slips her hand down her belly, and I watch her fingers vanish underneath her sweatpants.

Her sweatpants are baggy—I can't see the way her fingers are strumming her sex, but I imagine it must be good because her eyelids flutter. Her breath catches suddenly, as though she hit a particularly pleasurable spot. That sound nearly makes me break out of my pants.

But I don't. I'm aching, but it's a sweet ache—I love this. I love the way Kenzi looks wrapped up in ecstasy, and I want to savor every second of this. I slip my hands up her legs, which tighten around my hips in response.

She's so worked up. Her head bows, and she hiccups her breaths, rapid, sweet gasps.

I push her further. I tease her and nibble the sensitive skin on her throat. I draw a hand up her body and tug her sweater over her head. Her pigtail falls messily as I tug the sweater from her and toss it to the ground. I cup her soft breast in my hand and drag my thumb over her hardened nipple. I can tell she's sensitive, because the small touch makes her shudder.

"You're beautiful," I tell her, "do you know that?"

She drops her head against mine. "I need you inside of me," she moans. Her voice is breathy.

I don't need to be told twice. I need it, too.

I unbuckle my pants. I wiggle them off my hips as far as they'll go and tug my cock out of my briefs. I'm so aroused that even the small touch of my own hand makes the whole organ buzz.

I reach into my wallet and tug out a condom. I free the latex from its plastic and stretch it down my length. Kenzi watches the process and wets her lips with the tip of her tongue—she looks hungry, and I'm ready to satisfy her.

I tug her sweatpants and panties from her hips, and she squirms to get them off her legs. Once she's free, she climbs in closer. I guide my tip between her nether lips and sink myself into her heat. She moans and lowers her hips, taking me in deeper. Slowly, she slides down me until I'm buried inside of her, and she's snug in my lap.

I take the side of her face in my hand and kiss her. I

swallow her tongue in my mouth. She's sloppy, breathless, and she starts to grind herself in small thrusts in my lap.

"Don't stop touching yourself," I murmur against her lips.

She wets her lips. "There's a…uh. Vibrator. In the bedside drawer."

Her cheeks flush pink as she says it.

But I don't want her to be embarrassed. I want her to be free to tell me what she needs—because nothing in the world is hotter.

I slip my thumb over her bottom lip. "Show me how you use it."

She breaks into a shy grin. "Okay…"

She reaches into the bedside drawer, hand fumbling around for a bit, then pulls out a sleek, silver vibrator.

She moves her hand back between her legs, underneath her dark little patch of hair. I watch her nestle the silver bullet against her slit and right over her needy clit. She clicks a button and, when the thing jolts to life, she whimpers like it hurts her. "Fuck, I'm so sensitive," she swears.

"Can you take it?"

"Yes…"

She rubs her toy over her slippery lips, settling into the vibrations. I can feel the low hum of it and, every now and then, it brushes against the base of me. It's intense, and good, and it pulls a moan from me.

Kenzi shudders in my lap, growing tighter around me. She's getting closer, nearing her edge, and watching her dissolve into a frenzy is bringing me toward my peak as well. My own orgasm builds, and every little rut of her hips makes me dig my heels into the mattress. But I hold off. I want to wait for her.

"Faster, baby," I tell her.

She whimpers and clicks a button, quickening the vibrators. Her breath comes in gasps. She clings to me, and I scoop the back of her head in my hand and crush her lips against mine.

She cries out into my mouth, and her sex clenches around me tightly, followed by quick pulses. She rides out her orgasm, rocking in my lap, moaning softly. I lift my hips to meet hers, and when I let myself go, it feels like an afterthought.

The trust in her eyes. The moans from her lips. Those are the moments I savor. My orgasm feels almost secondary.

She clicks the vibrator off, tosses it to the mattress, and pants. Those green eyes of hers look hazy, like she just woke up from a great dream. She grins.

"God. You're good at that."

"You're a vision," I tell her.

There's a moment between us. I'm still inside of her, and she's wrapped up against me, and we practically share the same body like this. I feel spilled open.

"I love you," I tell her. It just comes out.

Kenzi looks down at me, and her eyebrows knit, like I'm speaking a different language. She opens her mouth, but—

Then we both hear the front door unlock, and Otto's small feet racing inside.

"Shit!" Kenzi says under her breath. In a second, she jumps off me and grabs her clothes, yanking them on. I follow suit.

"You have to go," Kenzi says. "They can't see you here."

"Your mom knows about me, right?" Kenzi gives me a look, and that's all the answer I need. "Ah. You want me to hide in the closet or something?"

Kenzi's eyes flit to the window, then back to me. Her mouth in an apologetic grimace.

"Seriously?" I ask.

"I'm so sorry…I just…this isn't a conversation I want to have with Otto, you know?"

As if on cue, the kid starts calling out, "Mum?"

"*Go*," Kenzi says, her voice urgent.

Copy that. I open up the window. My jacket it downstairs, but—c'est la vie, I guess it's taking one for the team. I'm halfway on the tree branch, halfway in her window, when I glance back and add, "I'll climb out the window. One condition."

"What?"

"Come to my parents dinner this weekend?"

"Yes!" she says, exasperated. "Fine! Now leave!"

"Sweet." I wink. "See you later."

And then I drop, shimmying down the tree. My car is parked across the street, so I slide into it and warm it up.

I got up and out of there so fast, my condom is still clinging to me. Awkwardly, I reach into my pants, snap it off, and put it…where?

There's an old coffee cup sitting in the console. Sure.

A minute ago, I was telling Kenzi I loved her. Now, I'm stashing used condoms in coffee mugs.

Life is weird.

I'm about to peel out when I see through her window—Kenzi has made it downstairs. She scoops Otto up, and the kid laughs in her arms.

The sight warms me, like taking a sip of hot cider on a snowy day. She's a good mom.

I might've told her on an impulse, but I realize now that I meant it. I really do love this woman. I want to be part of that picture. Me, Kenzi, Otto, Donovan. One big happy family. It could work, right? Why not?

I start up the car and slowly drive away, back toward my place.

KENZI

*I*t's only later that I realize what I've done. After dinner has been made and consumed, after Otto has taken his bath and gotten into his pj's. Only when the house is quiet and still and I'm lying awake, staring at the ceiling, does it hit me.

I agreed to dinner with Jason's family.

I'm going to have to sit across the table from *Mr. Fucking King.*

Jesus Christ, save me.

3 9

———

DONOVAN

*J*ason always loses his mind before seeing his parents.

The day of the dinner, he spends the whole day walking around the house, completely scatterbrained. He'll be making an omelet one second, and the next second I'll find him trimming his hair in the bathroom, omelet already forgotten in the kitchen.

"You're doing that thing," I tell him.

"What thing?" He's finally eating his (probably cold at this point) omelet, standing up at the kitchen. He's carried a bottle of shampoo in from the bathroom, and it sits beside him while he eats—*why*?

I'm about to point it out to him when there's a knock on the door. Jason walks, barefoot, to the door and opens it up.

Kenzi comes blustering in. "Hey!" she says. "I'm only here for a second—did I leave a hair curler here?"

Apparently, Jason isn't the only one with scatterbrain. "In the bathroom," I tell her. "Bottom right drawer."

Kenzi has been squirreling things away at our place. It's a side effect of spending the stray night over here. First, it was

188

just a couple of pairs of panties. Now, it's hair product. Makeup. A blazer.

"You're a saint," she says and rushes to the bathroom to retrieve it.

I stayed home on prom night. I imagine this is what it must be like for most people, though—a flurry of half-dressed humans running back and forth between rooms.

When Kenzi vanishes into the bathroom, Jason stares at the wall, his brain a million miles away.

"What's on your mind?" I ask him.

"Do you know where my black blazer is?"

"In the closet. Next to mine."

"Cool, cool." He looks down at his hands, which are suspiciously empty. "Where's my—?"

"Kitchen counter."

"I love you, man," Jason says, reuniting with his omelet.

"Love you, too," I repeat. I'm scrolling through my computer. Even though the glare of my screen, I can feel Kenzi's inquisitive eyes on me, lingering in the archway.

"What's up, buttercup?" I ask her, deadpan.

"How do you guys do that?"

"Do what?"

"Say...*those words?*"

A smile twitches the corner of my mouth. "What? *I love you?*"

"Yes," she says, voice cagey, as though the very words are infectious. "That."

I shrug. "They're just words."

"So you don't mean them?"

I close my computer. "You know me, Kenzi. I don't have a heart." I scan her body. "Are you wearing that?"

She narrows her eyes at me. "What's wrong with it?"

I shrug.

She breaks her composure and laughs. "I'm joking. I've got a dress."

"T minus 30," I tell her, and she salutes me before standing.

As we get closer to time, however, with the two of them fluttering around me, I start to feel the jitters take hold.

I'm a grown man. An esteemed doctor. I make my own money, and I pay my own taxes, and I do my own laundry.

I shouldn't be nervous. But I am.

I go into the kitchen and decide to distract myself by putting away the flurry that Jason left—his dirty dish still on the counter. I rinse it and drop it in the sink when I spy a plate of brownies on top of the microwave. Jason is an okay cook, but he has a knack for baking. I stress eat, stealing a brownie and eating it off a napkin to avoid crumbs.

It's not like I haven't met Jason's parents before. Hell, I work for Mr. King. I've sat at his desk. I've walked through diagnoses with him. I've attended galas at the hospital. So why does the thought of eating food across from him for an hour, maybe two, make me sweat?

Maybe because things have changed now. I've seen his son's O face. I've sucked his son's cock. I've made him cum with my name on his lips.

Worse than that, I've developed, I don't know. Nagging sort of *feelings* for the guy.

So I pick crumbs and ruin my appetite on sugary sweets.

Jason finally reemerges from the bathroom and steps into the kitchen. "Hey, you're loosening up," he says.

He looks good, but that's nothing new—*looking good* has always been effortless for him. Dark hair jostled, he's wearing a light button-up and creaseless gray slacks. The top couple of buttons are undone, teasing his curly chest hair.

"Kenzi's still changing."

"Cool," Jason says. He crosses his arms across his chest and leans back against this counter.

Even dressed up, I can make out the bare outline of *him*. Even his relaxed slacks can't hide that mammoth.

My fingers twitch with the want to undo his belt, and my blood starts to rush south. Why am I so horny right now? I force myself to ignore the dryness of my lips and steer my thoughts.

He nods to the plate of brownies. "How many of those have you had?"

I scowl. "Are you counting my calories right now?"

"No. But uh…you should know I made those for Maria."

"I only had one. She won't notice."

"No, I mean like…they're special. You know. Like…*really* special."

My throat feels thick and slimy. What. The. Fuck.

"*Pot brownies?*" I hiss. "You made her *pot brownies?*"

Jason lifts his hand in a half shrug. "She's been having trouble keeping food down, so—it's medicinal! It's fine!"

"No, it's not fine! You need to…put a sign on them! You can't just have pot brownies lying around!"

Jason chuckles. "Holy shit, dude. You're going to be fun."

I groan and put my head in my hands. "I'm fucked. I'm so fucked. I'm going to be sick."

I feel Jason's hand on my shoulder. "Hey. Maybe this is God's way of telling you to chill out, go with the flow—"

"I don't want to *flow!*" I snap at him. "You poisoned me!"

"It's not a big deal. You used to get high all the time when we were kids."

"When we were *kids!*" I grab him by the collar of the shirt and bring him in close—I'm bull-seeing-red mad right now. "This might come as a surprise to you, but it's *not* my idea of a good time to be stoned in front of my boyfriend's dad!"

Those blue eyes widen, and a small smile climbs his lips. "Am I your boyfriend?"

"*That's* what you got out of that?" I hiss.

"Is everything okay…?"

We stop and turn to see Kenzi standing in the middle of the room.

She's wearing a white shirred dress with a frill trim. Lace flowers pattern the skirt, which stops above her knees. The neckline draws a V to her breasts and ties off into a sweet little bow.

She's breathtakingly beautiful, and for a second, my chest tightens and my heart beats faster and my throat closes. And I don't think it has anything to do with the edibles.

Probably.

Kenzi blinks at us, confused. "What's going on?"

"He ate the pot brownies." Jason points at me, the boy caught with his hand in the cookie jar. Kenzi's mouth falls into an "Ooooh."

A sharp stab of anger between my ribs. That voice in my head: *Everyone's having a good time, and as usual, you're fucking it up.*

"I'm fine!" I snap. "You look like a fucking angel! Jason's ready! Let's go while I can form sentences!"

I genuinely mean the compliment, but I'm too pissed and bitter, and my mouth is full of silverware, spitting knives.

"Do you *want* to go?" Kenzi asks.

"Yes. No. I don't know."

Kenzi frowns. Then she steps over to the table, picks up a paper napkin, and plucks a brownie from the pile. She tears off a corner and pops it in her mouth. "Solidarity," she explains.

I don't know why...but that does help. My heart, which is bouncing around my chest like a cat on a 2:00 a.m. rampage, finally starts to slow down.

I exhale, and the breath takes some of my rage with it.

"Okay," I decide. "Let's go."

40

JASON

The King Estate is the biggest private residence on Hannsett Island.

The two-story mansion overlooks the beach.

The whole place is enshrouded by tall hedges that make it impossible for anyone to look in. I didn't realize what an effect those hedges had on my psyche until years later when I started meditating in earnest.

When I was in a bad place or feeling vulnerable, I'd close my eyes and imagine myself surrounded by hedges.

It was privacy. Security. But it did something else important: it kept people and things out.

The King family was local, but we weren't *one of the locals*. We were *better than* the locals. The hedges kept us apart from everything.

You get a distorted view of yourself—and your place in the world—when you live in an ivory tower.

But there are consequences to being that high up, too. The fall is steep.

I pull the car up to the hedges and punch in the security code. The iron gate slowly swings open, letting us in.

I glance in the rearview mirror. Donovan is staring hard out the window.

"You okay, bud?" I ask him.

"Great," he says, but his jaw is tight, like it's taking everything in him to keep it together.

Note to self: maybe tone down the potency of the brownies next time.

"Why does it smell like sex in here?" Donovan asks suddenly from the back.

The noise that leaves my throat is halfway between an "oh" and a groan. I grab the coffee mug culprit from the console and shove it under my chair.

"I'm not going to ask," Donovan says. "I *really* don't want to know."

"Hey," Kenzi says. "How're *you* feeling?"

Her fingers slip over the back of my neck. I shiver. That's a secret hotspot of mine—the sensation of nails lightly trailing up the nape of my neck sends a hot lick of pleasure through me.

I tighten my grip on the steering wheel.

"Honestly? A little nervous."

Kenzi drops her head against the car seat. "We don't have to make a big deal out of it."

"What've you told them?" Donovan asks from the back seat, suddenly sounding on edge.

"Just that I'm bringing a couple friends over."

"That's good," Kenzi says. "I think we should keep that line. No reason to make things weird with…hey, Mom, Dad, these are the two people I'm fucking."

"Yeah," Donovan agrees. "Let's not."

I bite the inside of my lip. I'm not great at keeping secrets —but they're right. To open that jar of worms would invite too many questions.

But it doesn't feel *right* to keep them a secret, either. It makes this feels dirty.

Which it's not. It's beautiful.

"If you're sure," I say, but even I know I don't sound convincing.

I don't know if Kenzi realizes the effect she has on me, because her nails are still absently tracing circles over the back of my neck.

I've got to stop her before I pop a boner in front of my parents, so I gently remove her hand and press an affectionate kiss to the backs of her fingers instead.

That makes her smile. My heart leaps.

I pull us up the driveway. My mother is waiting for us. She's bundled up in an olive-green coat, thick mittens, and a scarf around her face. Even from the car, I can tell her cheeks are rosy. How long has she been standing in the cold waiting for us?

She eagerly waves a gloved hand as I park the car in the driveway and kill the engine.

The three of us step out, and the first thing I do is scoop my mom in a quick hug. She's too short and I'm too tall, which worked out for me in high school when I could easily avoid her embarrassing gestures of affection. Now, I have to bend down to press a small kiss to the side of her face and tell her, "Happy New Year."

"Oh, Happy New Year, my darling. It's *so* good to see you."

Her grip is always too tight, and it hurts in a way I can't describe. Since her kids flew the nest, she doesn't have a lot to hold on to, and my dad is crap at emotional support.

I make a mental note to push him to get a dog.

"Come on in!" she says. "It's freezing!"

We all head inside. It's warm in here and brightly lit. I can smell the cooking from the kitchen—notes of roasted vegetables and onion lingering in the air.

My dad stands in the foyer, lips pressed in a thin smile. I nod to him. "Happy New Year."

He nods back. This is as close as we'll get all night.

"I brought some friends—you guys remember Kenzi?" I put both hands on Kenzi's shoulders to take her coat.

"My uh…mom used to be married to Terry Blake. We were here a few years ago."

"Oh! Yes!" My mom clasps her hands excitedly, even though I can tell by her glassy stare that she doesn't recall Kenzi at all. "Of course—how is your mother doing now?"

"Fine, actually…"

"Donovan." My father clasps Donovan's hand. "Always good to see you, son."

Donovan shakes his hand. "You too, Mr. King."

I'm not going to lie—the way my father looks at Donovan?

It's with pride. It's the son-I-never-had look.

And it stings. For reasons that feel like taffy on my molars.

Can't win them all.

But I've got to admit—as someone who always had top grades, the best time on the swim team, the best *everything*, it's hard to come second place in the eyes of my own father.

That's a burn you can't fix.

"I'm glad your friends could join us," my father says. There's something behind his tone, however, like a razor blade between the teeth. I can't place it. And then he continues. "We had a surprise guest stop in. She'll be joining us for dinner as well."

"Who—?" I start, but then the glass doorway to the back patio slides open, and she steps inside.

My tongue rolls down my throat. My testicles retreat into my body. My toenails recede into my skin.

"Nadine," I say, and the word cracks between my teeth like a tasteless, unsalted cracker.

When Nadine smiles, it's with all of her teeth. "So nice to see you," she says, addressing the crowd like a politician.

When she sees me, her gaze flickers over me, from head to toe. "All of you."

"Oh, no," Donovan groans audibly. "The wicked bitch of the west."

When he notices us all starting at him, he blinks.

"What? Did I say that out loud?"

41

KENZI

Jason's ex-wife is a goddess.

It's really hard to put into words the kind of presence Nadine carries effortlessly through the house.

She's easily the most beautiful woman I've seen. Ever. Dark hair. Olive skin. Perfect lips. A slender body fitted into a sleek, white dress. Fear a woman who drinks red wine while wearing a dress *that* white. She wears beautiful, big gold earrings that peek out from under her dark, wavy hair—is it L'Oreal? Or is she just *worth it*?

She smells like lilac and honeysuckle, and it's a smell that entices you to lean in.

I can see why Jason fell in love with her. Hell—*I'm* half in love with her and I only just met her.

Or maybe it's the pot brownie that's kicking in.

Even as I dig into this smorgasbord of food in front of me —pesto pasta, grilled asparagus, stuffed mushroom, lightly dressed salad, and a chunk of bread roll—I have a hard time keeping my eyes off Nadine, who is sitting across from me. Every now and then, she catches my gaze and smiles.

She does the same thing Jason does—holds eye contact effortlessly. It's a skill.

I imagine what they must have looked like together—every picture the perfect Christmas card. A power couple. Hashtag couple goals. To be honest, I hadn't put too much thought into Jason's divorce before, but now it's driving me crazy. What went wrong?

She's smiling at me again, and it takes me far too long to realize that it's an *expectant* smile…she's asked me a question, and now I'm sitting there like a dolt, fork in hand.

Reality to Kenzi. "Sorry?" I ask.

"What is it you do?" she repeats.

"Oh—well. I'm sort of…in between jobs at the moment."

"She used to manage a high-profile band," Jason says. "Serious, like…top billboards. But she had to drop it to take care of her son."

"*And* she writes the most beautiful songs," Donovan adds.

My neck feels hot, and I can't help a smile from slipping on my lips. What's worse than one supportive boyfriend?

Two. Talking me up at the dinner table.

How'd I get so lucky?

"What band?" Nadine presses.

"The Polaroid Boys," I tell her.

"Polaroid Boys. I think I know them." She waves her fork in the air thoughtfully. "They did that one…what was it. 'Heart Beat on Fleek'?"

"The anthem to my nightmares," I say.

She laughs. "I like this one, Jason. Keep her around."

As though I'm the new family dog—fun for the whole family! Great at parties!

It's not completely off base, either; I'm unemployed, living with my mother, and I'm high off edibles. I feel like a heathen in this crowd. An ugly duckling in the midst of long-legged storks.

I stuff more pasta into my mouth, and that helps for the moment.

As if sensing my discomfort, Donovan leans over and bumps his leg against mine. His leg feels nice, his pants like velvet. His eyes are glassy—do mine look just as bad?

"You have pesto on your mouth," he murmurs.

"You have mouth on your pesto," I murmur back.

We break into a fit of laughter that no one else understands.

JASON

As Mom clears the plates, Dad gets up from the table. I feel his strong grip on my shoulder, a squeeze.

"Come up to my study. It'll only take a minute."

Dad's study is non-negotiable. I grew up dreading the words *see me in my study*. His study was where I got repri-manded for less than perfect grades. It was where I got sent to when I'd pulled another foolish stunt over at the marina. It was where we sat down for big conversations, where I decided on where to go to college.

The last time I'd been called into his study was the night I told the family I'd proposed to Nadine. He'd closed the door and told me sternly, *Is she pregnant? Because you know we can handle that.*

"Oooh, he's in trouble," Kenzi says, and Donovan cackles. They're both flying high...but at least they're having fun.

"Be right back, losers," I tell them. The *loser* is meant to be a term of endearment, but it makes Donovan frown. Words come out different in the King house.

Nadine rises from the table as well, and even though she hasn't been instructed to, she follows my dad and me upstairs. It's then that it hits me—this is planned.

Whatever this is, it's something they've been cooking up. Together. I turn my bones to steel and inwardly brace.

Dad's study is upstairs, the last door on the right. The door is always closed. He opens it, and when I walk through, I immediately feel the temperature drop a couple of degrees.

He has his own zone and his own heating and cooling system in here.

It's—literally—his own private domain.

The doors close behind us.

The walls are the dark blue of Vincent van Gogh's *Starry Night*. He has a bookshelf and a filing cabinet on one side and a glass case of achievements on the left. Awards and honors the hospital has received over the years from the medical community. Framed photographs of him shaking hands with important people—politicians, society men.

My dad takes his place behind his desk—stained oak, decorated. His diplomas hang on the wall over his shoulders like bodyguards.

Nadine takes the chair on his left—a high back, usually my spot of choice, but it's fine. I settle into the one beside her. Neither of us look at each other.

My father strokes his beard once, as he always does before launching into a serious conversation. "Nadine," he starts, "we're so glad you could join us for dinner, as always."

"Happy to be here." She smiles and crosses one leg over the other, like she's the guest on a talk show.

My father's eyes shift to me. "I got the promotional images back from the production company. Take a look."

He pushes a folder across the desk, and I open it up. I fan out four shiny prints. They share the same header, "On the Cutting Edge with Dr. Jason King," and the subtitle, "As seen on the Dr. Mazie Show!" The images are different, though: there's a few of me with my hands in the middle of a pretend surgery.

It's so fake, so put-on, and the images make my stomach churn in a bad way.

Nadine leans in, and her arm brushes against mine. She taps her nail on a photo: one of me sitting on a stool, my sleeves pulled up at my elbows, stethoscope hanging around my neck, smiling for the camera. "That's my favorite," she says.

I'm not quite sure *why* she's here, or why she has an opinion in the matter, and it rubs me the wrong way. I close the folder. "So what next?" I ask.

"Next, they're flying a small crew to Lighthouse Medical. They're going to interview you, as well as a few staff members. If that goes well, they'll pitch the footage to their team."

Nadine's phone buzzes at her side. She shifts her attention, pulls it out, and starts going through it while my father talks.

My skin buzzes. He would *never* allow me to disrespect him like that.

But he doesn't seem to notice her. Instead, he leans in and continues. "It is, essentially, the final test, so needless to say, the interviews have to go well."

"Understood."

"This segment could bring in big investors," my father continues. "We could build out the hospital. Update our equipment. So it's important that we make a good impression. As a united front."

"What does this have to do with me?" I ask, even though I already feel the inkling, a trickle of dread sliding down the back of my ear.

My father comes out and says it: "I need you two to pretend to be married for the interviews."

"You've got to be kidding me," I scoff. "We're divorced."

"It's for the camera," my father continues.

"No," I say. "Absolutely not."

"It's important that we show a—"

"United front. Yeah. You said that."

My father is—as always—a stone. Impenetrable. Calm. Meanwhile, I've always been the uncontrollable one. The temper. My anger rises like a storm.

"Did you agree to this?" I ask Nadine. Even I can hear the snap in my tone, like a rubber band pulled too far.

She says it like it's nothing: "Celebrities do it all the time. Brad and Angelina. Tom and Nicole."

She doesn't even avert her eyes from her phone when she talks to me. It's the straw that breaks the camel's back.

"This?" I motion to her and her phone. "This is the kind of shit that drove me crazy. Can you look at me when you talk to me?"

Her dark eyes flicker to me and narrow. Like my father, she has no inflection when she says, "Are you angry with me, or are you angry with the situation?"

"Try all of the above."

"It's just TV, Jason," she says. "It's not personal."

They're cyborgs—emotionless, cut from the same cloth. They draw clear lines between business transactions and real life. They don't mind peddling lies to get what they want.

How can they both sit there so calmly while I feel like a ripped sail flapping in the wind?

"Our marriage," I growl. "Was that *not personal*, too? Just for show?"

"Nadine." My father's deep voice cuts through the heated conversation smoothly. "I think I should talk to Jason alone for a moment, if you don't mind."

Nadine's gaze fixes on me, but she rises from her chair obediently. "Calm down," she murmurs to me on her way out.

Calm down. My two least favorite words in the English language. I curl my fingers tightly around the arms of my chair and try to remember to breathe.

I am Jason King. Top surgeon at Hannsett Island. I am enough.

The door softly clicks closed behind her.

We're alone, and there's a little more space in the office. My rage has room to stretch, and my jaw unclenches.

"I know your relationship with her is complicated," my father says smoothly.

"It's not complicated," I tell him. "We're divorced. It's simple. And it's over."

"All I'm asking is for you to wear your ring and stand next to her and smile. For one night. Surely you have the capacity to think outside yourself for one night."

"I can't," I repeat. "I'm seeing someone."

Someones, technically.

My father's frown deepens. "Who?"

"It doesn't matter."

"Jason—"

"I can't do it. Okay? I'm a surgeon. Not an actor." I stand. "Can I go now?"

His lips tighten. I don't wait for him to respond. I turn and put my hand on the door handle.

"You're being selfish," he says. "You have been since you were a child. You always think of yourself first."

"I'm not. I'm just doing the right thing."

"Think about it," my father says.

"Sure."

I open the door and exit, closing it hard behind me.

I don't get too far down the hall, though. Donovan is standing there, arms crossed, shoulders hunched around his ears.

"Hey…you okay?" I ask.

He shakes his head. He's got that on-pins-and-needles look.

My old bedroom is right here, so I open the door for him. "Here…let's chat." I touch his arm, but he leans away from it. He ducks into the room instead, and I follow him inside.

They've changed it up. It's a guest room now. Sheets are made, the whole thing smells like Febreze. There are still traces of me, though. My shelf of first-place trophies—everything from third grade science fair to the college track team. A couple of old family photos. There's a picture of me and Nadine on our wedding day, which Mom must've framed and put in here while I was gone. Wishful thinking?

Donovan paces the short length of my room like a lion and slips his hands over the back of his head. "It was about me, wasn't it?"

"What?"

"Your father wanted to talk to you. Was it about me?"

"No—why would it be about you?"

"I don't know," Donovan snaps, "maybe because I showed up to family night high as a kite!"

"You do sound a little paranoid right now…"

A noise leaves his throat, almost like a growl. "He might just be *daddy* to you, but in case you've forgotten, he's also my boss. If I lose my job—"

I hold up my hand. "You're not going to lose your job."

"That's easy for you to say!" His lips press together. "You do this. All the time."

"What?"

"You make me feel like an asshole. You put me in these situations that turn me into the villain."

"You ate the brownies. All on your own. Believe it or not, I wasn't trying to sabotage you."

"Sabotage! That's the word. You're a saboteur." Donovan flops back in bed suddenly. His eyes flick over the ceiling. "Is this your room?"

I shift my weight. "Uh. Yeah. My old room."

"It reeks of latent homosexuality."

"Huh?"

"You have a naked man on your wall."

"That's...Muhammad Ali. And he's not naked. He's wearing shorts."

"I bet he didn't wear shorts in your dreams."

"No comment."

Donovan sighs loudly and rubs his hand over his face. "Ignore me. I'm just...stoned."

Carefully, I sit on the edge of the bed beside him. "I don't think you're a villain," I tell him.

"No?"

"You're a good guy." I pick at lint on my pants. "Hell...I admire you."

Now Donovan scoffs on a laugh. "You *admire* me?" he asks dubiously.

"Sure I do. You're a better doctor than I am. You fuck who you want. No matter what the consequences. You stay true to yourself. Even when it's hard. Even my dad likes you more than he likes me."

Another chuckle from Donovan. "Probably true."

"He went to your med school graduation."

"Yeah. He did."

"He didn't go to mine."

Donovan props himself up on an elbow, half sitting up in bed, and squints at me. "What?"

I shake my head. "Mom went. My brother went. Dad sent a card. 'Congratulations on your big day.' With a new credit card enclosed."

Donovan examines me. "You'll never be your own man if you spend your time trying to please your parents."

"Easy for you to say. Both of your parents loved you unconditionally. I've never known what love looks like without hoops you have to jump through to attain it."

"You sound like a circus animal."

"I feel like one."

"So what *do* you want?" His eyes are on mine. So dark. So

penetrating. They cut right through. "Not you—Leonard King's son. *You*. Jason. What the hell do *you* want?"

I swallow hard. My throat is dry. "I don't know."

"Yes. You do. You're just too afraid to take it."

I reach out and grab him. His surprised *mmf!* gets muffled against my lips.

But he doesn't pull away. He doesn't push me off. After a moment, his tongue finds my teeth, and he invites himself into my mouth.

The way his tongue curls against mine sends a jolt down my spine and straight to my cock. I hear myself groan as we sway together. Our bodies find each other as I dig my tongue into his mouth, drinking him in deeply.

"I'm too high to bottom," Donovan pants when we break for air, "just grind against me."

"Okay…"

Donovan rolls himself over, ungracefully, like a flopping fish. I press my body against his, sealing myself to him. His back, my chest. His ass, my hips. I push his hair back, and it's so straight, so stubborn, it sticks up like porcupine quills when I rub it the wrong way. I nuzzle against the back of his neck, inhale him, and nibble his shoulder, the bit his shirt leaves bare.

I roll my body against his, slowly, with purpose. I move the way I would if I was inside of him, and the notion makes me swollen with need. When Donovan pushes back against me, adding friction, it's not in tandem. I have a rhythm, but he has a purpose—to bring us both to sloppy climaxes, and fast. He slots his rear against me and wiggles, grinding on my cock in a way that takes the breath from me.

I regain control and press him tightly into the mattress. I grind on him, and he grinds against my bed.

The noises he makes are animal—throaty grunts and shaky *uhs* into the mattress. I don't even know if he's aware he's making them. His face is to the side, and his eyes are tightly closed, concentrated, mouth open in pleasure. He grips the bedspread under him, balling it. A sound escapes him, loud, and it sends a bolt of panic through me.

I try to remind him, "My parents are downstairs..."

"I don't care," Donovan growls, and the noise sends shivers down my spine. "Don't fucking stop."

He reaches up and grabs the back of my neck, holding me tightly, pinning me there. I want him. Badly. I want to feel our naked bodies together. But somehow this—even though we're both fully clothed—feels just as good. Seeing him unravel underneath me is almost more than I can take, and I don't want this to stop.

"Flip," Donovan says suddenly. He yanks my shirt, and I follow his lead, rolling onto my back on the bed.

Now, Donovan climbs on top of me. He drapes his body over mine, molding us together like wet clay. I can feel him now—his erection bulges, radiates heat. He ruts unevenly, and I feel his cock hunt on my pelvis before it nuzzles against my cock, and his jerky thrusts send such a hot friction through me it makes my throat dry.

I don't know where to put my body. I'm suddenly six feet of awkward. Where should I put my arms? My hands? They're stuck to my sides, useless. Yet Donovan gyrates over me as if it's the most natural thing in the world for him.

"Do you want me to fuck you?" he asks suddenly.

My brain freezes. I know the answer, but my tongue won't let me say it. So I sputter out a "Huh?"

"I said..." He twists his hips in a way that sends sparks from my groin to my toes. "Do you want me inside of you? Have you?"

"Have I...uh...?"

"Have you ever had someone inside of you?"

Somewhere on my shelf of trophies beside my bed sits a first-place award for debate team. But all my oratory skills go out the window at his question. I'm fumbling over my words. "I don't…uh…no…"

Donovan's hands plant on the mattress on either side of me. He bows his head so his body against mine. His voice tumbles into my ear. "I'll show you how good it feels. I'll hit places inside of you that you didn't know existed."

My neck burns. My face feels red hot. He's grinding me against the edge of my pleasure.

He continues, his voice weaving through my lust-fogged brain. "And when I find it…that spot inside you that makes you whimper…I'm not going to stop. I'm going to make you blow so hard, it'll turn you inside out. You're never going to want anything else but my cock, buried to the hilt."

My fists grab empty air at my sides, clenching then unclenching, fingers splaying.

"Donovan…" His name comes out as a warning. My voice is so hoarse, it's almost unrecognizable. "I'm going to…uh…"

Donovan's laugh is a warm puff of air against my collarbone. "I know."

He doesn't stop. He pivots his hips into mine—tight, rapid thrusts—and I know I should, but I can't hold back anymore. The moan that escapes me is loud, and he swallows it at the last second with his own tongue, sealing his mouth against mine as I spasm with pleasure underneath him.

My lap is wet, a stain I'm going to regret in a couple of seconds. But I can't think of anything but reaching that precipice again, and my fingers finally leap into action, gripping his hips as I hump myself through the last shuddery waves of it.

I can't stop moaning, and I bite his shoulder to stifle the sound. When I finally pull back, breathless, he has wet, pink teeth marks on his neck.

"Fuck," I swear.

"Yeah," Donovan agrees. "Fuck."

He kisses me again, and this time his tongue melts me.

I'm six foot five. I can lift two hundred pounds. But underneath Donovan, my bones are weak. When his tongue slides against mine, tasting like red wine and hunger, I'm as vulnerable as a rabbit, heart kicking in my chest.

I'm so lost in his kiss, I don't even hear familiar heels on the hardwood until it's too late. "Honeybear?" my mom's voice calls out, thin as reeds. "Is everything okay?"

She tries the handle—and I locked the door, Jesus-God-fuck I know I locked the door—but the panic fries every nerve in my body for that split second before the lock catches and keeps her out.

"It's fine!" I call out quickly. "Everything's fine. Just…had a little…uh…"

"*Accident?*" Donovan teases.

I slap my hand across Donovan's mouth. His whole body trembles with silent laughter.

"Do you need a hand?" my mom offers, and I want to die.

"Nope. I'm good. I'll be right down. Thank you."

Her kitten heels click away. When my mom leaves, I finally release him from my grip.

"You're right," he says once he's freed. "My life *did* turn out way better than yours, honeybear."

"Shut up and help me clean up."

KENZI

"*K*enzi."

Nadine's tongue catches my name, the way a magician pulls *is this your card?* out of thin air.

I blink. I've been zoning out—a bad side effect of the pot brownie I ate earlier. It makes me spacey, and it takes me a minute to reorient—that same feeling you get when you wake up in a bedroom you don't recognize and slowly have to put the puzzle pieces back together.

Jason, Mr. King, and Donovan all went upstairs. Mrs. King is in the kitchen doing dishes. After a couple of attempts to help with the dishes (and subsequently being thwarted), I returned to my chair, sipping my wine and spacing out.

Except now Nadine's is hovering beside me, honey-brown eyes on mine expectantly.

"Join me on the patio?"

Her fingertips brush my shoulder, and it sends goose bumps up and down my arm.

Stop being weird, Kenzi.

"Um. Yeah. Totally."

Nadine helps herself to the sliding glass doors—it occurs

to me then how comfortable she is in this house. She was, after all, in-lawed into it at one point.

Could I ever be that comfortable here? Or will I always feel like Cinderella, feeding foie gras to my mice friends under the table?

There's a wide pool here, outlined with stones, but it's covered up for the winter. There's a second, smaller pool—a Jacuzzi, I bet—that is also covered up, but looks active, a thin blue light peeking underneath the cover.

They have an array of outdoor furniture here, including comfortable lounge chairs. It's cold as hell, but the Kings have their own outdoor heaters, these long metal things that look like tiki torches, with yellow-blue flames flickering inside. Nadine and I converge around a heater, and she adjusts the knob, turning it up. It's surprisingly cozy, and my hands begin to thaw.

"Can we speak candidly?" Nadine asks.

"Sure," I say. My brain is empty. I'm feeling candid.

"You and Jason. Are you an item?"

Should I feel weird admitting this to his ex? I don't. If anything, it feels like we have something in common now. "We're a *something*," I say.

She seems to accept that answer with a nod. She glances off, across the way. "That's good. I'm glad he's happy."

I stare at her. She means it. Everything about her is so composed, so *pristine*. She fits into this house—and Jason's family—effortlessly.

So I have to ask… "What happened?"

She sizes me up. "What has he told you?"

I shrug. "Not a lot." I consider it. "I think…it probably hurts to talk about."

"Coming together was quite simple," she says. "My father runs Oxim, a multimillion-dollar pharmaceutical company. He worked closely with Mr. King. Our arrangement was good for business." She tips her glass of wine to her lips.

"Naturally, it helped that Jason is a fox. More than that, he's a sweetheart. Not many of those left."

I can't help but grin at that. "Yeah. He is all of those things."

"We were good for a time. But ultimately, he wanted something I can't give him."

"Mm." I nod knowingly. "A penis."

She arches a perfect eyebrow. "No. A *heart*."

"Oh."

Well—that one feels like a punch in the tits.

Nadine continues. "My career always comes first. And I would do *anything* to get what I wanted. I couldn't date a man who prioritized me above all. The dynamic was…uneven."

"Huh."

The conversation has taken a turn. I feel a strange knot twisting in my throat, and I take a swallow of wine to push it back. The heat from the open flames feels too hot suddenly, and I can feel myself grow flushed. I want to jump into the enclosed pool. Let the icy water chill me until I don't feel anything at all.

Nadine looks at me, and her perfect smile returns. "He seems happy with you, though. Perhaps I was the caustic bitch he needed to get over to find someone like you."

Or maybe he traded one caustic bitch for another.

We're interrupted by a hiss—the sound of the sliding glass doors opening and shutting.

"So this is where the party is." Donovan's voice breaks through the haze of my self-loathing, and immediately, I feel my spirits lift.

He and Jason come over to join us. Donovan takes one of the chairs across from us, but I'm feeling needy. I take Jason's hand and give it a squeeze. Rather than pulling away, he leans into it, perching on the arm of my chair and moving his hand to my back. "You good?" he asks.

"Mmhm," I hum, leaning my head on his thigh. I feel small and safe here.

Donovan has a bottle of red dangling from his fingers. He pours himself a glass, and when Nadine extends her own glass, he tops her off as well.

"What have you boys been up to?" Nadine asks.

Donovan's dark eyes swoop over Jason intently. "We just had a heart-to-heart."

With my cheek pressed to Jason's thigh, I noticed his pants are black—weren't they blue when we came to dinner? "Did you change pants, or am I going crazy?" I ask.

"We had a wine spill," Donovan answers. "He had to rub it out."

Even in the dying light of the sunset, I can see Jason go bright red, his ears positively pink.

Jason changes the topic. "What've you girls been talking about?"

"You, mainly," Nadine says—which isn't a lie. "Your Kenzi is a real charmer, here. I would hold on to her, if I were you."

"Because you're so good at that," Donovan adds, a sharpness in his tone. "Holding on to things."

She purses her lips. "Donovan, aren't you and I ever going to be friends?"

"Don't count on it."

Say what you will about Donovan—but he is ride or die, all the way.

"How about a toast?" Jason lifts his glass to break the tension.

"To old friends and new," Nadine says.

"And everything in between," Donovan adds.

We click glasses and drink on it.

JASON

For a minute, it's actually nice.

Nadine, Donovan, Kenzi, and I chat. Kenzi has her head on my thigh, like a cat. Even now and then, Donovan catches my eyes. Our, uh, *thing* upstairs might've satisfied me for the moment, but it's also ignited a new desire in me, and every time he makes eye contact, it's hard not to clear the distance and put my mouth on his.

But soon enough, my parents come out, and any *want* for Donovan goes immediately on mute in this presence. It's replaced by this wall—a feeling of being on guard.

Everyone—including my parents—is a little tipsy, which means it's the time of night when my dad regales everyone with his work stories. HIPAA be damned.

"Oh, Leonard." My mom pets my father's chest. "Tell them the story about your *special* summer patient."

He chuckles. "I'm sure they don't want to hear about it."

"I do!" Kenzi says too enthusiastically.

The corners of my father's mouth lift. "Alright. He was in the oncology wing. He's a transvestite, so he wants me to call him *she*."

My blood starts to hum. "Trans," I say. "You can just say *she's trans*. Transvestite isn't a word used anymore."

He lets out an impatient breath. "Anyway—we have this sort of terse back-and-forth about pronouns, of all things. Finally, I turn to him and say, *Well, ma'am, I've got bad news about your testicles*."

For some reason, this makes both my parents laugh. I feel like someone has stuck a wire underneath my skin and touched it to an open socket.

My mother sighs. "The gays are just so *PC* about everything." Her eyes flicker upward, and she remembers her company for a moment because she says, "No offense, Donovan."

Donovan shrugs. "None taken." To his credit, he does look calm about the whole thing. *Blasé bastard.*

I can't let this go. "Hold on—yes," I snap. "Offense is taken. Mom. You can't say things like that."

She knits her eyebrows at me. "Why not?"

"How would you feel if I called you a man? In the middle of a *cancer diagnosis?*"

My father puts his hand on her knee protectively. She makes a vague motion with her glass of wine. "Oh, does it matter? Donovan just said he doesn't mind."

"I don't," Donovan said.

"Okay—but did you stop to think that maybe Donovan isn't the only queer person here?"

My mother blinks at that. Then she turns and stares for a long, hard time at Kenzi. Her mouth opens, and she lets out a small "*Oh.*"

Kenzi puts her hand on her chest. "What, me? Oh, no, I'm not—um—well, I mean, with the right person, *maybe* I'd think about switching teams, you know? Never leave doors closed, I say..."

"It's me," I blurt out. My blood is hot, my temper has

flared, and I'm in The Zone. I'm seeing red, and I can't stop the words from flying out of me. "I'm bisexual. And I'm dating Kenzi and Donovan. Does anyone have a problem with that?"

For once, everyone goes silent. I can feel my father's stare, his glare like a shot from a nail gun. My mother opens her mouth, closes it, and then opens it again. A fish on dry land.

"Well...no," she says finally. "Of course not, darling."

My father shifts in his spot, and his chair scrapes across the concrete. I can hear the soft lapping of water on the lip of the pool. If Nadine is surprised, she doesn't show it; she glances down at her phone, checking the time.

Kenzi claps her hands together loudly. "What do we have for dessert?"

45

DONOVAN

The King residence is a maze.

There are about twenty different bathrooms here. I pick the one under the stairs. The walls are turquoise blue, and there are small jars of seashells in here—the kind you'd find at a beachside hotel—and the whole thing smells too much like potpourri. I check my eyes to make sure they're not completely bloodshot.

I also need a second to breathe.

On one hand, I've discovered I have a new kink. Jason King, moaning and flushed red underneath me, unleashed something primal inside of me.

On the other hand, being claimed by him, in front of his family, was also something I didn't know I needed...until it happened. The whole night feels like a fugue state. Like I'll wake up and tomorrow I'll be back on my knees, scrubbing Mr. King's boat, while Jason and his friends call me *dick boy* from the bow.

I dab some water between my eyes and on the back of my neck. Then I exit to rejoin the crew.

On my way back to the patio, I hear voices from the

kitchen. I slow down the hall, pausing next to one of the many family photos hung on the wall.

"—I hope you haven't forgotten our arrangement."

Mr. King's voice is low, threatening. Gone is the amiable, polite host from before.

"Of course not." Is that…Kenzi? I glance around the corner. They're alone in the kitchen, and she's carried a stack of dessert dishes to the counter. Mr. King has her cornered—quite literally—at the sink.

The way he's talking to her makes my blood go cold.

"But you and Jason—"

"I haven't told him about Otto," Kenzi says firmly. "And I won't."

For a moment, the silence that hangs between them is thick.

"Tread very, very carefully," he tells her. "You'll do anything to protect your son. And I'll do anything to protect mine."

With that, Mr. King takes his exit, leaving Kenzi and going back outside to the patio.

Kenzi lingers, however. I watch as she white-knuckles the kitchen counter, frozen in place. Her chest rises and falls quickly with each breath.

I can't watch her suffer alone anymore. I step out from behind the wall, entering the kitchen. "Hey," I say gently.

Immediately, her hand flies to her chest. "Jesus, Donovan. You scared the crap out of me." Her eyes flicker over me, and then she squints. "How long have you—?"

"Long enough." I lean against the counter beside her. We don't look at each other, but our arms touch. "So that's why you haven't told Jason yet."

"Otto needs the care he's getting right now," Kenzi says softly. "If he didn't have it…I don't know what we'd do…"

She sounds terrified, close to tears. I've never heard her voice like this.

I reach out and weave my fingers through hers. Her hand is trembling in mine. "We'll figure it out," I tell her. "Together. I promise."

There's a hiss as the sliding doors open and shut. Immediately, Kenzi retracts her hand, and her back goes stiff.

But it's only Jason. He steps into the kitchen, a small smile on his lips. "Hey. You guys okay?"

Kenzi matches his smile. "We're great." Her walls have gone up again. She's behind a defense I can't climb.

"Cool," Jason says. "You wanna get the fuck out of here?"

I chime in. "Please."

46

KENZI

We don't get quite the same treatment leaving the King residence as we did entering. Rather than the all-smiles greeting committee, we get a couple of tight-lipped grimaces, quick pats on the back, and *hope to see you soon*s that sound less than genuine.

Mr. King has daggers in his eyes, and I can't wait to be outside of range.

We make it through the cold and into Jason's car, and Jason has to let the car run for a minute in park, blasting heat on the window shield to clear the crystals.

The second we're in, Donovan lets out a whoop from the back. "Hands down, the strangest dinner party I've ever been to," he says.

Jason lets out a bit of a laugh. "Yeah, it was…a lot."

The window clears enough, so he puts the car into gear and pulls us out of the parking lot. I'm not sad to watch the King mansion vanish in the distance. Jason has a mile-long stare, though, as he watches the road ahead.

"How're you feeling about it?" I ask and slip my hand over his leg.

"Which part?" he asks.

I shrug. "Seeing your ex. Coming out to your family. All of it, I guess."

The dim light from the headlights casts intense shadows over his face, and I can see the muscles in his jaw tighten as he picks his words carefully. "Lighter," he finally says. "Scared. But in a good way."

"Scared...about what?" I press. "Are you worried about what your parents will think?"

This, too, takes him a second to consider. "No," he says and sounds surprised by his own response. "Honestly? I don't give a rat's ass what they think."

"So what are you nervous about?"

He rubs his hands over the steering wheel once. "That was the first time I've ever said it out loud to anyone. Even myself. Honestly...I'm not even sure I know what it *means* to be bisexual."

"It means you're greedy," Donovan says from the back.

I roll my eyes and give Jason's thigh a squeeze. "It doesn't have to *mean* anything. You're the same person you were two hours ago. You're just...a more honest version of the guy you were before."

"*Honest*," Jason says, and the word seems to carry some weight the way he says it. "Yeah. I like that."

Guilt, the ever-present crab on my shoulder, gives me a pinch. I rub the back of my neck to ward the feeling away.

"What do you want to do now?" Donovan asks.

Jason seems to think about it; then, suddenly, he veers. We come to a quick stop at the side of the road, where he parks the car. "I want to go for a swim," he says, as though it's the most obvious thing in the world.

Then he unbuckles and gets out of the car.

Donovan and I exchange a glance. "Are we...supposed to follow him?" Donovan asks.

"I am." I unbuckle my seat belt, and the car complains with small beeps as I get out of the passenger side.

We're right on the Bayside. I take my shoes off and step off the edge of the road and onto the sand. I have to tread through dune grass, its tendrils capped in ice, until I get to the beach.

Jason is already at the edge of the water. He kicks off his loafers and, without hesitating, dives into the surf. Nice suit and all. When he resurfaces, he lets out a shout. But he's grinning.

Something inside me unlocks. He is brave, and bold, and *fucking insane*, and I want to be insane with him.

Donovan steps in beside me. "Truth or dare?" he asks.

Donovan and I glance at each other, and the look in his eyes is all I need to know that we've both come to the same decision.

"*Dare*," we both say simultaneously.

We ditch our shoes. Donovan drops his blazer, and I lose my shawl as we run at top speed into the ocean. The second the water hits my legs, it feels like shards of ice against my skin. It sucks the breath completely out of my lungs, and I cry out—a sharp, shrill noise.

"It's better once you're in!" Jason calls out, engulfed to his chest. "I promise!"

I trust him. I force myself through the initial blast of pain and shock and—

I take the leap. I jump into the swells until I'm up to my shoulders in it.

And Jason is right. Once you're in? It's not so bad.

It's freeing. My clothes cling to me uncomfortably, but I feel invincible.

Donovan is in the water with us. He's catching his breath, but his eyes are alive.

I swim out to Jason. He grins at me. "You good, Trouble?" he asks.

"Never been better," I tell him, and I mean it.

I don't know how long we stay in the water. But I feel

amazing while I'm in it. We're wild animals. We're unbound, like points of light in the sky. We're free.

It only hurts when we get out, and the chill in the air eats through my soaked dress. The three of us grab the clothes we've left scattered across the shore. We dash to the car and jump in—wet and sandy, shivering and laughing. Immediately, Jason blasts the heat, and I stretch my fingers over the vent. My hands are bright red, fingers numb.

"H-h-holy shit," I say between chattering teeth. "That was insane."

Donovan reaches between the seat dividers and clasps Jason heartily on the shoulder. "Some endurance training, Phelps. Was that some special ops Doctors Without Borders training they put you through?"

At that, Jason winces slightly. His hair is wild at his forehead, his wet shirt plastered to his chest, nipples peaked with the cold. "So...in the theme of *honesty*," he says. "I never joined."

Donovan gawks. "Hold on—do I have frostbite in my ears?"

Jason leans back in his seat, tilting his head back and closing his eyes. I can see the silhouette of him—the sharpness of his chin, the bob in his pronounced Adam's apple as he speaks.

He starts: "The Doctors Without Borders bit...I made it up for the Dr. Mazie show. I *wish* I had joined. But the truth is, they asked me what I'd been doing and I just panicked. I made up a story I made up so I wouldn't have to tell anyone where I really was."

"Where *did* you go?" I ask.

"After I finalized the divorce with Nadine, I felt...like a failure. I rented a hotel room in Jersey and didn't contact anyone. For weeks. I drank myself stupid, slept, and watched Die Hard like...twenty times."

He can't look at either of us. He exhales a deep sigh. "I just didn't want to feel anything. My heart hurt. I was so embarrassed. I couldn't face my family. I couldn't face anyone. I've literally never failed at anything. Second place is as good as last place in my family's book. Divorce is fucking unheard of among the Kings. I didn't want to be a loser."

For a second, neither Donovan nor I say anything; we just let the hum of the car heater fill the empty space. Jason looks so vulnerable right now—cracked open under the moonlight—and my chest aches for him.

Finally, Donovan returns his hand to Jason's shoulder and gives the other man a squeeze. "Jason," he says seriously. "I've got something to say...and I want you to really hear me, okay?"

Jason nods. "Okay..."

"As someone who has spent his *entire lifetime* as a loser... it's about time you joined us."

There it is. That hopeful grin slowly returns to Jason's face. "Yeah? I'm part of the losers' club?"

"You're damn right," I concur. "Trust me. It's way more fun here."

47

KENZI

We go back to their place. Between frantic bouts of kisses and touches, the three of us shed our clothes all the way from the living room into the bathroom, leaving little piles like Hansel and Gretel.

In the shower, sand and salt water roll off me. The hot water brings my limbs back to life. My fingers throb as they move from freezing cold to burning hot, sensation tingling through them.

And through me. Jason's lips on my shoulders. Donovan's hands on my hips. Cleansing me. Resurrecting me.

We towel off, but we're still dripping wet when we stumble into the bedroom.

It's strange—even though we spent the whole night together, I feel like I haven't seen them in so long. We wear different masks with other people around; in front of Mr. and Mrs. King, the three of us had to be conservative, judicious. Here, in the privacy of our own home, we can love openly. Want openly. Crave each other openly, fully, desperately.

A version of myself that has spent all night caged up inside of me has finally been released.

Jason lifts me up, and I wrap my legs around him as he carries me to bed. He kisses me, and I can taste the abandon on his lips. After tonight's excitement, he's a lighter man. Brighter. There's nothing holding him back.

Donovan comes behind him and kisses Jason's shoulder. Jason twists his head to catch Donovan's lips in his own. The sight of them kissing always making my heart flip. But there's something...*different* about them tonight. They're easier with each other. More relaxed. I don't know what shifted, but I do know it's a good look on them. I feel a fluttering between my legs just watching them.

"I want it," Jason murmurs, so quietly I almost don't hear him.

"You want *what*?" Donovan pries, encouraging.

Jason wets his lips briefly, nervously. "Uh...you. Inside of me."

Donovan glances at me. "Do you mind if I borrow your boyfriend?"

He's being coy. I play into it. I trickle my nails up the nape of Jason's neck—the way I know he likes it—and I feel him shudder lightly under my touch. "Only if I get to watch," I reply.

"Even better—you get to help. Pass me a condom and lube. Pretty please."

I dig both items out of the bedside drawer—a condom and a small, clear bottle. When I hold it up, Donovan nods and opens his palm for me to drop them in.

Jason lies down on the bed, still as a cadaver. He's quiet. Unnaturally quiet for talkative Jason. Is he nervous? I remember my first time suddenly—how I let Jason take the lead. How Donovan sat beside me, holding me, reassuring me. How *safe* I felt with my two best friends there with me.

And now it's my turn to be the rock.

I flop down and snuggle up next to Jason. "Nervous?" I ask him.

He chuckles lightly. "A little."

"Do you think I'm incapable of being gentle?"

"Yeah. Kinda."

I slip my fingers through Jason's hair. "How does this feel?"

He closes his eyes into my touch and hums contentedly. "Good."

I allow myself a minute to admire Jason's body—the linebacker's chest. His skin looks honey-colored under the dim light of the bedside lamp. I trace the black dove ink across his chest and then trickle my fingers down his toned abdomen.

"I'm going to start with my fingers," Donovan says. "It might be cold at first." He drizzles lube into his palm, snaps the cap back on, and then his hand slips between Jason's legs. "Ready?"

"Yeah," Jason responds. Donovan's eyes lock on Jason, watching his face, and the muscles of Donovan's arm flex as he inserts a finger in the other man.

Jason's eyes shut, and his eyebrows knit. His jaw clenches a little.

I nuzzle against his neck and nibble his earlobe. "Relax," I whisper to him. "Breathe."

He does, exhaling deeply.

"How does that feel?" Donovan asks.

"Uh…strange," Jason says.

"Bad strange or good strange?"

"Good. I think." Jason wets his lips. "I can take more. Keep going."

"Alright…here's another finger."

Jason groans at that one. I kiss and suck his neck and glance down at Donovan. Donovan is still watching Jason, carefully monitoring his face for any sign of discomfort. With his free hand, he takes Jason's cock and starts to pump.

"Fuck," Jason swears and arches into Donovan's touch.

His manhood swells under Donovan's grasp, swiftly moving from half-mast to full.

"Good?" Donovan asks.

Jason buttons his bottom lip between his teeth briefly. "Yeah…" he murmurs. "Really good."

There's a hitch in his voice that makes me throb. I squeeze my thighs together to relieve the pressure.

"You're doing so well," Donovan coaxes, reassuring. "I think you're ready for me."

"Yeah…" Jason sighs. "I want it."

Donovan removes his hands from Jason, which makes the other man groan. He's already hard, and he unwraps the condom, slipping it over himself. He positions himself between Jason's legs and slowly eases inside of him.

Jason half whimpers. "Is that okay?" Donovan asks.

"Yeah," Jason mutters. "Yeah…really good…just…slow…"

Donovan returns his fingers to Jason's cock. He thrusts inside of him, slowly, and pumps him in time.

Jason lets out a noise that sounds like *nyuh-huh.* His eyes are screwed shut, his jaw tight. His neck glows red. He looks like he's in pain—or pleasure? It's hard to tell.

But goddamn, it's arousing.

I can't help myself. My fingers dive into my panties, and I find my slippery wet slit. Immediately, I start flicking my clit. My pleasure bundles and tightens.

"Fuck—stop," Jason says suddenly, and Donovan freezes.

"Am I hurting you?"

Jason shakes his head.

"Do you want me to pull out?"

Another shake of his head.

"Use your words, Hotshot."

Jason hides his face in his hands. "I…uh. Don't want to cum yet."

A light grin ghosts across Donovan's lips. Donovan's eyes

catch on me. They slide over my lewd state appraisingly. "What do you think?" he asks me.

"You two are beautiful," I breathe.

"Isn't he being so good?" Donovan pries. He takes Jason in his hand and pumps him, slowly. Jason throws an arm over his own face, muffling the sound of his moans.

"Mmhm…" I rub myself faster.

"Don't you think he deserves to taste your sweet cunt?"

My breath catches. "Yes…"

I slip out of my panties and crawl over to Jason. He's ready for me, and he holds my thighs when I sling a leg over his chest and lower myself down onto his face. I can feel the warmth of his breath, then the way he nuzzles my cunt, kisses it. Finally, his tongue sneaks between the folds of my slit and lashes across my seam.

"Yes," I whine, "that feels so good…"

Immediately, I'm rocking against his lips. He drinks me in greedily, his tongue bold and hungry. When I open my eyes, I catch sight of Donovan. Watching me. Intently. As if he's memorizing every moan. Every bite of my bottom lip. Every flutter of my eyes.

Jason's tongue is sloppy with need, and his desperation is infectious. Every lick, suck, and nibble sends me closer to the edge of insanity.

I collapse forward and knead my fingers into the muscles of Jason's stomach. My pleasure has made me weak, and I can barely keep myself upright.

Just when I need it, Donovan's strong grip slides over the side of my face. His fingers fist my hand, and he leans forward so his forehead touches mine. I lean into him, and I can feel his breath beating against my lips. We're moving in tandem now; he is the moon, and I am the tide, and I'm swaying into his orbit, following his lead.

"Good," Donovan says, "you're doing so good. Give me

everything." And I don't know if he's talking to me, or Jason, or both of us, but with his permission, I unravel.

A pitchy sound leaves my throat as my orgasm crashes against Jason's mouth. I whine and rock against him, everything in me throbbing. Nuzzled against Donovan, I can hear the hitch in his own breath and his soft, low groan. I feel the vibrations of Jason's moans against my slippery wetness.

We're cresting together—all three of us. Tripping like dominos, crashing and sighing.

I climb off Jason's shoulders, and he pants. Jason's body is slick with sweat, his skin furnace hot. I see white trails of him across his abdomen and dripping down Donovan's fingers. We cuddle him between us, Donovan and I. I want to wrap him up, and I squeeze tightly to this man I cherish so deeply.

He's still trying to catch his breath, panting in the darkness. He laughs. It's the best sound.

"I love you," Jason blurts out. "Both of you. I love you like oceans. I love you to the moon and back again. I love you so much my chest aches—like physically hurts—when I think about you."

His admission hits me like a bag of bricks, and it knocks the air out of me. "I…" I start to speak, but my throat closes up before I can get any further.

His cum, I can swallow. His admission of *love*? It gets stuck like a chicken bone.

Words clot in the back of my throat, stubborn and solid and refusing to go any further.

I look at the other man in bed with us. In the dark, Donovan's eyes flicker like steel.

"Love you, too, big guy," he interrupts. He says it for both of us, saving me from my own fumble. "It's been a long day," he adds. "Let's sleep it off."

Then he reaches over the both of us and flicks off the lamp, and the room floods with darkness.

4 8

KENZI

tto's favorite shirt has a giraffe on it. The giraffe is wearing roller skates. It's getting too small for him now, the sleeves exposing most of his wrists now, but he loves it so much that I can't bear to throw it away.

So I fold it with the rest of the clothes. Donovan and I sit side by side on the love seat, a pile of clean laundry between us, and we're stacking neat, folded piles on the table.

I told him he doesn't have to help—but Donovan does it anyway. The truth is, the repetitive motions help. Last night weighs on my mind. I can't stop thinking about how Jason confessed his love, so openly and warmly. And how, the second he said it, it wasn't joy that filled my heart, but fear.

"Can I ask you something?" I say to Donovan.

"Go ahead."

I hesitate, and then I just come out with it: "Do I have a heart?"

His eyes arch. "That's your question?"

"Humor me."

He scoffs on a laugh. "No. You're a cold, soulless queen like me. It's why we get along so well."

My face goes hot. I snatch up a pile of shirts and stand up with them. "Asshole."

I don't get far, though. Donovan leaps up after me and grabs my arm. "Hey. What's wrong with you?"

Those dark eyes ground me. I feel my anger crest and topple down. "What if…Jason hates me when he finds out I'm…heartless. That's why he left Nadine, isn't it?"

"He left Nadine for a lot of reasons," Donovan reasons.

"He's so…open. True." The backs of my eyes sting. I have to put the stack of clothes back down. I wipe my eyes with the back of my hand, doing my best to stave off the sudden wave of sadness. "And all I do is keep secrets. He told me he loved me last night. And I froze. I feel like such a heartless bitch."

"Hold on," Donovan says. He touches my throat, running two fingers up and pressing in underneath my jaw. "Here. You do have a heart. I can feel your pulse. And that's coming from a doctor, so you know it's true."

We're close like this. His dark eyes look so earnest. Have I ever noticed how beautiful those eyes are?

Like caramel. So easy to fall into.

I find myself falling. Leaning in closer. He does the same, his breath on my lips, when…

"Mummy?"

We pull apart. Otto stands there, rocket ship pajamas on.

Quickly, I go into mom mode and put on a smile. "Hey, buddy. Couldn't sleep?"

But his expression makes my stomach clench. He looks confused, like someone who's woken up from sleepwalking. "I…think I had an accident," he says.

But when he steps closer, my heart drops.

His pants are wet, but they're stained the color of rust. Like blood.

Immediately, I scoop him up into my arms. "You're okay," I reassure him. "It's going to be okay."

"I've got the car," Donovan says and snatches up the keys.

* * *

Donovan is the one who gives me the news.

Donovan: "His kidneys are shutting down."

Me: "But I thought the dialysis was working?"

Donovan: "It was. But it only slows the process down—it doesn't cure him. Unfortunately, the damage to his kidneys was already extensive when he got here."

Me: "So what's the next step?"

Donovan: "He needs a transplant. We've got him on the list, but…there's no saying when he'll get a match for sure. Until then, we'll keep him on dialysis. He needs to stay here for a couple of nights for observation."

Me: "Okay."

Donovan: "It's okay to be scared."

But I don't feel scared. I don't feel anything.

My soul is ice water, and I'm a million miles under the sea.

PART IV

THE TRUTH: JANUARY, 2019

4 9

DONOVAN

Kenzi doesn't leave Otto's side.

I do everything I can to ease his discomfort and flush the infection from his system, but in the end, it comes back to the same result: he needs a new kidney. Fast.

When I work, it's through a haze. All I can think about is Otto.

I barely register when, halfway through my shift, Leonard King comes up to me and taps me on the arm.

"Donovan. A moment."

I follow the other man to his office. I've worked in this hospital for almost ten years, but I could probably count on one hand the number of times I've been inside Mr. King's office. He's in his own tower, cut away from the rest of the hospital.

I'm immediately uncomfortable, but I sit down across from him anyway.

Sharks can smell fear. I don't want him to catch the scent.

He presses his fingertips together, tenting his hands. "How is Kenzi's boy doing?"

"Not great. Otto's kidney enzymes are down from yesterday. He's going to need a transplant soon."

"How long?"

"I give it two weeks. If everything goes smoothly."

"And if it doesn't?"

I shake my head. "The infection could spread. Damage his other organs."

King closes his eyes and tilts his head back. It's as though he's lost in thought, but the act itself is performative. There are no furrows in his brow.

"A shame," he comes out with, finally. "How is his mother handling it?"

I feel a prickle of warning here. Why does he want to know about Kenzi? I keep it vague: "As well as anyone can."

A smile cuts across Mr. King's face. "I remember when you were kids. You two were practically glued at the hip, weren't you?"

"I guess some things don't change."

"You have a special relationship with her. And Jason."

My mouth clamps shut, jaw tightening. So *that's* what this is about. "All due respect," I say, "if you want to know about your son, you should probably ask him."

A sharp smile crosses his lips. "This isn't something I can discuss with him. He hasn't been himself since he started living with you."

Ants are crawling across my skin. I'll be polite—because he's my boss—but I don't have to sit here and listen to this shit.

If he wants to believe I'm the bad influence that turned his son queer, that's fine by me. I couldn't care less. But I don't have to put up with it.

"What do you want?" I ask, because I'm done beating around the bush.

He blinks. "This isn't about what I want," he says. "This is about what's best for everyone involved." His leather chair groans as he leans back into it. "I would like to help Otto. I have strings I can pull to ensure he gets what he needs. Under one condition."

"What condition?"

"You leave Hannsett Island. Tomorrow."

A burning in my throat, like cyanide. I can't unclench my jaw.

He continues. "I've written you an excellent recommendation for Lenox Hill. They're a great hospital. I'll expedite the transfer."

"But—"

"Your father's debts have been washed clean. So have yours. You've served the Lighthouse well, and I commend you for your work here. Lenox is eager to have you."

Being set free is a strange sensation when you never felt like you were in a cage.

"All due respect, sir…the Lighthouse Medical is where I was trained. It's where I've always wanted to be. My patients are here. I don't want to be anywhere else."

"The change will be good for you," he continues. "For all of us. For Otto and Kenzi, especially." He reaches into his desk and pulls out a sheet of paper. He pushes it across the table to me, along with a pen. "I have your transfer documents already filled out. All you need to do is sign."

Hannsett Island is my home. The Lighthouse Medical Center is the only hospital I ever wanted to work in. The thought of leaving Kenzi and Jason right now makes my stomach churn.

But there's a second thought, a mantra, repeating over and over in my head:

Otto needs this. Otto needs this.

"What about my patients?" I ask.

"They'll be in good hands," he reassures me.

I stare at the black line on the document.

"And these *strings* you're pulling—"

"That's for me to worry about. Nothing illegal, if that's what you're asking."

Honestly? It doesn't seem beneath him to go straight for some black market trade.

When I don't move, King presses. "Alternatively, you could stay. We could wait three to five months for another kidney to come available, if Otto lasts that long. Kenzi could lose her son, but I suppose these things happen. You know what that feels like to lose family, don't you—?"

I swipe the pen off the desk and scribble my signature across the black line. As soon as it's done, I drop the pen and put my hand back in my lap. I don't want him to see my hands are shaking.

"You're making the right decision," he says.

"Are we done?"

He nods. I rise. My heart is pounding. I can't get out of this room quickly enough.

But I pause with my hand on the door handle. There is one thing I can't let go—

"Just so you know," I tell him, "your son's sexuality isn't an illness that you can cure."

His eyes don't leave mine. "No," he says, his voice shockingly calm, "but I can remove the tumor."

His words are a knife between the ribs, but I push on. "Jason is a great guy. And if you spent less time trying to control him and more time supporting him for who he is, you'd see that."

He says nothing at that. I walk out of his office, feeling as though I'm stepping out of a nightmare.

KENZI

I keep it together for Otto.

It seems like we'll be here at least overnight for observation. When I'm with him, I try to keep it light-hearted and fun. He's uncomfortable. Kevin—he says—is being a bully.

The only thing worse than seeing your child suffer...is being helpless to do anything about it.

I wish Kevin was real. I wish I could call his mother up and unleash on her. I wish I could banish Kevin from our existence. I wish I could take Otto and run far, far away and leave Kevin stranded here.

But I can't. Otto is in the hands of the doctors at Lighthouse Medical now.

He's strapped into a dialysis machine, tubes and wires churning through my boy. Pearl sits in the chair opposite us, her nose in a Nora Roberts novel. I sit in the chair next to Otto and pet his dark hair back. "How're you feeling, buddy?"

He lifts his arm, and IV lines follow. "Like a cyborg."

I let out a small laugh, because somehow, through all this, he still has a sense of humor.

There's a knock on the door, and I glance up to see a doctor I don't recognize enter the room. She has a warm smile. "How are we doing?"

"Holding up," I tell her. Otto gives her a thumbs-up.

"That's what I like to hear." She steps inside and shakes my hand. "My name is Dr. Esmeralda. I'll be your attending doctor."

"Oh—sorry. There must be a mistake. Dr. Donovan is our doctor."

Her lips thin, but her smile remains intact. "Unfortunately, Dr. Donovan is no longer with Lighthouse Medical. I'm taking over his patients. Including this strong man here!"

"Hold on—what do you mean, he's no longer working here?"

"Just that. He's transferred to another hospital in New York."

"*Transferred?*" Pearl balks.

"I can assure you, I've been through Otto's paperwork, and we'll keep him on track—"

I grab my jacket and sling it over my shoulders. I turn to Otto and say, "Hey, how would you feel if Grandma Pearl stayed with you for a bit?"

Otto nods. "Okay."

I kiss his forehead. "You're my strongest boy." Then I turn to my mother and promise, "I'll be right back."

* * *

I interrogate Jason, but he knows nothing. He does give me the keys to their place, though.

Donovan isn't home. There are some notes scribbled on a notepad though—the ferry departure times for today.

The wheels of the rental car squeal as I jet it down the road.

I'm beating the speed limit, but I don't care. The next ferry leaves at 5:15.

It's 5:04 now.

I swerve around cars going too slow. I lay on the horn. It's a miracle when I pull up to the parking lot in one piece, the car spitting gravel under its wheels.

The ferry blows its horn. Last call for passengers.

I kill the engine and race out. I've left my coat, and the cold nips here, this close to the island's edge, but I don't care.

Because I *see* him. Donovan. Bag slung over his shoulders. Handing his ticket to the ferryman before trudging up the ramp. The wind kicks through his hair, which looks ginger blond in the light.

"Donovan!" I call out before he can board the ferry.

He stops in place and looks at me. The muscles in his jaw go tight.

I'm short of breath, and the cold air makes my lungs feel like I'm breathing through ice. I stop at the bottom of the ramp, and he doubles back to meet me.

"What the hell are you doing here?" he asks.

"What are *you* doing?" I counter. "You're leaving? *Now?*"

His eyes narrow. "I was going to call you."

"When? When you were in New York and I couldn't do anything about it?" He paces away, jaw set. I throw up my hands. "Jesus Christ, Donovan, just talk to me!"

He steps close, and his voice is low, intense. "I promise, I will explain everything. But I can't talk about this. Not here." His eyes flicker side to side, as though he's looking for someone. Or someone's looking for him? When they meet mine again, he says: "Right now, you need to trust me."

"You can't abandon Otto." My voice cracks. My vision goes hazy. "He needs you."

I need you sits on the tip of my tongue, but the words clot.

Donovan glances at his feet. *Finally* showing some emotion. A hint of shame. "He's a strong kid. He'll be alright."

My jaw clenches. "Truth or dare."

His eyes darken. "I'm not playing this game with you."

"Truth or dare."

He throws up his hands. "Dare!"

"I dare you to tell the truth for once."

"What do you want me to say?"

"Do you love me?" Silence from Donovan. His lips press together tightly, sealing the words in, so I continue. "Is that why you never pick truth? Because you're afraid to confess it…you love me. You have. Ever since we were kids. I didn't get it before, but now—"

"Stop." It's not angry—his tone sounds defeated. His eyes close briefly, as though he's in pain. "Please, stop."

"Why?" I ask. "Because it's true? If it's true—if you really love me—stay. Stay for me."

His eyes open again, and he stares at me. I can't decipher the darkness behind those browns.

"I don't love anyone but myself, Kenzi," he says. "You should know that by now."

Cue my heart, shattering into a million pieces.

I can't speak. There are words—words I want to say, balled up in the back of my throat.

But they won't come out.

The ferryman comes between us and starts to close the gate. "Are you coming aboard, ma'am?"

Otto is in Hannsett Island. Jason is here.

But my heart is on the ferry, clutching his bag.

I shake my head. I step back behind the yellow line and hug my arms to my chest.

"I love you," I tell him suddenly. The words hurt. Like something has been torn out from inside of me, stitches ripped open.

Donovan's eyes go wide. He looks like I've slapped him. For a minute, he just stands there, staring at me.

"Say something," I prompt, because this dead air between us is too painful, and he feels so far away already.

"I'm sorry" is the last thing Donovan says before he turns and boards the ferry.

The cold suddenly sinks into my bones, chilling me from the inside out. I can't move, though—I'm rooted to the ground as I watch the ferry launch off, churning dark water below as it goes. Donovan stands there for a while, watching me. Then he turns and vanishes inside.

He's gone. And I'm left all alone.

51

———

KENZI

I ride back to Lighthouse Medical in a daze.

I stay with Otto. I listen as Dr. Esmeralda explains that they'll be running tests for the next couple of days. She uses phrases like *mitigate the damage.*

I have my armor on, and I can barely hear her through the plates of steel.

But when Otto falls asleep and there's nothing but me and the sound of my own anxieties bouncing around inside my skull, it becomes incredibly hard to keep myself in one piece.

Pearl stays with Otto, and I excuse myself for just a minute. My vision blurs on the way out—the door becomes a foggy shape, and I barely make it through before my cheeks grow hot.

The sanitized floors vibrate in my vision. Every time I blink, the world gets a little hazier, like going to the eye doctor: *What about this? Can you see now?*

I bump into a solid form. I rub my eyes and try to turn away. "I'm sorry—"

"Hey." Jason's hands move to my shoulders. He holds me to him, keeping me in place. "Are you okay?"

My bottom lip won't stop shaking, but my throat feels like a steel trap and refuses to let any sound escape. It's all I can do to shake my head.

He pulls me against him. Pressed to his chest, I inhale him deeply: patchouli, mint.

A dam breaks. I'm shuddering, and I can't stop it—like I've got hypothermia. Jason wraps his arms around me and tightens. I'm safe in his boa-constrictor grip, and finally, the tears start to fall.

"I'm so scared," I sob. "What if—"

"No," Jason says firmly. "No *what-ifs*. It's going to be okay. Everything is going to be okay. I promise."

"Donovan left, he just left—I told him I loved him and he still left."

Jason holds me and presses a kiss to my hairline, when I hear a small voice state, "It's my fault."

Immediately, I pull back and wipe the tears from my face. Otto is there, looking so small in his little hospital gown, his expression grave.

"No, honey—" I crouch down, and my face feels hot, and I know I must look like a wreck, but I force my voice to steady and tell him firmly, "You did nothing wrong. Okay?"

"Not me," Otto says, "Kevin. He chases everyone away."

My heart crumbles. I suck in a breath of air, but I can hear the shake in my lungs.

"Hey, buddy," Jason says suddenly. "You know what I think?"

"What?" Otto asks.

"You're the coolest kid. I know it. Dr. Donovan knows it, too. Whatever he's got going on, that has to do with him. Not you."

There's a sense of conviction in Jason's voice that Otto and I both need right now. He's the solid ground on which we can stand. Jason hangs in the doorway, then adds, "I was about to get some pizza from the dining hall. Does anyone in this room like pizza?"

Quickly, I swipe tears from my eyes. "Pizza sounds heavenly."

5 2

JASON

They stay at the hospital for three nights.

Pearl comes in and out, bringing clothes, bringing food. I try to help where I can.

Nothing from Donovan. I've called, texted, but he's a ghost in the wind.

I don't get anything from him but a voicemail informing me to *trust him* and a reminder to water the house plant.

I try not to let it get to me, but it's hard. It's like breaking the inside of your lip and trying to ignore the bump.

I've got to be strong. Kenzi needs me. Otto needs me.

She puts on a smile for Otto and keeps her voice light and jolly, but a light has gone out behind her eyes.

She's spent. And I can't blame her.

I keep myself busy. The day of Otto's release, I do a clean appendectomy. The surgery is flawless, the stitches tight, and it feels healing, somehow. Like in removing the bad organ in another human, I'm cleaning out something rotten within myself, too.

Sometimes, it's better to get rid of something toxic than try to hold on to it.

I finish my shift and knock lightly on the door to their

room. Kenzi opens up. She's wearing a thick gray sweater that swallows her. She looks glassy-eyed and tired. "Hey. Otto's napping."

I see the kid in bed behind her. It breaks my heart every time to see him looped up to machines.

"I talked to Dr. Esmeralda," I tell her.

"And?"

"I've got good news and bad news. The bad news is, he's not getting any better."

Kenzi hugs herself tighter. "The good news?"

"He's stable enough to go home."

"That is good," she says, her voice sounding hollow. "He misses his own bed."

I take her arm in my hand and give it a small squeeze. "I'm finishing up here. Want me to come over? Keep an eye on him."

She nods, and a little hair tumbles out of her messy bun. "Yeah. I'd like that."

* * *

We pick up bar food at the Anchor and drive to Kenzi's place.

Missus P sets the table, a meal of bar burgers and fries, but no one seems very hungry. Eventually, Kenzi takes Otto upstairs to give him a bath and put him to bed.

Kenzi's mom is clearing the table, putting the dishes in the sink. I roll up my sleeves and button them above the elbow.

"Can I lend a hand, Missus P?"

"You do one better and lend both of your hands, Jason. That wine won't open itself."

"Yes, ma'am."

I find the corkscrew and take the bottle of red from the counter, uncorking it. Then I pluck a glass from the cabinet and pour her one. She wipes her hands on a dish towel and then takes the glass with a "thank you" before stepping out of the way so I can pick up where she left off.

I load dishes while she sips. "That boy is her whole world, you know."

"I know. Otto is a great kid."

"God forbid, if something were to happen to him…"

"Nothing will happen to Otto on my watch. I'll make sure of it."

She sighs, then says, "I'm just…*saying*. Worst-case scenario being what it is. Kenzi will…need someone."

"I'm not leaving her side for a second. I promise."

She examines me. "Someone raised you right. Which is strange, because I've met your father."

I load the last of the dishes and wipe my hands. "Yeah, well, Kenzi and I have something in common."

"Which is?"

"We both have pretty cool moms."

She lets out a laugh at that. Then she taps the side of her glass. "I'm taking this into the bath with me. You be good to my daughter."

"Good night, Missus P."

She gives my arm a pat as she drifts past me and heads upstairs.

She's a class act. It occurs to me, out of nowhere, that I'm more comfortable in Kenzi's kitchen, with Kenzi's family, than I am with my own.

I break my own rules and pour myself a half glass of wine.

"Can I get one of those?"

I glance up. Kenzi descends the stairs and collapses into one of the flimsy chairs around the kitchen table. She's changed out of her hospital clothes and into equally cozy non-hospital clothes: gray sweatpants and an oversized blue sweater with snowflakes knitted into the collar. Her thick hair has gone frizzy, and her eyes are half-lidded. She looks *exhausted*. But—and, I swear, I'm not trying to fetishize this kind of soul-weary fatigue—there is something beautiful about her right now. She's vulnerable. Too tired to keep up those ten thousand walls she usually has around her. She's soft and tender, like a bruise, and I try to be gentle with her.

I pour her a glass and slide it across the table. She wraps her fingers around the stem and takes a small sip, but it's mechanical. Her eyes stare into an empty chair across from her, so I fill the spot.

"How're you holding up?" I ask.

"Not great," she says. "I'm a bad mom. A bad friend. A bad…everything."

"You're not bad," I reason.

Those green eyes narrow. "My son's kidney is failing. Donovan is who-knows-where. And I'm…barely holding it together."

Her voice is hollow, feigning apathy, but her eyes are brimming with tears.

I give her a moment, letting her roll around in her own misery. Sometimes, it helps to hold space for self-pity. Then, after some thought, I say, "I had this patient come in one time…he was a street performer, who dressed up and did these juggling acts. Well, his act went awry, and he had a chainsaw lodged between his shoulder and his clavicle. I extracted the blade, sewed him up, and recommend he stop juggling chainsaws. He said the chainsaws weren't the problem. Chainsaws, knives, you name it, he can juggle it. The culprit was just a plain, normal hacky sack that he'd decided to throw into the mix just to give people a little perspective. It threw his whole game off, and the whole thing came tumbling down."

Kenzi smiles, just a little, and tucks her chin into her palm. "So what's the moral of the story, Guru Jason?"

"The moral of the story is…you're juggling a lot. And I see it. Frankly…you're doing the job of twenty people right now.

Mother. Daughter. Nurse." I reach across the table and lace my fingers in hers. I give her hand a squeeze. "I think it's okay to cut yourself a little slack."

She rubs her thumb over the back of my hand, and I see those tears well up again. She lets go of my hand to brush them away. "God, this must be terrible for you. Spending your off-duty time coaxing me out of my depression."

"Kenzi. I want you to really hear this. I wouldn't be here if I didn't want to be. I *want* to be here. I promise. Whatever you need. I'm here for you."

She stares at me for a second, and then she crosses the table to stand beside me. Before I know it, she's climbing in my lap, straddling me.

I let out a muffled noise as she crushes her lips against mine, hard. "Ah—this isn't…you don't have to thank me for being here…"

"You asked me what I need," she said. "I need this. I need you."

"I need you, too…"

My need for her is a blood rush, pulsing hot. Kenzi is a hit of straight dopamine, and when she curls her tongue inside my mouth, I feel a lick of pleasure that runs down the center of me, knotting in my lap. I've tasted Kenzi's hunger before, but this is different; the way she's kissing me is desperate and uncontrolled, like she's trying to climb completely inside of me. She grips the back of my neck, her nails grazing in that way that makes me groan in her mouth. Her body is warm and slots perfectly against mine, and when I cup her ass to pull her closer, she wiggles against me in a way that suggests she needs this as bad as I do.

My lips feel swollen when we break for air. "Should we move this upstairs?" I suggest. After all, Otto doesn't need to walk in on me mauling his mom in the kitchen.

Kenzi grins. Her palm slips underneath my shirt, fingertips playing on my abdomen. "What, are you afraid you can't keep quiet?"

"No. Afraid *you* can't."

I suck her bottom lip into my mouth, drawing it between my teeth before releasing, and as if to prove my point, she gasps.

"Yeah," she purrs, lust-drunk. "Upstairs is good."

I cradle her in my arms, and when I stand, she winds her legs around my hips. She hooks her arms around my shoulders and presses small, needy kisses under my jaw, down my throat, as I carry her upstairs. We pass Otto's room and Missus P's, and I carry Kenzi to her own room—the last one on the hall. I close the door behind us, flick the lock, and lower her onto the bed.

We're ravenous here. It occurs to me that we're unbalanced—we've gotten so used to the three of us in bed, now we're passionate enough for three people, not two. She rips the buttons of my shirt, I throw her sweater across the room, and to my delight there's nothing underneath—just the round swell of her breasts, pink nipples hard for me. We tear at each other's clothes and roll around in bed, kissing, pawing, sloppy, until we roll right off the bed. My back hits the ground hard, Kenzi on top of me. Kenzi quickly covers my mouth with her hand, and I vibrate with silent laughter as she stares hard at the door, listening for any sounds of life.

"Don't make a sound," she whispers and then kisses the back of her hand where my mouth should be. There's a brief pressure on my face as she pushes up to her feet, and my body misses her warmth. But, obediently, I lie there, quietly, as Kenzi gets up and puts on her sweater once more so she can crack open the door and glance down the hall. She stays there for a couple of seconds, then closes the door again and goes into her bathroom instead.

"Coast clear?" I ask when she returns.

"Thankfully." She has a condom between her fingers, and

she tosses her sweater back on the floor. She climbs down with me, and I watch her undo my pants and then lift my hips to help so she can yank them down my legs, along with my briefs. My pants are at my ankles now, awkwardly trapping my legs, and my stiff cock, now freed, springs back against my navel.

"I want to put it on," she explains as she rips the packaging.

"Hot," I say as I lift onto my elbows, and it comes out sarcastic, but I mean it. I genuinely find it hot when, instead of inconveniently fumbling with the wrapper between kisses and touches, the condom becomes part of the sex act itself.

Kenzi takes me in her hand and, slowly, massages me from base to tip. I bite back a groan and try to focus on breathing to keep my noises to a minimum, but it's hard. Her touches coax out an ache buried inside of me, and I grant myself permission to savor this. She strokes me until I'm fully swollen, bow-taut, and only then does she roll the condom over me. She gives me a couple more pumps like this, and I can feel less of her, but the sight is no less erotic, her touch no less exciting, and when her eyes meet mine, those emeralds burn.

"Come here and kiss me," I tell her, and she climbs over me and does. I slide my hands up the backs of her soft thighs, over her cotton panties, and squeeze as we kiss. I pull her against me and gently roll us over, so now she's underneath me. We're wedged on the carpeted ground between the bed and the window, but neither of us seem to care. All my thoughts dissolve at the tip of her tongue, which dances over mine in a way that turns my dick into a second heartbeat.

I roll her panties off her legs and plunge myself inside of her. Kenzi gasps, and I remind her to "be quiet, Trouble." She's soaking wet for me, and she whimpers softly into my mouth as I slide inside her easily. She hooks her thigh around me, her heel pressing into my rear, encouraging me deeper, and I fill her to my hilt.

She's beautiful now—lips swollen and wet, face red, chest rising and falling rapidly as she pants in quick, shallow breaths. I rut against her, savoring her, but she hooks her hand at the back of my neck and begs, "Harder."

So I give it to her. I stabilize myself with one palm flat on the floor, and I swing my hips into hers. She arches back and reaches up for one of the pillows, snatching it off the bed and bringing it to her face. Kenzi screams into the pillow as I fuck her so hard, I can hear our hips slap together.

I need to see her face, though, so I yank the pillow from her and catch her mouth in mine instead. She lets out a series of whimpers against my lips, and her fingers curl at my chest, at my back, nails digging in.

"Put your hand on my throat," Kenzi says breathlessly, between thrusts.

Now here's the thing: I don't usually engage in physical play. I'm six foot five. Two hundred and ten pounds. I'm a walking brick house. I know how easy it is for me to seriously hurt or bruise someone—even if I don't mean to.

But the look in her eyes tells me she wants this. My hands —like everything else about me—are big. I wrap one of them around her throat, and my fingers spread far.

Gently, I squeeze. I know the muscles here; I avoid her larynx and press my thumb and fingertips in at the sides of her throat instead. Her carotid arteries are here, but putting pressure on them for a short time is marginally less dangerous than crushing her larynx.

I watch her face intently for any signs of discomfort. "Is this okay?" I ask.

She nods—at least, as best as she can with her throat in the vise of my hand. She grips my arm and squeezes. "*Harder*," she says, her voice raspy.

I increase the pressure. Her heels dig into the backs of my

thighs, climbing me, and she arches against me as she struggles for breath.

I hold my own breath with her—I'm not going to make her hold hers any longer than I can. But the way she's struggling makes me uneasy. Quickly, I release her completely from my grasp.

She looks up at me and blinks. "Why'd you stop?"

I press my lips together. "You looked like you were struggling."

She takes my hand again, guiding it back to her throat. "It doesn't matter. Keep going."

"It *matters*."

She shakes her head and insists, "I don't care. Choke me."

But there's something wrong about this. I can be as kinky as the next guy—but the look in her eyes, it's off. She's not *here* with me. I deflate slightly, my arousal taking a nosedive, and shake my head.

"What are you doing?" I ask.

She looks at me like I'm crazy. "Having sex."

"No. You're not. You're hurting yourself, and you're using me to do it."

Kenzi turns her head and looks away. Her face turns red, but she doesn't speak, shame, maybe, or sadness trapped in her throat.

And maybe I'm the asshole here. Maybe someone else— maybe *Donovan*—would have choked her until she was black and blue, fucked her hard enough to make her bleed, and satisfied that masochistic itch inside of her.

Maybe these are my own demons—all the fights I got into as a kid, all the times I used my body to hurt people and then swore I wouldn't do that again.

But the disconnect in her gaze unnerves me, and we've reached an impasse.

"I love you, Kenzi," I tell her, my voice intense. "You know that, right?"

She still won't look at me, but her bottom lip quivers at that.

I hover over her. Gently, I lean down and press a soft kiss to the side of her face, then another under her ear. "I love you," I murmur. "All of you. Even the parts you don't like."

Suddenly, she grips the back of my neck. Tight. "I love you, too," she whispers in my ear.

She says those words, and immediately, two things happen:

My heart swells twenty times larger in my chest.

I nearly cum, right then, just from hearing it.

"Say it again."

"I love you…"

I moan and kiss her. She kisses me back—and this time, she feels solid, real. She feels like *Kenzi*. She's not a ghost of herself, and she's not desperately clawing at someone who isn't there. She's mine, and she's here, present with me. I cup her face and stroke my thumb over her cheek and feel the wetness of her tears there. She wraps her arms around my shoulders, clinging to me, and we start again, making love now, as one.

We kiss and slide together, holding each other, tasting each other. I tell her I love her, again and again, and when she says it next, we crest together, and this hot, intense pleasure catapults from my soul into hers.

We ride it out, kissing, panting, and I've never felt closer to her.

53

KENZI

When I wake up, Jason King is naked in my bed.

I want to say the light of day brings out his blemishes—an ugly wrinkle or an old, unsightly scar.

But it doesn't. He's perfect. Every inch of him. His strong jaw. His tousled raven hair. His stacked physique, dove tattoo sweeping over his chest and peeking out from under the thin sheet. His protective arms.

He's so sweet, so kind, so full of unconditional love, and I hate him for it suddenly.

Why can't I be satisfied with this beautiful man in my bed, with the biggest heart known to mankind?

Why does my love need to have porcupine quills to feel real?

Quietly, I slip out of bed. I brush my teeth, tease the sex-knots out of my hair, and slip into clean clothes. Then I sit on the edge of the bed and rub my hand gently over Jason's bicep. He stirs, blinking out of his deep slumber, and when he sees me, he grins.

"Hey," he says.

"Hey." I try to match his smile.

He props himself up on his elbow. "You're up and at 'em."

"I have to make breakfast."

"No. You don't." He pulls himself out of bed—and even in the cold morning, *dear Lord* is he impressive. He finds his clothes on the floor and steps into them, pulling his pants around his hips. "You hang out. Relax. Everyone likes scrambled eggs, right?"

I bite my lip. There are thorns inside my chest, and I feel the urge to say something cruel.

"I thought about him last night," I say casually. "Donovan."

Jason looks up at me as he ties the laces of his shoes. "I know."

"Does that bother you?"

"No," he says plainly. He tugs his shirt over his arms. "I was thinking about him, too."

His words vibrate through me. He catches the side of my face and presses a kiss to my forehead instead when I tilt away from his mouth.

And in that moment, I *do* think of Donovan. And something he told me. He'd said—*is it possible that you're looking for reasons to hate Jason...because hating him is easier than telling him the truth?*

He was right. Jason has done nothing wrong. It's the lie that's poisoning us. This venomous sac that has latched itself to my heart and spoils everything it touches.

"I'm going to get Otto ready," Jason says, fingers on the doorknob. "Come down when you're ready."

"Jason." He stalls and waits. My tongue is stuck to the roof of my mouth, but I have to get these words out. "There's... something you need to know."

* * *

I tell Jason everything.

I tell him about taking the pregnancy test when I was eighteen, after the first time the three of us had sex. I tell him how I went to his father for help. I tell him how I struggled with the secret, how it ate me up alive for the rest of the summer. I tell him about running away from Hannsett. About keeping Otto away, all those years.

And then I tell him about coming back. I tell him about the deal I struck with Mr. King, and how he made me swear that I would never tell Jason, *or else*. I tell him about how Donovan found out, but how I made him promise to hold my secret, too.

The words come spilling out of me, everything I've kept enclosed in my chest for so long. Jason doesn't say anything. He just sits on the bed beside me and listens, occasionally furrowing his eyebrows with displeasure, occasionally glancing at the floor as though lost in thought.

His eyes are on the rug, with a faraway look in them, when I finish. For a minute, we're both silent, letting the weight of the words sink into our bones.

"Otto is my son," he repeats, as though he has to hear the words in his own tongue for them to make sense.

"Biologically," I say, as though that makes a difference, as though this is still something he can opt out of. And maybe there's a part of me—a selfish part of me—that's protective of these past twelve years where it's been only Otto and me against the world.

Maybe there's a part of me that's still struggling to let other people in. Even Jason.

I wet my lips and measure my words before I speak again. "I understand if you hate me, or—"

"*Hate* you?" His dark eyebrows furrow. He looks at me and then takes my face in his hands. "Thank you," he says suddenly.

The shock hits me in the chest. "For what?"

"For taking such good care of our boy."

Our boy. The minute he says the words, whatever fortress I had left around my heart is blown apart. I grip his wrist and choke back a sob. He pulls me into his arms and presses the sweetest kiss I've ever felt to my forehead.

"I'm going to take care of you," he says. "Both of you. From here on out. I promise."

He covers my face in kisses. I feel safe with him. Safer than I deserve.

"What do you need right now?" he asks, and the sincerity in his voice breaks my heart.

"Um…" I bite my lip. "Breakfast did sound nice."

He lets out a laugh. "Yeah. That I can do."

He tucks a strand of hair behind my ear, and this time I'm the one who grabs him and kisses his mouth. Jason is strong —oak-tree strong. The kind of strength that has roots. I need him now, more than ever, his ability to ground me, keep me sane.

His pocket starts buzzing. "Sorry," he says, "it might be the hospital."

"Take it," I urge.

Those blue eyes still look apologetic as he lifts his phone to his ear. "Yeah?" He's quiet for a minute as he listens. "Are you sure? Okay…that's great news. We'll be right in."

My heart is drumming against my rib cage when he hangs up. I put my hands on his thigh and squeeze. "Was it the hospital?"

He nods. A light smile comes over his mouth. "A kidney just came in. It's a match for Otto."

For a second, I can't breathe. "Are you serious? I…thought you said it could take months…?"

"I did." He frowns, and I can tell there's something bothering him. But then he turns to me and says, "I'm going to go to the hospital. Check it out."

"We'll come with you." My heart is buzzing. "If it's good…"

"If this works out…Otto could get a new kidney today."

I didn't know if I could feel happiness again. But I feel it now. It soars through my chest, and I fling my arms around Jason and hug him tightly. "Oh my God…oh my *God*. We'll get packed. Right now."

54

JASON

Kenzi, Otto, and Missus P pile into the car. As I drive them to Lighthouse Medical, there are ants under my skin.

I keep it together for Kenzi. She's happy. And hopeful. And she deserves to be both of those things.

But something about this doesn't feel right.

"How long does the surgery take?" Kenzi asks from the passenger's seat.

"Six hours. Maybe more, depending."

"On complications?"

"On anything. It's just a delicate procedure."

"But it's safe, right?"

She's asking a million questions, and I reach over to give her thigh a squeeze.

"I'll give you the full run down at the hospital. Okay?"

She smiles, tightly, but I can tell she's anxious.

"Can you stop the car?" Otto says from the backseat. He's been quiet this whole drive and I blink in surprise.

"You okay, bud?"

"Just—stop. Please."

I glance at Kenzi. She smile falls and she looks just as confused as I feel.

I pull the car to the side and, the second it stops, Otto unbuckles his seatbelt and jumps out.

"Otto!" Kenzi starts to get up, but I put a palm up to stall her.

"Give us five?" I ask.

Her eyes are wild, frantic. "But—"

"Five minutes. That's all."

I squeeze her hand and then release it. Reluctantly, she hangs back.

I get out of the car. I know where Otto's going.

He's climbed the rope separating the road from the dunes and he trudges through a narrow footpath that's almost completely snowed over at this point. I follow him and we wind through the trees.

The clearing opens up at Donovan's "Screaming Rock."

Otto goes to the edge, but he doesn't scream. He just sits down on the ground, hard, and stares out at the long stretch of ocean below.

His puffy jacket makes his movements awkward. He digs a small rock out from the hardened dirt. I watch as he launches the rock through the air to the ocean below.

"Otto." I say his name, but he doesn't turn around. He just pries out another stone.

I step over and sit down beside him. The morning cold freezes the inside of my throat and I can see my breath in front of my lips.

"Do you want to talk about it?"

He shakes his head. His blue eyes are cast down. He looks like he's holding back tears.

"I miss Dr. Donovan," he says then.

"Yeah…I know you two had a special relationship." I glance out to the water. "I uh…I'm not really good with kids."

Otto looks up at me, blinks. But he's listening.

I continue, "My dad...he wasn't really good with kids either. When me and my brother were growing up, he didn't know how to play with us. Support us. I guess what I'm trying to say is...I'm not going to get this right all the time. But. If you'd let me...I'd really like to be there for you."

Otto looks at me. Those blue eyes are glassy now.

I slip my hand to his shoulder and give a light squeeze. "You're a strong kid. Really strong. I'm proud of you, bud."

He sniffs and glances away. "Thanks."

His small body leans against mine, and I can hear him sniffling. I draw my fingers through his hair.

"It's okay," I murmur to him. "It's going to be okay."

* * *

At the Medical Center, I drop Kenzi, Missus P, and Otto off in the waiting room.

Transplants are my specialty. So I'll be performing the surgery on the live donor. Which makes it my job to screen the donor.

Making the call to be a live donor isn't easy. The recipient is getting better—the surgery, if successful, will most likely have a positive outcome on their life.

With a live donor, you're removing the organ of an otherwise healthy person. It's risky. It can, and often will, have lasting consequences. It can also be the most rewarding thing a person can do with their lives. They are, in my opinion, the real heroes. But it makes it all the more important that I make sure the donor knows what they're getting into, and that they're prepared for what's ahead of them.

I check in with the front desk, and they let me know that my donor is waiting on the second floor. I scale the steps and head into a private conference room.

I'm not entirely prepared to see the person waiting for me, though.

He's an older gentleman—in his sixties, maybe. His gray hair is long, tied back in a familiar ponytail. He's wearing a Hawaiian shirt—even in the dead of winter—and a too-big smile.

"Mr. Blake?" I ask.

"Jason!" He stands, jovial, and shakes my hand. "Or should I call you Dr. King now? Boy, it's been a minute, hasn't it?"

"Sure has."

It's been nearly a decade since I last saw Terry Blake. He used to own a boat at the marina. And, for about a year, he was married to Pearl Stratton. The first time I met Kenzi, she was a smart-ass eighteen-year-old, tired of watching her newly married mom and Mr. Blake make out on their boat.

And then he and Pearl got divorced—though as far as I could tell, it wasn't particularly contentious, it just *didn't work*. He still showed up now and then to play golf with my father, but eventually, he faded from the picture.

I hadn't thought anything about it then. Until now.

He shakes my hand a little too long, and I notice the sweat on his palms. "It's good to see you," I tell him as I retract my hand and take a seat. "I've been wondering what happened to *Sweet Harmony*."

"Ah—had to sell her." He shows all of his teeth when he smiles. "You know how things get."

"Sure." He sits across from me, crosses one leg over the other, then seems to rethink it and puts both feet on the ground. I smile. Try to put him at ease. "What prompted you to want to be a donor?"

He goes somber, which is a strange look on him. "I heard Kenzi's kid was having a time of it. Hell of a thing. And I thought to myself, dammit, Terry, you've never done one good thing in your life. Here's a kid who needs you. Step up to the plate!"

"That's admirable of you. And your doctor walked you through the potential consequences?"

"Oh, they've given me the whole spiel. Took my blood, did the workup. Said I'm a great match for the kid. When do we get going with this anyhow?"

He won't stop fidgeting. Alarm bells are ringing in my head. "In a minute. Since I'm the surgeon, I like to have a one-on-one with my patient beforehand so I make sure you understand the outcomes. There's infection. You could develop a hernia from the site. Of course, there's always the risk of a fatal complication."

He's starting to sweat. His grin is more of a grimace now. "But you're the best surgeon there is, right?"

"Even good surgeons know the risks."

"Yes, yes. I'll sign whatever you need me to sign. Agree to the terms and conditions, all that."

He fishes a tissue out of his pocket and starts using it to dab his forehead. He's lost some hair at the top of his head, and there's a balding patch in the back.

"One more question," I say smoothly. "How much is my father paying you to do this?"

The smile slides off his face completely, and it tells me everything I need to know.

* * *

My father's office is on the top floor. Glass walls, often with the shutters drawn. The biggest office in the building, and one of the best views of Hannsett Island.

The King needs his tower, after all.

I don't bother knocking. I just push inside and let myself in.

"We need to talk," I say.

Not *can we talk?* Or *when is a good time for you?*

Now. We need to talk now.

My father lifts his eyes from behind his desk. He must

sense the shift in the temperature, because he says, "Patterson, I'm going to have to call you back."

He hangs up his call, setting his phone down. Immediately, I launch into it. "You tried to buy Terry Blake's kidney. That's coercion. Organ trade. You could see prison time for that."

A laugh leaves my father. "What stories has he told you? That man was always half out of his mind…"

"Stop!" I demand. "Tell me the truth! For once!"

My father's mouth draws into a thin line. He opens his hand and gestures to the seat in front of him. "Sit down."

I don't. I'm done with him pulling my strings like a marionette. I plant my palms on the table and look him in the eyes. "You've been controlling my life from day one—"

"And look where's it got you." His eyes are a thunderstorm, his voice low and dangerous. "The top surgeon in the Northeast."

"I did that," I snap. "*Me*. With my own two hands and a scalpel. Not you."

He goes quiet. "Is that what you think? You were a spoiled brat. Partying on my boat. Getting drunk. Having sex. Do you think I didn't know? If I hadn't pulled the strings I did, you'd be nowhere. Nothing."

"Not nothing. I'd be a father. Otto's father."

A bitter hiss of a laugh leaves him. "So she told you. I knew she'd crack eventually, the two-faced bitch—"

"*Two-faced*? Her? You've been lying to me for years!"

He rises from his chair quickly. I remember how much that used to scare me—the way he's looking at me right now. How it used to make me feel so small. How I used to sink backward, cowering underneath him.

I don't even flinch now. I stand my ground, calmly.

For a second, I see a look of surprise flicker across his face. His jaw tightens. Sternly, he tells me, "Everything I've done, I've done for you. So you could, one day, fill my shoes. I would have done anything to see you succeed, and I regret none of it. You're a father now, and one day, you'll understand—"

I cut him off. "You're right," I tell him, "I *am* a father now. And I'm going to make damned sure I'm not anything like you."

I push up from the tips of my fingers and straighten up. I'm taller than him. I have been since my limbs shot up in high school. But I never *felt* like the bigger man…until now.

For the first time in my life, I see how small he is. How fragile and insecure. The fear behind those cloudy blue eyes.

The last thing I see is his slack-jawed expression as I exit his office and close the door behind me.

* * *

I pick up a phone in the hallway and call downstairs to the OR. "Stop prepping Otto Stratton," I tell the nurse. "The transplant is canceled."

"No. It's not."

From nowhere…there's Donovan. I blink, because he must be a mirage. He's a fucking sight for sore eyes, tucked away in his leather jacket and black pants. Hair messy. Soft, dark eyes.

I want to hug him. I want to kiss him. But I don't.

I just got finished cutting one toxic person out of my life. I'm not about to let a second one in. And right now, Donovan is a big question mark.

"Donovan." I keep my voice even as I put down the phone. "What are you doing here…?"

"Keep prepping Otto," he repeats, confident. "Surgery is on."

I clench my jaw. Of course he's going to fight me on this.

"I don't know if you remember…but you left. Pretty dramatically. You're not his doctor anymore."

"You're right. I'm not." Then he lifts his arm. There's a plastic hospital band loose around his wrist. "I'm his kidney."

55

KENZI

"Goodness, it takes the doctors a long time to do things, doesn't it?" Pearl says. "They tell you that they'll be right back, and then thirty minutes later…you're still waiting."

She digs into her purse as though she's looking for something, huffs with exasperation, and then folds her hands neatly back into her lap.

Pearl, Otto, and I are tucked away into an exam room together. *Waiting.* We've been here maybe ten minutes, but it feels like ten hours.

I pull out my phone and shoot Jason a text:

[Me:] What's going on? Are we doing the transplant today?
[Me:] Anxious minds want to know.

It doesn't take long before my phone vibrates in response:

[Jason:] We've gotta talk

[Jason:] Come to room 204

[Jason:] Just you

I tuck my phone into my pocket and get up from the chair. Otto is sitting on the exam table, his legs swishing, and I run my fingers through his messy hair. He needs a trim.

"I'm going to step out for just a minute. Do you need anything?"

"A kidney?" he asks hopefully, putting on a cheese-smile.

"I'll see if they have one in the vending machine."

He gives me a double thumbs-up. Morbid humor is the best we can do right now to keep everyone's spirits alive. I press a kiss to the top of his head and dip out of the exam room.

I have to retrace my steps a couple of times to get where I'm going—after spending so much time in the pediatric center, I forget how enormous Lighthouse Medical actually is. I have to cross a bridge between buildings and finally find a room labeled 204.

It looks like an exam room, and I'm not 100 percent sure I'm in the right place, so I knock lightly first.

"Come in," I hear from inside. I crack open the door.

And *he's* there. Not Jason. Donovan. He's sitting on the table, slumped into his leather jacket, but he straightens up when he sees me, looking just as surprised to see me as I am to see him.

"Hey..." he says. Cautiously, the way one might approach a deer.

I see red. Immediately, I fly into the room and launch at him.

"What the hell is wrong with you?" I snap.

He hops off the table and holds up his hands, as though trying to calm me. "I can explain..."

"*Explain?* You *left!* Otto was stuck in the hospital and *you left.*"

"I know. It's complicated."

"Uncomplicate it. Tell me the truth. For once."

His lips screw downward. "Jason's dad made a deal with me. If I left…he'd find Otto a kidney. I guess *polyamorous, bisexual son* wasn't at the top of his Christmas list. He assumed taking me out of the picture would rectify the issue."

"So that's why Otto got bumped up the list."

Donovan nods. He hooks his thumbs into the loops of his jeans. "I didn't want to get you involved, which is why I couldn't tell you. I wasn't sure what exactly he had in mind… but whatever it was, I knew it wasn't legal. You're entangled enough as it is. I couldn't take the risk. Not until it was properly reported."

I blink at Donovan. "You reported Mr. King?"

"The second I left. Someone like that has no business treating patients. The Board of Medicine is looking into it… it's the start of a long process."

For a minute, I'm speechless. This is *a lot* to take in, and I have to glance away from Donovan to process it. Because when I see him and those trusting, dark eyes, it takes everything in me not to grab his face and kiss the living hell out of him.

"I'm sorry, Kenzi," he says, his voice low and earnest in a way it almost never is. "I can't imagine the hell I put you and Otto through."

I bit my lip. "Yeah. It was hell. But if anyone knows the persuasive power of Mr. King…"

"Well, he's going to have to persuade himself out of a jail cell soon." His voice is darker, bitter, a little more like the Donovan I know.

It's then that I notice the plastic hospital band around his wrist. I touch it, running it between my thumb and forefinger. "Are you hurt?"

"Uh…no…" His lips press together, and he's almost shy, suddenly. Then his eyes meet mine, and he says, "I'm your new live donor. If you'll have me."

Cue all the air leaving my lungs. "What?"

"I got my blood work done. Made sure I was a match to Otto. Even my therapist gave the stamp of approval. My kidney is clean, my brain is clean…we're good to go."

"If this is some…dramatic apology…"

"It's not. I promise. I'm not that good at apologies."

I look him in the eyes now. I *have* to see his expression. "Donovan…are you sure?"

When his eyes meet mine, I see nothing but sincerity in them. And confidence. He's made up his mind about his decision. "All my life, I've just wanted…a family. I've already lost my mom. My dad. If something happened to Otto…I…well…" He clears his throat and turns, briefly thumbing the edge of his eye. They've gone glassy. He finally finishes with "Your family is my family."

I slip my hand over his chest. "I thought you didn't have a heart?"

He looks back down at me and takes my wrist in his hand, rubbing his thumb over the skin there. "I don't. But I do have a kidney."

5 6

JASON

The OR is my kingdom.

And, today, Donovan is in it instead of watching from behind glass.

I have to make the switch in my brain. I have to treat this like any other transplant. If I let my mind rest on the fact that I'll be slicing open my lover first and my son second, I won't be able to focus.

I go through my checklist. My blades are ready. My team is prepped.

I am Jason King. Top surgeon at Hannsett Medical Center. This surgery will go off without a hitch.

Except Donovan, I notice, is trembling.

"Are you cold?" I ask.

"No."

"You can back out of this anytime, you know," I tell him. "Even now. Just say the word and we'll stop. No one will blame you."

Donovan's gaze meets me. "I know. I can be ready and nervous, right?"

"Right."

His eyes flicker away from me and land on my table of

sterilized tools—a handful of different-sized blades. "It's not the procedure," he says. "Going under the knife, it just… brings up weird things for me."

"You want to talk about it?"

"Not particularly." He seems to think, then says, "Do me a favor?"

"Anything."

"Just don't cut me open to the fucking Beastie Boys."

Even here, lying flat on the operating table in a hospital gown with the spotlights on him, he still has the energy to rib me.

"I'll do you one better." I nod to my tech—my hands are sterilized—and tell her: "Press play."

She turns on my music. Otis Redding fills the room.

"Kenzi made the playlist," I explain. "Based it on your records at home. She titled it, *Don't fuck it up.*"

Donovan laughs at that, a genuine chuckle. "Love it."

The anesthesiologist nods to me. "We're ready when you are, Dr. King."

I stand next to Donovan. "You want to hold my hand?"

He's quiet for a second, and then pride gives way to need. "Okay."

I lace my fingers with his. I hold his hand as the anesthesiologist fits the mask over Donovan's mouth and nose. He inhales, and his eyelids fight it briefly before slipping closed.

I wait until he's completely lost consciousness before I unwind my fingers from his and gently set his hand back down on the bed.

"Alright," I say, calm and in control. "Let's get to work."

KENZI

*O*tto, Pearl, and I are waiting with bated breath when the exam room door finally opens up.

A doctor I haven't seen before steps in with a big smile and far too much energy. "Hey! I'm Surgeon Elliot Caulder." He glances at me and Pearl. "I'll guess you two are twins. And this must be Otto, right?"

Otto nods shyly. "Yep."

"Great. I'm the pediatric surgeon, and I'll be assisting in the surgery today. Before we go any further, I'm going to need help from my handy assistant…" I only notice now that he has a hand behind his back, and when he pulls it forward, I can see that he's holding a plush teddy bear with a bandage over its head. "This is Rex, our recovery bear. If you'd like, you can hold him while I go over the procedure with the adults."

"I'm twelve," Otto says, deadpan and unimpressed. "Not a baby."

"Alrighty!" Dr. Caulder pulls up a chair in front of me and Pearl, the bear sitting in his lap. "Let's talk."

"How's Donovan?" I ask.

"As far as I've been told, the surgery is going smoothly.

They're about halfway through, which is when we want to get started prepping Otto. That way, the kidney has less time floating around before it's transplanted. Now, a couple things you should know—"

He walks us through it. Complications that can arise during the surgery. Complications that can arise *after* the surgery. And then, once he's prepped us on everything from kidney rejection to shark attack, he clasps his hands together and says, "I'm going to give the three of you a couple minutes, and then we'll come in and start prepping Superman here."

He gives Otto a fist bump on his way out, which Otto half-heartedly returns.

Pearl hugs Otto tightly and tells him how brave he is.

It's strange. I spent so much time wanting this moment, *waiting* for this moment. But now that it's here…the thought of putting my son's life in the hands of a surgeon is terrifying. Even if that surgeon is Jason King.

I pet Otto's long hair back from his forehead. "I really should've trimmed this."

He blows at his bangs. "I like it."

I press my lips together. "How are you feeling?"

He shrugs. Then he admits, "A little scared."

"I know." I hold him. I don't want to let him go. "I love you, little man."

"You're my bacon, Mum," he says, and I don't even want those words to leave my ears.

* * *

The surgery takes over ten hours.

Jason opens Donovan, removes the kidney, and then carts the organ over to Otto's room, where he stitches it inside my baby.

I only know this because doctors come by periodically to keep me in the loop with small, hopeful updates.

As the clock ticks on, I start to feel like my soul has completely left my body. The only thing keeping me grounded is Pearl, who slips her hand in mine and holds it.

We sit in a private waiting room and watch the minute hand click on the clock on the wall.

I can't eat. I can't sleep. I take Jason's advice and replay a recording I made in voice notes over and over again. It's a simple sound, just my own voice telling me, "It's okay. It's going to be okay."

It's two in the morning, and just when I think I'm going to completely lose it, a familiar face rounds the corner.

Jason is sweat-soaked and pale, and for a second, my heart lurches in my chest and nearly climbs out my mouth.

But then he smiles, that crooked, boyish grin of his. "Surgery was a success," he says. "Otto is coming out of sedation now. He'll be out in a few minutes—"

I don't let him finish what he's saying. I launch myself at Jason and wrap my arms around him. I hold him as tightly as I can, curling up into him, and he hugs me back, holding me.

"Thank you," I whisper, and my voice comes out as a sob. "Thank you, thank you…"

* * *

Otto is drowsy. Otto complains that he can taste the saline. But Otto is *alive*. My boy is alive, and his body is no longer poisoning him from the inside out, and everything is going to be okay.

I can't stop looking at him. I can't get close enough to him. I can't stop touching his hair, to the point where he swats my hand away with a whined "*Mum.*"

For him, he just woke up from a long nap, and now he's got a strange scar up his abdomen. For me, I feel like I've been stuck in the foxhole in the middle of a war zone for the past ten hours.

Eventually, Otto and I fall asleep curled up in his hospital bed.

I don't know how long we sleep for. When I wake up, I notice it's dark outside the window, and the curtains are drawn. They've turned off the overhead light, too, but there's still a light from the adjoining bathroom, and the light that filters in through the box window in the doorway.

Pearl sleeps in a cot beside the hospital bed.

Otto's arms are splayed about in all directions which is, somehow, his most comfortable position to sleep in. By some miracle, he hasn't pulled out any of the IVs or wires attached to him, and I'm soothed by the consistent beep of his heart monitor.

I hear muffled voices in the hallway. Through the door window, I can see Jason talking to another doctor. Jason rubs his hand over his mouth, his forehead creased with concern.

Carefully, I peel myself out of the hospital bed. My clothes are wrinkled, and they feel stiff and uncomfortable. I hang my legs off the side of the bed, slide into my shoes, and quietly exit the room, closing the door behind me.

In the bright light of the hallway, I feel a little strange and out of place—like a little girl who crawled out of bed in her pj's to interrupt the adults' raucous nighttime party.

"Hey," I say, and both turn to look at me. I hug my arms around my chest. "Everything okay?"

Jason glances at the other doctor and then pats him on the shoulder, which seems to be his cue to leave. He turns to me then and says calmly, "It's Donovan. The surgery went smoothly, but his blood pressure dropped during recovery, and—"

My ears block the rest of his noise, turning it into a fuzzy tangle of sounds. I can't hear any more doctor-speak. I know the sympathetic turn of the eyebrows. The pinched corner of his mouth. The way he clasps his hands to keep himself from nervously rubbing them together.

I know what he's saying, what he's *really* saying.

Something went wrong. Donovan is in trouble.

"When can I see him?" I ask, breaking through the fog.

"Now," he says. "If you'd like. We haven't been able to get him to wake up yet, but you're welcome to see him."

"Please."

Jason slips a hand to my back.

He guides me through the hospital. This building never sleeps—many rooms are dark, turned out for the night, but there are still plenty of nurses and doctors at their stations, checking in on patients, working at the computers.

He leads me to a room and opens up the door but lingers by the doorway instead of coming in.

Just when I thought I couldn't possibly have any more room for anxiety, it swoops in again, birds low-diving in my stomach. Donovan is lying in the hospital bed, strapped up to monitors and tucked under a white blanket. He's *Donovan* alright, but the nothingness in his face terrifies me. If it wasn't for the slight rise and fall of his chest, I wouldn't be certain he was alive at all, and that thought chills me.

"Do you want me to stick around?" Jason asks gently.

"No…it's okay. I need a second."

He nods and then gives my arm a small squeeze. "I'll be right out here if you need me."

Then he closes the door, giving Donovan and me some privacy.

There are a couple of chairs in the room, and I pull one up to sit beside Donovan's bed. His skin looks so pale, like wax. I find myself transfixed on his chest—the hospital gown opens low, and I can see his necklace bunched up. His mother and father's wedding rings close to his heart.

I reach over and trace one of the rings with my fingertip. "Hey…it's me," I say, the words sounding strange out loud. I feel like I'm leaving a voicemail instead of talking to a living, breathing human. But in case he can hear me, I push forward. "You've got to wake up...Otto is recovering well. He wants to thank you for his new kidney. We couldn't have done any of this without you."

I press my lips together and then get to the truth of it. "*I couldn't have done any of this without you. My whole life I've been afraid to fall in love...terrified of trusting other people. Then I found you and Jason. You loved me. Without any strings. And that...scared the hell out of me.*" I take a breath. "But more than that...it scares me to think that I could lose you and you'd never know how I felt. You're the other half of me. You get me. In a way no other human ever has. You're my best friend...my soul mate...and I love you."

The words don't sound strange, or forced, or wrong. They sound *right*, so I lean forward on Donovan's bed and reach over to draw my fingers through his hair.

"*I love you*, Donovan..."

Suddenly, he moves. His eyebrows knit, and his mouth curves downward. "Ow..."

"Donovan?" My heart jumps in my chest. I leap forward and catch the side of his face in his face. The backs of my eyes burn with unfallen tears. "It's okay, I'm here...what's wrong? Do you need me to get Jason?"

"No." He shakes his head. "You're...leaning on my catheter line..."

Immediately, I sit up, removing my arms from the bed. "Oh...my God. I'm so sorry."

He lets out a wheezed laugh. "It's okay. It was less painful than your heartfelt declaration."

A laugh escapes me now, too, even though my eyes are glassy. "Jerk."

"Slut."

He looks up at me. Those deep, dark eyes look at me like they see straight into my soul.

"You scared me," I whisper. "I thought I lost you."

"I'm not going anywhere. Ever."

Then he hooks his fingers through mine. He squeezes. I squeeze back.

"How's Otto?" he asks, a hint of alarm trickling into his voice.

"Great, thanks to you. They say he's recovering well."

"I'm glad to hear that."

He looks back at me, those eyes flickering over me. "How are *you*?"

"Better, now."

He pauses for a moment. "I want to kiss you," he says, "but sitting up hurts, so if you're into that sort of thing, you're going to have to meet me halfway…"

Immediately, I lean over and catch his lips gently in mine. He lets out a soft sigh into my mouth. I feel complete. Like, finally, the last piece of the puzzle has slid into place.

Our strange little family is whole again.

DONOVAN

I can't walk far, and I'm still shaky on my feet, but I convince Kenzi to wheel me through the skywalk to the pediatric ward.

I put my hands on the wheels, halting us as soon as we get a couple of feet from Otto's room. "Lock the chair," I tell her. "I'll walk it from here."

She arches an eyebrow. "Are you sure about that?"

"Yeah. I don't want to freak him out."

She clicks down the lock on the chair. "I'll give you two a minute."

I ease myself up to my feet. The pain makes me wince. The skin around my incision feels taut and tight. I force myself to straighten up as much as I can to walk into Otto's room.

He's sitting up in bed. He's got his rocket ship pj's on. He looks bright-eyed, though. Alert. *Healthy.*

His eyes get wide when he sees me. I offer a smile. "Hey. Can I come in?"

"Sure," he says, then goes quiet again.

I sit down on the far edge of his cot. "How are you feeling?"

"Good. A little sleepy."

I nod. "Listen…I heard you got a little upset when I left. And I just want to let you know…nothing like that is ever going to happen again."

His eyebrows knit, and his mouth screws up, as though to say *duh*—and it's so bizarre, because sometimes, he really does have Jason's expressions. "I know. I have your kidney. You're *literally* stuck with me."

I can't help but laugh at that. He might have Jason's eyes, but he has his mom's weird sense of humor. "Yeah, I guess I am."

I shift and my shirt must ride up, because he points at my side and says, "Can I see it?"

"Oh…yeah." I roll up the edge of my shirt just enough so he can see the gnarly stitches going down. "What do you think?"

Suddenly, his eyes light up. "Hey! We're matching again."

He pulls up his shirt to show the scar.

He's so excited about it—so excited to have the same scars as I do.

It plucks a string in me. Maybe I'm still hopped up on morphine. Maybe I've got the hospital blues. But whatever it is, I feel the prickly sting in the back of my eyes.

"Can I give you a hug?" I ask.

He nods. I pull him against me and wind my arms around him. The top of his head smells like hospital bed and graham crackers.

"I love you, buddy," I tell him, praying he doesn't hear the croak in my voice. "You know that, right?"

"Love you, too," he mumbles and clings to me.

JASON

’m running on empty. But I don't stop running.

I visit Otto to check in on his progress. The first twenty-four hours of the transplant have the highest risk for complication, but his vitals are good, and his recovery is going well, even if he is a bit groggy from the medicines. Otto wakes up enough to admit to me privately that he would like the recovery teddy bear, after all.

I go to pick up the teddy bear (we have a whole bunch of them waiting in pediatrics) and, on the way, run into Kenzi, who needs some clothes from home.

So I drive back to her place, pack a bag of clothes, and bring them back to the hospital.

Check in on Donovan and give him a teddy bear.

Donovan: "What the fuck is this?"

Have a teddy bear thrown at my head. Donovan is recovering his strength well.

Give the teddy bear to its true owner. Otto is back asleep, so I tuck it into his arm.

Deliver the clothes to Kenzi, who is grateful.

Go to check in on Donovan again. He's stubborn and not

taking his morphine. Instead, he's curled up, gritting his teeth.

Stroke Donovan's hair until he settles back to sleep.

Do the rounds and check back in on my daily line of patients.

Once everyone's cleared, go to the bunks. Collapse in the bottom bunk, still fully clothed, and set my alarm for two hours. Fall asleep with the phone still in my hand.

Wake up with a body behind me. Kenzi is the big spoon, with her arm tucked around my middle.

In this moment, everything is worth it. I hit the snooze button and allow myself a precious thirty more seconds to savor this feeling.

When my alarm goes off a second time, I get up to do it all over again.

DONOVAN

*O*tto goes home after a couple of days.

They keep me hostage for four days longer.

By my last day, I'm ready to break out. I hate being on this side of things. I feel like I'm keeping warm a bed that would be better suited for someone else. Anyone else. I have patients who need me. I want to see Otto running around. I want to shower in my own bathroom and sleep in my own bed.

Luckily, on my final day, they loosen the reins a little. I'm allowed to shower. Get out of the hospital gown and into my own clothes. At this point, I'm almost completely unplugged, save the heart monitor on my finger and the IV drip in my arm which dispenses morphine if I need it. I've ignored the line as much as possible, but the first couple of days, the pain was blinding. And then, when the pain got better, something worse seeped in—an ugly, black depression.

Not about the surgery. Something else. Being in bed like this, helpless…it brought up too many bad memories. Memories of watching my mother fade away. Memories of when I'd decided enough was enough. Memories of my father plucking his own IVs out and growling in that deep voice of his, "Screw it, if I'm dying, I'm doing it in my own damn home."

I'll admit it—when the thoughts got loud, I hit the morphine a few times just to knock myself out.

Boredom will kill you. Silence. It's the top reason retirees kick the bucket, and I know if I don't leave here soon, I'll lose my mind.

My cry for help is met by a familiar face. The door opens and Kenzi steps inside.

"Happy discharge day," she says.

"Happy, happy."

Then she locks the door behind her. And pulls the curtain around us.

I knit my eyebrows. She answers the question in my expression with "Just checking to make sure you're fit for discharge."

A smile twinges at the edge of my mouth. "Are you a nurse now?"

"I am today." She climbs into bed with me and cups my face in her hand, drawing her thumb across my cheek. I've been clinically pawed at by nurses and doctors, but I haven't been intimately touched in over a week, and the warmth of her palm makes my heart pick up speed. "Hmm…bright eyes," she diagnoses. She runs her hand down my chest and rests it there. "Strong heartbeat." Her fingers trip downward, until they hug my growing bulge, and she smiles. "Ah…seems that *all* your organs are in working order."

She kneads me through my jeans, and my lonely need quickly swells. I expel a hiss. "What are you doing?"

Those green eyes meet mine. "Something I've wanted to do for over ten years." She takes off her shirt and lets it drop to the bed. Her breasts hang free—beautiful drops of creamy soft skin across her chest. "Do you want me to stop?"

"Not for a second," I say, and I can hear the catch in my own voice.

She kisses me, and our tongues collide.

Something unlocks inside me. A deep, bottomless well of need, and I pull her into my lap and ravish her with my tongue. She sighs into my mouth and unzips my pants, tugging my cock out. I'm unbearably hard for her, and she slips me between her legs, grinding on it first so I feel the slippery heat of her folds. She's slick, and then I'm slick with her, and she slides me inside of her, gasping loudly as I fill her.

"Oh fuck," she whispers, her head bowing against me as she lowers herself onto me, slowly, until I'm completely sheathed in her.

"*Fuck*," I agree, because she's so tight, so hot, and she feels better than I could've possibly imagined.

There's an annoying bleeping in my ear, and I'm so swept up in Kenzi that it takes me a second to realize *I'm* the annoying thing beeping. My heart rate, that is, rocketing upward on the monitor. I growl and, frustrated, use my teeth to tear the tape around my fingertip, snapping the monitor off.

Now the monitor screams. I fumble—one arm trying to hold Kenzi in my lap, the other arm wrestling with the monitor. I punch in a couple of buttons to shut it up, but I'm too forceful with it, and the whole thing upends, clattering to the ground.

Kenzi's hand flies to her mouth, and she breaks into laughter.

"Fuck it," I say. "They can add it to my hospital bill."

"How long do we have before someone comes to make sure you're not dead?"

"I'd give us five minutes."

"Hmm, what can we get up to in five minutes…?"

"Let's find out."

I swallow her in my arms and kiss her so roughly, I'm sure both our lips will be bruised later.

This hospital bed has left me feeling like a ghost of myself, but with every soft moan that falls from Kenzi's lips, I feel myself come alive more and more. The current state of my body can't keep up with the force of my desire, though, and as I hook an arm around her to thrust upward, I'm awakened from my lust-stupor by a sharp bolt of hot pain in my side.

I grimace and growl through it. Immediately, Kenzi stills, and her eyes go wide with worry. She lifts my shirt, gingerly touches the space around my stitches, and says, "Shit, sorry—are you okay?"

"I'm fine," I tell her, but even I can hear the strain in my voice. "Just…maybe we go slow."

"I can go slow," she says, pushing away the dark strands of hair that have fallen in front of her face.

For a second, the two of us catch our breath. Recalibrating.

And then…something shifts in the energy between us.

I'm buried inside of her, and she's completely naked on top of me. But when we kiss again…it feels shy. Her lips brush against mine hesitantly, curious, and I apply pressure back, consenting, wanting.

We feel like two people kissing for the first time.

I share her breath. She shares mine. We savor each other in a way we haven't before. I worship her—touching the smooth curve of her thigh. The fullness of her hips. The warmth of her breasts. And, finally, cradling her face, fingers dipping into the thickness of her hair.

There is not an inch of this woman that I don't cherish. I have a hard time forming the words, but I tell her so in lingering touches. The brush of my thumb behind her ear. I drop my head against hers and close my eyes so I can listen to the hitch in her breath. I focus on the softness of her skin and each slow undulation of her body. She balances herself on top of me, and her fingers dig into my thighs every time she lowers herself back down again.

We're in sync now. Flowing. I keep one hand in her hair, encouraging her pace, and my other hand I move to her mouth. She parts her lips for me, and I slip two digits in, wetting them on her tongue, and she sucks gently before I draw them back. I drop my hand between her legs and find that small bundle of nerves that makes her gasp.

The pain in my side has mostly gone away—it's just a low, dull throb now—and fuck it, because this moment is too goddamn good and I want to savor every second. I rub her in just the way she likes, and I can feel her thighs start to tremble and her body grow tight around me.

I close my mouth over hers in the exact moment we crest together. It's almost blinding—the pure pleasure of it—and I moan and she whimpers and we sink into each other, unable to get close enough. She ruts her hips against me, shivering as she comes down from her high, and I hold her tightly and feel our bodies pant, breathing out of rhythm.

There's a light knock on the door. "Dr. Donovan?" a nurse tries. "Everything okay?"

Quickly, Kenzi covers her mouth, quaking with laughter.

"Everything's fine!" I call out. "Just a machine malfunction. Thank you! Come back later!"

I wait until I hear the click of her shoes vanish down the hall before I release my hold on Kenzi. She laughs into my shoulder now.

"Fuck," she says, the both of us still hazy. "That was…uh…"

"If you say better than the first time, I'm going to push you off this hospital bed."

Her laughter escalates, her breath hot on my shoulder. This time, I join in, laughter escaping me.

I feel lighter than I have in years.

DR. MAZIE SHOW

FADE IN:
                INT. LIGHTHOUSE MEDICAL CENTER -
DAY

CLOSEUP on the statue of a man holding the world. The tagline says: "A guiding light in the dark."

CUT TO:

INT. OFFICE ROOM – CONTINUOUS

DR. JASON KING, Chief of Surgery, wears a button-up, a white coat, and a dazzling smile.

INTERVIEWER
    So, tell us, what is a day in the life of a surgeon at Light-

house Medical like?

DR. JASON KING

Stressful. Constantly. You have to be the type of person who thrives under pressure. For me, that's my sweet spot. I get bored easily.

INTERVIEWER

So you see it as a challenge?

DR. JASON KING

Well--yes and no. *Yes*, the work is challenging at times. You have to be a perfectionist to get in this field. Anything less than perfect can have major consequences. But it has to be more than an empty search for perfection. You have to have heart, too. You have to care about your patients. That's someone's life in your hands. It has to be more than a number. It has to mean something.

CUT TO:

INT. THE OPERATING ROOM - CONTINUOUS

DR. JASON KING

This is where the magic happens. Operating table. Monitors. We've got a viewing area so family or residents can stay and watch. This place feels really sacred to me. Some people go to church. This is my altar.

CUT TO:

INT. THE DOCTORS' MESS - CONTINUOUS

DR. JASON KING
  This is where the doctors go to recoup. We've got a kitchenette and bunks in the backroom. I've spent more nights
there than I can count. Oh--and this is Dr. Esmeralda, one of
our senior staff members. She's the best of the best.

DR. ESMERALDA
  Who are you calling senior?

DR. JASON KING
  She's been working here twenty years. So basically, she
started when she was five.

DR. ESMERELDA
  Flattery will get you nowhere.

CUT TO:
  INT. THE CEO'S OFFICE - CONTINUOUS

DR. JASON KING
  This is where our CEO works--he's dedicated to the
principles and ethics of this Medical Center.

DR. KING opens the door and speaks to a man out of view.

.   .   .

DR. JASON KING
Hey, we've got the camera crew here.

CEO ADAM DONOVAN is wearing a suit and tie. He
frowns at the camera.

ADAM DONOVAN
What's this?

DR. JASON KING
For the Dr. Mazie Show. Remember?

ADAM DONOVAN
What do you want?

DR. JASON KING
Just say hi.

ADAM DONOVAN
Hi. Now get the **** out of my office.

DR. JASON KING
He's uh--a little busy.

CUT TO:
INT.   PATIENT   INTERVIEWS,   OFFICE   -
CONTINUOUS

. . .

PATIENT #1: MARIA SERVARIO

I went through my worst days and my best days at this hospital. They become family after a while.

PATIENT #2: KENZI STRATTON

Jason and Donovan saved my son's life. That's no exaggeration. I don't know what we'd do without them.

PATIENT #3: PEARL STRATTON

You know, I was once in the running for Real Housewives of Long Island, but then I divorced my husband and, well, I suppose I became *ineligible* or something. But the camera still loves me, don't you think?

CUT TO:

INT. JASON'S OFFICE - CONTINUOUS

INTERVIEWER

What was your most difficult surgery?

DR. JASON KING

Uh--I had to operate on my partner and my son in the same day. Kidney transplant. One of the hardest things I've ever had to do.

INTERVIEWER

Were you nervous?

. . .

DR. JASON KING

Before. Absolutely. But once the surgery started, I just told myself, this has to be successful. There's no room for failure. I believed I could do it, I took my time, and I did it. The surgery went smoothly.

INTERVIEWER

What do you want people to know about the Lighthouse Medical Center?

DR. JASON KING

It's not enough to be a good doctor. I cut into people, sure, but at the end of the day, I'm the one opening my heart to them. No matter who they were before now--they're here. They need help. And I've made it my mission to take care of as many people as I can.

INTERVIEWER

One more question. Your father left quite a controversial legacy. How would you like to be remembered?

DR. JASON KING

As a good father and a compassionate partner. If I can do those two things right, nothing else matters.

PART V

AT LAST: SUMMER, 2019

6 2

KENZI

here's nothing like summer on Hannsett island.

Sunlight shines down, shimmering like tiny glass shards across the clear water. It's a scorcher of a day, so I'm laid out in a purple two-piece bathing suit and a white, airy sun shirt that keeps my shoulders from completely going red. My face is protected by a wide-brimmed hat, a pair of sunglasses, and a hell of a lot of sunscreen.

There aren't a lot of places to hide from the sun, after all, not when you're out in the middle of the bay. *Dock Buoy* bobs listlessly, attached to a mooring ball.

I've spent my Saturday afternoon hard at work at the second half of Diana Gabaldon's *Outlander*. Life could be much worse.

I finish my chapter, dog-ear the page, and let my gaze travel. I'm curled up on one of the benches near the steering wheel by the end of the boat, and from my vantage point, I can see Jason pace across the deck. There's an awning between us, but every now and then, he passes where I can see him. He's wearing nothing but a pair of swim trunks, and in my stolen corner, I let myself admire his sculpted body:

305

the outline of his biceps, his rippling abdomen, that perfect V that settles around his hips.

He's talking intently to someone on the phone. I can't hear what they're saying, but he's got his business voice on, low and serious. I watch as he hangs up the phone and pauses briefly to stare across the water. We're not far from Hannsett Island—only a mile or two out, maybe—but you still get a good view of the island from here: the towering lighthouse, the medical center, and the boats swaying in the marina beside it.

When Jason comes back to the cockpit, I pull my knees up and rest my book in my lap.

"All good?" I ask him.

"Yeah." He hangs from the archway that leads down below and tucks his cell phone into one of the hanging storage pockets. "That was one of the producers from *The Dr. Mazie Show*. They loved the footage. Wanted to offer me a regular segment."

"And?"

He shrugs. "I turned it down. That was my dad's vision. Not mine."

"I'm proud of you."

He grins then. "They *did* say that they'd be interested in doing a spin-off reality show about a polyamorous doctor...*Paging Dr. Poly*. What do you think?"

I wrinkle my nose. "Gag."

He laughs. "I know. That's what I said."

He sits down on the landing beside me. I play my fingers through his hair. "Is it a curse to be so handsome?" I ask him.

"You have no idea."

I nuzzle my nose against his. He smells like peppermint and sea salt.

"Speaking of big things..."

"I like where this is going..."

He snorts a laugh. "Mind out of the gutter, Trouble. I was thinking about South Africa."

I knit my eyebrows. "Not where I thought you were going with this."

"Donovan has things on lock at Lighthouse Medical. So… I'm thinking it's about time I put my money where my mouth is."

"And your money is in South Africa?"

He shrugs. "Doctors Without Borders. It's always been a dream. I can take a couple months. Really help people."

I open my mouth. Close it. "What about Lighthouse Medical?"

There's one of his cocky side-grins. "What're they gonna do—fire me?"

Sometimes, I forget that my boys are at the top of their game. Prime time.

Jason is, after all, the top surgeon in the state—and Donovan took over the post as the director of Lighthouse Medical since the great Leonard King "went into retirement."

Aka, he's on house arrest in his mansion on Hannsett Island.

Justice isn't always cut-and-dry, but I was never interested in revenge—I was interested in *freedom*. And we have that now. We have the freedom to be the people we want to be. To *love* the people we want to love—as unconventional as our strange little family might be.

Jason turns back to me, and his blue eyes flicker over me, sizing me up.

"You want to come? We can bring Otto. Introduce him to the elephants."

I bite my lip. "Can I think about it?"

"You, pretty lady, can do anything you like."

He tilts his head to kiss me. It's upside down and our lips mismatch, but it's ever-so-sweet.

Our public display of affection is followed by a chorus of "Ewwwww!"

Otto and his best friend, Diego, Maria's son, are at the front of the boat, swinging from a hammock attached to the jib and the mast.

"Hey!" Jason calls out. "Don't make me come over there!"

"Or what?" Diego taunts. He's a brave little boy, petulant at times, but I think his boldness rubs off on Otto, who is normally such a wallflower of a boy, in a good way.

"Or it's overboard with yah!" Jason leaps into action, and in two long-legged strides he's on the other side of the boat. He grabs Diego, hoists him out of the hammock, and dangles him over the edge of the boat.

Diego screams with laughter. "Otto! Help!"

Otto clambers out of the hammock and goes to rescue his friend. In only the past couple of months, he's shot up. It's like the new kidney packed a wallop of growth hormones. If he keeps this growth spurt up, he'll be as tall as Jason by the time he hits high school.

As it is, he's tall enough to "rescue" Diego. The two boys then proceed to "defeat" Jason by pushing him overboard. He pulls a perfect dive. When he hits the water, they cheer, and I roll my eyes.

Boys. I'm surrounded by boys.

"Diego! Play nice!"

Well, not entirely surrounded—Maria is my lone female compadre. Like me, she's taken the precious downtime to read and sunbathe. She does it from her rental sailboat, *Cisne*, which is latched onto ours with a series on complex knots and ties. When she catches me looking at her, she rolls her eyes and huffs, "Boys!"

Yes. *Boys.*

Donovan appears, popping up from below deck. He comes carrying a paper plate with two halves of a sandwich on it. He sits down on the landing between the cockpit and the stairs and holds out the plate for me. "Sandwich?"

"What's in it?"

"Good stuff."

I take a half and take a bite. He's not wrong. Turkey, tomato, lettuce, Havarti cheese, red onion, mayo, mustard, avocado...*good stuff.*

I hum contently and dig into my half. "You know me well."

Donovan gets comfortable in the small nook, pulling up his legs. He's wearing jeans and a soft dark T-shirt—far be it from Donovan to wear anything lightly colored, even if it is ninety-something degrees out. "What'd I miss?"

"Jason's talking about going to South Africa for a month or two."

"Did he try to recruit you?"

"Sure did."

"Sounds fun. New places. New people. You did say you wanted to travel."

"I did." I shrug. "But...believe it or not...I think I'm staying."

"Oh yeah?"

"Yeah. I've gotten kinda used to this place."

Out of the corner of my eyes, I see Donovan work hard to try to hide his pleased smile. "Huh" is all he says.

I hear the sudden rush of water as Jason emerges. He climbs up the short ladder on the back of the boat and into the cockpit. He's soaking wet, his hair matted to the back of his neck, his trunks clinging in ways that make it hard *not* to stare.

"Oh! Lunch!" Jason exclaims, as excited as a kid. He steps beside Donovan and helps himself to Donovan's half, taking a bite.

Donovan narrows his eyes, edging away. "*Watch it.* You're dripping. Everywhere."

"Fuck, that's so good." Jason returns Donovan's sandwich and sucks mayo off his thumb. "Can you make me one?"

"I did, and it's downstairs—*argh!*" Donovan attempts to scramble back as Jason steps over him to go below deck, dripping as he goes.

I can't help but laugh. They might be at each other's throats more often than not, but they're also an *endless* source of entertainment.

Before too long Jason pops back up, a little drier than he left, and says, "Hey, you guys wanna see something cool?"

"Always," I tell him.

He climbs over Donovan (again) and sits down on the bench opposite me. There's a small console between us, with wings that can be propped up to form a table. Jason puts his sandwich plate in his lap, and in his other hand, he extends a picture frame toward me.

"Happy thirteen-year anniversary," he says.

Donovan and I exchanged confused looks. "Anniversary of *what?*"

"You know. *The first time.* The time that produced…that kid." He tilts his head toward Otto.

"How the fuck do you remember these things?" Donovan counters.

"It was a week after they released *Batman Begins* in Hannsett Theatre."

Donovan groans. "I *hate* that you know that fact."

I sidle up next to Donovan and hold the frame out for him to see. "Check it out."

Honestly, I didn't think there was any photographic evidence of the summer the three of us spent together—this was a time before Instagram and selfies, after all.

But there we are. The three of us. Teenagers. We're at the marina's pool. I'm in a bathing suit with a plaid shirt thrown over top. Jason sits beside me, arm looped over my shoulders, posing for the camera in that obnoxious way boys do—

he's either throwing up the peace sign or a gang sign, it's hard to tell. Donovan, dressed in black, black hair, black nails, black glare, looks moodily at the camera as though he's prepared for it to take his soul.

More than anything, I'm struck by how *young* we look. We thought we knew everything then. But we were children. Innocent in our own way. Young, dumb, and in love with ourselves in that self-absorbed way all young adults get to be.

"Holy shit," Donovan says, "We look like puppies."

"Where'd you get this?" I ask.

Jason shrugs. "I've had it. I just thought it was time to put a nice frame on it."

I hear twin feet patter across the boat. "Whatcha looking at?" Otto asks, hanging behind me. The two boys seemed to have smelled something more interesting going on this side of the boat. They're both in their swim shorts, and I can see the crescent of Otto's scar that goes down his side. It's healing well, but to my boy's credit, he's never been ashamed of it—instead, he seems to have no problem showing it off. His badge of courage.

I shift to the side to make room and hold out the picture frame. "It's me, Jason, and Donovan…a very long time ago."

"Whoa, cool," Otto says, holding the picture so he can get a better look.

"That's *Dr. Donovan?*" Diego asks, and his mouth drops open dramatically.

"It was…a phase." Donovan slips his hand to the back of his neck self-consciously.

Otto examines the picture. "Mum, can I get a lip ring?"

Simultaneously, Donovan and I answer, "No."

"This is very special, Jason," I tell him, and I prop the photo up on the center console so the teenage versions of ourselves are staring down at the adult versions of ourselves. "Thank you."

"Yeah, well," Jason says, wide smile threatening to crack across his mouth, "muskrats for life."

I link my fingers with Donovan's and echo, "Muskrats for life."

* * *

We have dinner together—our family and Maria's. We make hand-rolled pizza and burn it on the grill attached to the back of the boat. Personally, I'm a fan of the crispy bottom and the places where the cheese melts and hardens around the crust. Donovan tosses up a salad as well, and for dessert, the boys put marshmallows on sticks and make s'mores over the open flame.

Otto and Diego have pulled out their sleeping bags across the deck of Maria's boat, and it's not even 10:00 p.m. before Otto is drifting off, curled up in his sleeping bag. The salt air really takes it out of you. I slip my fingers through his hair and says, "Hey, buddy, I think it's time to head to bed."

He pulls the covers up over his chin. "I want to sleep out here," he complains.

Maria glances over at me and smiles. "It's fine. They can come inside if they get cold."

Out here, on the water, the stars are brighter than ever. Tiny pinpricks scattered across the sky. I don't know what kind of a life I expected for Otto, but for a while there, I wasn't sure he would see much of anything beyond the four walls of his hospital room. My heart feels so impossibly big knowing that he gets to experience *this*—rocked to sleep by the sway of the boat, under the stars beside his best friend.

"Thank you," I whisper to Maria, and she shrugs as if to say *no problem.*

We clean up our places and say good night. I kiss the top of Otto's head, and he's so tuckered out, he barely is able to murmur a "love you."

It's a bit of a balancing act to go between the two boats—Jason goes first, lifting his leg over one railing and then climbing over the other. He extends his hand toward me and helps me over, and then does the same to Donovan until we're all back aboard *Dock Buoy*.

Downstairs, there are dishes in the sink, the radio still going. Jason goes to the sink and rolls up his sleeves. "I'll wash, you dry?" he asks me.

"Done."

Donovan fiddles with the music until he finds a station he likes—a nice, groovy ambiance. I can't help but smile as I stack plates in the drying rack.

"What's that smile?" Jason asks.

"Just…memories. I was just thinking about that summer. When we were kids. The first time I had dinner with your family, and you and I came downstairs and cleaned up."

"I remember," Jason says.

"I wanted you to kiss me. So badly."

"What, like this?"

Jason pulls me against him suddenly, and I don't even care that his hand is wet at the small of my back because his lips are on mine now. I feel the graze of stubble against my cheek, and I melt under the heat of his kiss.

"Yeah…" I murmur. I can feel my heart beating between my legs already.

Jason's hand slides down my back and cups my ass, giving it a squeeze. I wind my leg around his invitingly.

It's not always easy for the three of us to find stolen moments. Now that I have my two men all to myself, I'm feeling ravenous. And, by the change in Jason's breath and his hard length against my hip, I can tell he is, too.

"This," Donovan says, "is why the dishes never get done."

He stands behind Jason and draws his hand up the back of Jason's neck, into his thick head of hair. It's a weak spot for Jason, and a small groan leaves him. "Fuck the dishes," Jason mutters.

He's too tall, and when Donovan tugs lightly on his hair, his lips are officially out of my reach, but I lift to nuzzle underneath his chin. I graze my lips down his throat and slide my tongue over the bump of his Adam's apple, which bobs in response.

Is there anything more fun than getting Jason wound up? I don't think so. The hitch in his breath makes me drench my panties, and I feel the soft fabric cling to me as I draw my fingers underneath his shirt, tracing the V of his abdomen, the rippling muscles there.

"Should we uh…" Jason swallows, barely able to form words. "Bedroom?"

"Yes, please," I agree.

The three of us abandon the sink and move into the main cabin instead. I start to pull off my shirt, but then I feel Donovan behind me. He draws his fingers down my arms, catches my wrists, and locks them behind me.

Jason sits down on the edge of the bed in front of me. He smirks. "C'mon, Trouble. Don't you know a girl shouldn't have to take off her own clothes?"

I give a little struggle—not looking to escape, just to test the strength of my bonds. Donovan grips my wrists tighter, and I feel his lips and teeth graze my throat. "I wouldn't," he purrs darkly, and the sound goes straight between my thighs.

"Or what?" I breathe.

"Or we're going to keep teasing you until you break," Jason tells me.

And, *oh*—Jason reads the room well. Because my heart pounds in my chest as he slowly unbuttons my blouse. The two sides of my shirt fall open. My bra unclasps at the front, so he undoes that, too, so that my breasts are on full display in front of him.

Those blue eyes drink me in. "Fuck, you're beautiful," he

says, and my nipples tighten into small, hard peaks under his gaze.

He crooks his finger and draws a knuckle down my stomach, then loops his fingers at my pants. He undoes my shorts, sliding those off my legs as well. He examines me, his hands running up my thighs, coaxing them apart, and a bizarre thought pops into my head: I wonder how his patients keep from soaking themselves anytime he puts his hands on them. I know I wouldn't be able to. Something about the thought of Jason clinically examining me while I throb and try not to moan makes my cheeks flush hot.

His thumbs stroke the very edges of my panties between my thighs, teasing. "You're soaking wet," he observes.

"Is that your professional diagnosis?" I ask.

"It's a symptom," he plays along. "My diagnosis is that you're a horny girl in need of two men to claim you."

He kneads his knuckle against my slit, and even with the fabric between us, I feel the burn of pleasure. My knees start to buckle, my hips rocking forward to meet his touch, but Donovan's strong grip on my arms keeps me upright.

"Second opinion?" Jason asks.

"I'd say you're on the money," Donovan confirms as he ghosts his lips up my throat and nibbles my earlobe.

I fight back a whimper and let my body relax against Donovan. I'm helpless to move my arms, but when I reach back with my palms, I can feel the denim of his pants and the swell of his need underneath. I cup his groin, massaging, and he grows harder under my touch. He lets out a low growl in my ear, and the sound sends a shudder through me.

I'm at their mercy, and Jason teases me. He pulls my nipple between his fingers until I gasp and then does the same to the other. When he finally puts his mouth on my breast, my nipples are sore and sensitive, and the gentle wet heat of his tongue makes me burn. I moan, squirming under his caresses, and my thighs clutch together, aching for any friction.

"Please," I beg, "I want it so bad." I give Donovan a squeeze, hoping he'll give me what I need.

I watch hungrily as Jason undresses and sits back on the edge of the bed.

"Do you want him?" Donovan asks me.

"Yes," I breathe. Jason's body is perfect, and my eyes follow the swoop of his dove, down to the tone of his belly and his gorgeous, thick cock.

"Do you want his cock inside of you?" Donovan presses, and my thighs squeeze once more.

"More than anything."

Jason peels off my panties, and Donovan releases me, pulling off my clothes the rest of the way. I immediately climb into Jason's lap, starved for him, and I crush my mouth against his and wrap my legs around him. I nestle in close and reach down so I can grind my naked pussy against the hard length of him, rubbing him between my slippery lips. He sighs into my mouth, and we tangle up in bed, touching, humping, ravishing each other.

I can hear Donovan's clothes rustle as he undresses. His cold rings kiss my bare back as he leans down to kiss my shoulders.

Jason rolls us over so I'm trapped underneath him—this huge mountain of a man. I feel so safe here, though, so adored as he takes both my wrists in one hand and pins them above my head. He reaches down between us, and I hold my breath in anticipation, releasing it in a sharp gasp when he presses inside of me, filling me.

"Oh, God…" I whisper as he mounts me, rolling his hips against mine.

Donovan climbs over Jason, the three of us stacked like dominos, and I hear Jason grunt and feel his fingers tighten in mine. "Fuck," Jason moans between his teeth.

"Do you need me to slow down?" Donovan asks.

"No," Jason pants, "keep going."

Now the three of us are moving as one—a single wave, flowing and ebbing, in and out.

Donovan is steady and controlled above us, precision and steel.

I'm an ocean of need and want, spilling out.

And Jason is between us—Jason, our beating heart.

I link my fingers in his, holding his hand, and cry out when my orgasm takes me, exploding around him. He covers me in sweet kisses—my lips, my cheeks, the backs of my eyelids—as I come down. They spill over with me, the three of us moaning, throbbing. I feel Jason hot inside of me, and I squeeze my thighs around him, encouraging.

"I love you," I murmur at his lips—words that used to be so impossible now tumble from me so easily. I free a wrist and reach up, sliding over Jason and then Donovan, feeling Donovan's hair, digging my nails into Donovan's back. "I love you, I love you…"

We fall apart finally. We're panting, slick with sweat, and I'm cuddled between them.

"Fuck, I love the both of you so much," Jason says.

"Love you, too," Donovan adds. I lay my head on his chest and hear his heart pound at me. I draw my hand down his body and feel the raised skin of his half-moon scar along his abdomen.

"It's always going to be like this," I say, "isn't it? No matter where we go. Or what we do. We always come back to each other."

"Always," Jason says, winding an arm around me and kissing my shoulder.

He rests his hand over my stomach—over the small bump that's four months in the making. That was conceived in a hospital bed, in the middle of winter, at the peak of our insane roller coaster of a relationship.

A hint of life that I don't have to keep as a secret. There are no more secrets between us now.

Donovan pushes my hair back from my forehead, and his leather band brushes against my skin. "Muskrats forever," he murmurs against my hair.

I link my fingers in his and reach my other hand over my stomach, winding my fingers with Jason's.

I belong here, between the two of them. And now we get to expand our family…together.

THE END

* * *

Note from Adora: Thank you for reading the Truth or Dare duet! I hope you had as much fun with Kenzi, Donovan, and Jason as I did.

Please leave a review to let me know what you think. Reviews are lifeblood for authors like me!

Now keep reading for a special bonus epilogue that takes place a couple years in the future when Jason, Donovan, and Kenzi decide to officially tie the knot…

Thanks again for being a loyal reader!

XOXO,

Adora

PART VI

EPILOGUE

KENZI

"It's a beautiful day for a wedding," Maria sighs.

I hum in agreement. "Not a cloud in sight. The sun is out. The water is flat. The—"

"Bilge tank is backed up," Jason cuts in.

"What??"

Jason grips the safety line and swings his leg over the yacht's edge to hop off the boat and onto the dock.

The SS Galant is an elegant, mid-sized yacht. Behind those tinted windows is a small crew that has pulled together the perfect wedding reception. They've cleared the deck for our vows and decorated inside with a buffet and a dance hall.

It's the perfect location for our on-the-water wedding.

Except for this one set back.

We were supposed to embark thirty minutes ago. Instead, the entire wedding party has been baking on the hot, wooden dock.

It's honestly a pretty comical sight.

My mom, Pearl, and her new husband are in their crease-less suits, sitting on floatation cushions. He's holding a beach umbrella up to keep her pasty white skin from burning.

I'm in my full wedding gown, sitting on the bare dock

wedged between Maria and Donovan, who looks incredibly dashing in his traditional black suit and incredibly irritated with the dark frown stamped on his expression.

I'd be laughing my ass off if I wasn't getting splinters in my dress.

Jason disembarks the SS Galant and crouches down in front of us.

"Well," he reports, "the good news is, they can clean it up. The bad news is, the entire place is going to smell like… uh…*bilge water.*"

Translation? Our ceremony has *literally* gone down the toilet.

"Shitty way to start a wedding!" Otto cackles.

"Otto!" I snap. "Language!"

He pinches his mouth in a frown.

He sullenly sits on the dock next to his best friend, Diego, and bounces his two-year-old sister, Joan, in his lap.

My sweet, sensitive little boy is developing into a terrible teenager, complete with a bad mouth, a bad temper, and a bad attitude.

Even if he *is* good at puns.

"What are our options?" I ask.

"We can move everything on deck," Jason offers.

"Air fresheners," Donovan suggests.

"Fuck," I mutter under my breath, but not low enough.

"Mom! Language!" Otto retorts and Diego chuckles.

Will puberty ever end?

"There *is* another option," Maria ventures. "How many people can *Dock Buoy* fit?"

* * *

It's not a yacht. It's better.

Dock Buoy is Donovan's thirty-two foot sailboat.

It only has one bathroom and one and a half beds. The

engine shudders the entire boat. The kitchenette is comprised of a mini-fridge and a hot plate.

But with our wedding party of less than ten humans, it's perfect for us.

Still, it's not exactly the all-out wedding party that Jason was hoping for, and I feel a twinge of pain for him as I watch him gazing out mournfully at the sea as *Dock Buoy*'s full sails carry us through the channel.

Jason came from wealth, and his love languages are: physical affection, words of affirmation, and money. It doesn't matter than Donovan and I would've been happy getting married in our living room. Jason likes doing big, showy displays of affection for us.

The yacht wasn't just a wedding-day extravagance—it was his way of saying: *I love you both and this day is important to me.*

It took me a while to get comfortable with Jason's particular brand of unconditional love.

I'd grown up thinking love was a toxic thing. Something that broke people. Hurt people.

Jason's chest-first, full-hearted declarations of love, occasionally, overwhelmed me.

I remember in that first year, when the three of us were fumbling through the infancy of our poly relationship, I hit a snag. I felt my body shutting down every time Jason was inside of me. My bones would go rigid, my chest would get tight, and I'd have a hard time getting off. He noticed. When he asked me about it, I broke down. I confessed that every time he was in me, I felt a well of anxiety that he'd get me pregnant again.

When Jason got me pregnant with Otto, our union created a wonderful boy…with a myriad of health issues.

Otto is my gift. My beautiful, perfect child. I wouldn't have him any other way. But the thought of going through the medical scares, and the painful testing, and the fear that

I'd lose my child all over again…it scared the crap out of me.

Selfishly, I didn't know if I'd survive that again.

Jason didn't bat an eye. He scheduled a vasectomy. That day. To make *me* comfortable.

Jason has, and always will, give nothing less than 110% to his lovers. I learned that then and I see it now, the pensive look on Jason's face. He's worried he disappointed us which, in Jason's brain, is grounds for full tar and feathering.

Well, that won't do.

Donovan is helming the ship, so I take a minute to sidle up next to Jason. He's wearing a beautiful all-white suit, tapered to his slim hips and his broad shoulders. He has his legs pulled up on the long cushion, so I part them enough to slide into his lap. Immediately, his arm curls around my middle, accepting me against him.

"It was a nice thought," I tell him.

"But crappy execution. Literally."

He puts his head on my shoulder like a puppy dog.

My forlorn perfectionist.

I rub my hand up his thigh and squeeze. Nothing but muscle there. *How'd I get so lucky to get married to the most stacked surgeon alive?*

"I'm sorry it didn't work out."

"Me too."

"*But* on the bright side…a yacht wouldn't have this view."

I nod to the foredeck. Diego and Otto are sitting against the mast, their shoulders pushed together, grinning over some video they're watching on Otto's phone.

Joan is up there with them, because she cries any time she's not by Otto's side. She's stuffed in her puffy lifejacket and tied with a safety harness to the mast. She waddles around like a puffin and points to the sea. "Otto! Look! Seagull!"

"Cool!" Otto says with faux enthusiasm.

"Otto! Seagull!"

"I see it!"

"Otto! Look! Seagull!"

"I heard you, little monster."

"Hey, Joan," Diego says, entertaining her, "What noise does a seagull make?"

"Cah-caw!" Joan says.

The boys chant together: "Cah-caw! Cah-caw!"

I feel Jason grin against my shoulder. "You're right. The view is good."

"Kids! Smile!"

Twelve (Pearl's husband, also known as Anthony, I guess) aims his phone at me and Jason. We both put on smiles as he snaps a picture.

He's taken on the role of unofficial wedding photographer.

"Beautiful!" he beams enthusiastically. I don't think I've ever seen that man anything less than utterly excited, and I wonder what kind of Viagra-infused energy drinks Pearl is mixing into his oatmeal.

My thigh buzzes and I feel Jason shift to pull his own phone from his pocket.

The expression on his face darkens when he sees the caller ID.

"Everything okay?" I ask.

"Yep. One sec."

He untangles from me and steps out of the deck, walking the thin railway to the foredeck and out of listening distance.

JASON

I pick up the phone to the sound of crying.

"Jason," my mother weeps, "don't do this."

My heart is a rock in the ocean.

Sinking fast.

I quickly put distance between myself and Kenzi, walking towards the bow of the sailboat. This is our perfect day, after all, and I don't want anything to ruin it.

This phone call is quickly damaging my mood, though.

I pinch the bridge of my nose. "Mom. Please don't cry."

She gives a shuddering sob. "This isn't you. Remember Nadine? Amy? You used to be such a…a…"

Asshole. I used to be such an asshole.

A bully who was afraid of all this longing inside of him. Who took it out on the people he loved. People like Donovan. People like Kenzi.

I hurt them. And I have to live with that.

"…A *perfect* boy," my mom finishes, finally finding the word.

I keep in touch with my mom.

I don't talk to my dad.

Sometimes, I think I can get through to her. I want her in my life.

But when she pulls shit like this, she makes it impossible.

"I'm happy," I tell her. "Happier than I've ever been. They make me happy. Both of them."

I say each word slowly and clearly so she can hear it. *Really hear it.*

She hiccups and goes quiet.

"You want that, don't you?" I ask. "You want me to be happy?"

"Yes, but…not like *this.*"

My throat goes tight.

My dad is under house arrest for a myriad of bribery and medical malpractice charges, but, sure—

I'm the disappointment.

All because I had the audacity to fall in love with two people.

"Your dad is here, and—"

"*Mom.*" My throat goes tight. "Don't put him on."

The phone switches hands anyway.

"Jason," he says, and even hearing his voice is like ice trickling down my spine. Every bone in my body goes rigid. He can't do anything to me. He's miles away, trapped in his house with an ankle monitor, while I'm out at sea with the people I love.

But fear lives in the body, even after it's left the brain, and my muscles have been conditioned to sit up straight, tighten my jaw, and *act like a King* when he's around.

I don't say anything. I can't. My throat is in a vice.

He continues: "There are somethings you can't turn back from. Trust me. I know."

Even in the two years since I last spoke to him, he sounds older than I remember. Slower. Tired.

"This world doesn't take kindly to people who break the

rules. I just want you to think about what you're doing," he says, pretending to be someone who *cares* about me when I know what this is—he's only ever cared about the King family image. And here I am.

His once-perfect child. Getting married to the man and woman of my dreams.

"Don't ruin your life—"

I can't hear any more.

I *won't*.

I hang up, which is something I should've done two minutes ago.

My hands are fucking shaking.

"Dad." I glance over my shoulder. Otto and Diego have stopped playing with their phones. Otto is staring at *me* now, concern etched in his forehead. "You good?"

The angry thrumming in my heart starts to slow.

This is my family now.

This is all the family I'll ever need.

I get an idea.

I motion him over. The two boys rise and stand beside me.

Otto has shot up over the past year—he's almost as tall as I am now, and that's saying something, because I'm the tallest guy I know. I drape my arm over his shoulders and point out past the boat. "You see that buoy over there?"

It's a red, floating device, about the size of a barrel. It clinks as it rolls in the water. It's designed to navigate ships away from shallow waters.

Otto sees it, and he nods. "Uh-huh."

I hold out my phone. "Think you can hit it with this?"

Otto blinks up at me in surprise, and then a crooked grin crosses his mouth. "You serious?"

"Dead serious. Go."

He bites his lip in concentration. Then he takes my phone, reels back, and chucks it as hard as he can.

It's liberating, watching that fucking thing sail through the sky.

The phone hits its target. It cracks into the buoy with a metal clang like a church bell, then bounces down into the dark depths of the ocean.

"Bullseye!" I shout, pumping my first in the air.

Otto's grin widens, thrilled with himself.

I give him a high-five and high-five Diego too for good measure.

"Check out the strong arm on that guy!"

Otto makes a muscle. "Read it and weep," Otto says, and Diego guffaws a laugh.

I recognize the deep, long-suffering sigh that comes up behind us.

"You know, phones aren't a renewable resource," Donovan says.

I step away from the kids to slip my arm around his shoulders. I cuff the back of his neck in my hand affectionately. "It was important. Trust me."

"Your parents?" Donovan guesses.

I shrug. "One last ditch effort to save my soul."

"You should've told them I sucked that out of you long ago."

"That's not the only thing you sucked—"

Donovan clamps his hand around my mouth. He's correct to do so.

Occasionally, I forget we have kids aboard.

When he releases his grip, I ask: "Who's steering?"

He nods his chin towards the deck. I squint in the dying sun and see Pearl waving at us from behind the large steering wheel.

"Anthony, look!" she says, deliriously happy. "I'm the captain!"

"Ah." I nod. "So *that's* why you're the favorite son-in-law."

"Gotta compete with Mr. Perfect somehow."

Perfect. The word grates on me now.

Donovan—the guy who doesn't like to be touched, who flinches with physical contact—must see that I need it, because he winds both arms around my middle and pulls me tightly against him.

I close my eyes and sink into his embrace.

They're wrong. My parents are wrong.

This isn't wrong. This is right.

Kenzi and Donovan are the only people who ever let me be myself.

What could be more *perfect* than that?

I rest my head back on his shoulder and exhale a hefty sigh.

"Hey, Donovan?"

"Hm?"

"Can you lift me onto the bow so I can shout that I'm on top of the world?"

"Absolutely not. I know how that story ends."

"I'd make room on my lifeboat for you."

"You better."

This is our life. Gentle digs. Affectionate ribbing. Underneath it all: *love.* The love I have for this man is vast, endless, and deep enough to drown in. It takes the breath out of me.

"Strong!" Joan shouts. "I'm a strong bull too!"

Those little chubby feet slap across the deck. She stomps over to us, pulls Donovan's phone out of his pocket, and then stomps over to the edge of the boat, as far as her harness will allow.

Then Joan chucks his phone over the edge. With a *ploink,* it drops into the water.

Er. *Whoops.*

"Sooo...I kinda forgot she's in that monkey-see, monkey-do phase."

I can *feel* Donovan fuming behind me.

"In good news," I add, "she *does* have a strong arm for a two-year-old. I don't know, I'm thinking—baseball all-star?"

"You're so lucky I love you," Donovan grumbles.

He's being factious, but I answer honestly:

"Yeah. I am."

65

DONOVAN

e drop anchor in Cape Stone, a couple hour sail from Hannsett Island. It's remote here, a quiet little inlet, and by the looks of it, we're the only ship here tonight.

We crack open some champagne, feed the kids, get everyone squared away, and then—

It's time.

Maria got ordained just for the occasion. She stands at the bow of the ship, book in hand. Jason and I stand side by side with her. Jason looks calm as a cucumber. But me—

I'm sweating.

"Relax," Maria says. She gives me a wink. "You look great."

"Thank you," Jason replies, stealing my compliment.

I narrow my eyes at him. "Don't make me push you overboard."

"I dare you."

That nearly makes me smile. It reminds me of that night that got the three of us here in the first place—one single game of Truth or Dare that changed everything.

I force my expression to stay neutral and shrug. "Later."

He grins. That goofy, golden boy grin.

I want to bruise his lips with my own.

Music starts up, a soft violin song played over the speakers.

Jason and I both turn our gaze to watch as Kenzi walks the length of the deck to join us.

My breath catches.

The sun shines brightly over her, making her dress nearly glow. It's a soft, loose, floral dress that trails lightly behind her. Her normally long and wild hair is pined back, revealing her stunning face. Those eyes look incredibly green with the clear, blue water behind her.

Pearl walks with her. She dabs her eyes as she releases Kenzi's arm.

"You look…" I can't finish it. My throat is too tight.

"Beautiful." Jason helps.

Kenzi's eyes shine. "You too."

She stands in between the two of us, and Maria starts the ceremony.

She says a few words about the meaning of love—how it looks different for everyone. She speaks about how grateful she is to have witnessed our love grow into what it is today. It's a moving, personal speech, and by the time we get to each say our individual vows, the three of us are already emotional.

Kenzi says her vows first. She sob-speaks them, and can barely get her words out without her voice trembling.

Jason brings some much-needed levity with his declaration. In true Jason form, his speech his heartfelt, sweet, and funny, and he has everyone chuckling.

After they say their vows, they slip on their rings.

I'm wearing both of mine now—an elegant, dark double band. It feels good to have the both of them wrapped snugly around me.

Kenzi is wearing her diamond ring from Jason. Jason is wearing his single-band that matches my own.

Now it's my turn.

I'm shaking. This is not my strong suit.

I hate public speaking. I hate being the center of attention. Even in this small, intimate crowd of our friends and family, I hate having eyes on me.

But I love Jason and Kenzi so much, and I need to tell them that.

I need them to know the things that are normally so hard for me to articulate.

I take a deep breath, count for three seconds, then exhale.

Mostly, I think Jason's meditation techniques are bullshit. But that one does center me.

Grounded, I finally speak:

"Growing up...uh. I was a weird kid. I didn't have a lot of friends. I kept people at an arm's length. But I was very close to my family. My parents taught me what love was. That love could be quiet. It could be a look or an action. My dad wasn't good with words...something we have in common. But every morning, he made my mom her coffee, exactly how she likes it, and brought it to bed for her before going out to work.

"When we lost my mom, I learned a new word for love. That sometimes love was just...a soft place to fall."

I swallow. Memories burn the backs of my eyes. But I want to continue. I *have* to.

"Then when I lost my dad...I lost my safety net. I wasn't sure I'd ever have that again. That...soft place. I put up walls. I grew armor.

"Then the two of you came back in my life and knocked them all down."

I force my gaze to lift from the floor now. I look at them —the two loves of my life. I want to look them in the eyes when I tell them this next part.

"You taught me to love again. Both of you. Then Otto and

Joan expanded my heart even more. It's not always easy. Love is scary and hard and it comes with its own unique challenges. Balancing kids. Career. Hell, some nights, who gets the remote is an all-out war. But even when you annoy the crap out of me—"

"Was that for me?" Jason says. "I feel like that was directed at me."

"—You're still my family. And I couldn't have chosen a better family. So…"

I reach behind my neck and feel for the clasp. It's a hard thing. It's a simple, thin chain, but it carries both of my parents wedding rings on it.

Now, I unclasp it and put the rings in my palm. I pull away the chain, freeing them.

I haven't taken this necklace off since I was a teenager. Except once. To get the rings resized for this occasion.

"I love you," I tell them. Those words that so often get stuck in my chest. "Both of you. You are and will always be my soft place to fall."

With that, I relinquish the rings. I fit my mother's ring on Kenzi's finger and my father's ring on Jason's.

"With that," Maria says, "I now pronounce you…"

Jason doesn't even wait for her to finish. He grabs the back of my head and pulls me into a hard kiss.

I choke on his affection. My chest feels broken open and everything is spilling out. I sink into the strength of his kiss, needing it.

He releases me and Kenzi comes in next. Soft, warm, loving lips. I taste the salt of her tears…or maybe they're mine.

My heart aches with gratitude for these two people in my life.

Jason dips Kenzi when he kisses her next. Everyone breaks into laughter and our family and friends cheer.

I close my eyes for a single, quiet second.

They'd be happy for me. I know they would. I can feel it.

I'm drowning in love, and I don't ever want to breathe again.

KENZI

It's over. We're married.

We did it. The three muskrats. Three sloppy, hormonal, insecure teenagers who have grown into three confident, beautiful, *married* adults.

As for legality—well, who cares?

We'll deal with the minutia later.

Right now, all I know is I have two husbands, and I couldn't be happier.

The ceremony breaks apart. I glance at the most *important* man on the boat—my Otto. He has a wide grin on his face as he watches us. He looks so dapper, so grown up.

I pull my son in for a hug and kiss the top of his head. "So? What did you think?"

"You guys are the weirdest," he grunts.

I roll my eyes. Joan tugs on my dress, so I lift her into my arms and she settles down.

"But," Otto adds, "I'm proud of you."

My chest swells. "I'm proud of you too, bug."

Diego stands beside Otto. He can't look at me. His eyes are wet and he ducks his head to cover a sniffle.

Otto blinks at his friend. "Bro, are you crying?"

"No," Diego chokes.

Then Otto does something unexpected.

He threads his fingers through Diego's and gives the other boy's hand a squeeze.

Oh. There he is. My sweet, sweet boy.

My heart does a flip.

There's a *pop* as Twelve opens up a bottle of champagne. The celebration has begun.

We eat, and drink, and enjoy the company of our friends and family. The sun begins to set, streaking brilliant bands of red and gold through the sky.

The wedding party peels away. They board the dingy to go to shore, and now Jason, Donovan and I have the night to ourselves.

Before they disembark, Twelve turns to me and shakes his phone. "I caught the whole thing!" he says excitedly. "Beautiful, just a beautiful ceremony."

"Thanks, Twe—"

I almost call him *Twelve*. Then I stop myself.

He and Pearl didn't *have* to show up. They don't have to support us and our unconventional union unconditionally.

I see that with Jason's parents. I see how quickly they turned away from him.

If my Otto can be a sweet boy, well, I guess I can be a *sweet girl.*

"Thanks, Anthony," I correct myself. Then I shake his hand.

He beams. I help him off the boat, the last man to board the dingy.

Donovan's arm brushes against mine as he steps beside me. Together, we watch Maria guide Diego through the steps of starting up the dingy. I wave and my baby Joan waves back. My heart catches like a fish on a line, and the boat putters off.

"Did I hear you say *Anthony?*" Donovan asks.

"You sure did."

"Wow. Little Kenzi is all grown up."

I elbow him in the side. "Dick."

"Slut."

Our eyes connect. There's a playful gleam in his.

I haven't seen that light in some time.

Between work, and kids, and the constant daily battles of *life*…when was the last time the three of us had a night all to ourselves?

"Are you thinking what I'm thinking?" I ask.

"Cake under the stars?"

"It's like you read my mind."

"Hmm," he purrs. "It's like we're *married* or something."

He grips the front of my dress and yanks me closer to him. Our noses touch and I can't help the grin that spreads across my lips.

I try on another title: "Husband."

"*Wife.*"

His lips brush mine. I curl my fingers into his shirt.

He tries to deepen the kiss, but I lean back on my heels. His breath patters against my lips.

We have all night, and I want to tease him.

Already, I can feel him thickening against me.

"Do you like my dress?" I ask.

He grunts. "No."

I gasp on a laugh. "*No?*"

"I hate it. Too distracting. I haven't been able to take my eyes off of it all night. We should probably rip it off of you."

I swivel, subtly grinding my hips against the swell of his want. Leaning in, I sigh, taste the heat of his mouth.

"Be good and maybe I'll let you."

Arousal radiates from him. Barely contained and heady.

Fuck romance.

I want it to hurt when he consummates our marriage tonight.

The wooden boards creek. Donovan and I snap out of our trance and turn our heads towards the sound.

Jason wears a wolfish grin. "Don't stop on my account."

He's carrying a plate with a giant cake slice on it. Big enough for the three of us.

"Cake! My hero."

I twist towards Jason without leaving Donovan's body. I press myself back against him so I can slot my rear against his hips.

He reacts with a sharp intake of breath and it sends a hot thrill through my blood.

I think he has more than *cake* on his mind when he murmurs darkly: "Let's eat."

JASON

When I come upstairs, Donovan and Kenzi and nearly chomping at the bit for each other.

I love the way they look at each other. The longing in their eyes.

There's a spark between them, and it lights a fire in me.

The three of us sit down on the long, built-in seat along the cockpit. Kenzi goes for the fork, but I snatch it away.

"The lady shouldn't feed herself on her wedding day. Donovan?"

He takes my cue. He takes her wrists in his hand and pins them down to her sides, immobilizing her.

Screw the fork. I pick up a chunk of cake between my fingers and feed it to her. She takes it in her mouth and then moans sweetly.

"*Fuck,* that's delicious."

I take a bite and put it between my teeth. I lean in towards her to feed her from my mouth. She takes it, but it's messy, and she laughs through the process.

"No!" she squeals. "It's too soft!"

Together, we're making a mess.

I smash another piece and feed it to Donovan. He takes it,

and then sucks the frosting from my hand. Those dark eyes meet mine. He slides his hot, wet tongue slowly, intentionally up the length of my two fingers, and I feel it as though there's a direct line from my fingers to my cock.

God. I want to be in his mouth. Badly.

But I'm enjoying this. The intimacy. The slow build of heat between all three of us.

I want it to last all night.

Donovan adjusts his grip. He pulls both of Kenzi's arms behind her back and traps her wrists in one large hand. His other hand reaches underneath her dress.

His eyes find mine. "Don't stop feeding her."

There's the Donovan I know. Electric. Demanding. In charge.

I break off another piece. Kenzi gasps. Her long eyelashes flutter.

Donovan's hand is working underneath her dress. Even in the dim light, I can see the cords of the muscles in his arm, moving and flexing as he finger-fucks her.

Her mouth is already open when I put the cake it. She nibbles the pads of my fingertips.

Donovan nuzzles his nose in her hair, his mouth to her ear. "Do you like your cake?"

She's dopey with lust. She bites her lip. "Uh huh…"

"Swallow."

She chews. Swallows. Obeys.

My cock aches at the sight of her like this. Soft and pliable for us.

He encourages her, his voice low: "What do you like about it?"

"It's…um. Sweet."

I push another bite passed her lips. She moans and her eyes fall closed. Her head falls back, pushing her chest forward. Her hard nipples stand out underneath her dress.

She won't let go of my fingers. She nibbles them. Sucks on them.

Fuck. I'm so hard, it hurts, but I can't tear my eyes away from the scene.

Kenzi, a lust-drunk kitten. And Donovan, puppeteering her, each movement from his hand making her swoon.

I can't stop myself. I kiss her.

Kenzi whines in my mouth. Her tongue is sloppy and her kiss is needy.

I circle my arms around her and reach up to pull down the zipper of her dress. I push down her dress and her bra, freeing her breasts.

They look so fucking good in the moonlight. I push my finger into the icing, then paint a heart around one her nipples. When I take her breast into my mouth, it's sweet.

I suck. Her soft, warm flesh fills my mouth. I roll my tongue over her hardened, sensitive nipple, and then I tug it between my teeth.

She shudders. Her whole body writhes.

"Oh, God," she whispers to the stars, her head craned back as Donovan kisses and sucks on her throat.

We feast on her like animals. Hungry, wild animals.

"Don't stop," Kenzi gasps with quiet urgency. Her body suddenly goes still and stiff and her legs lock around Donovan's wrist.

I suck on her other breast. I nibble and lick as she begins to vibrate.

"Oh, *God*," she repeats, breathless. "Yes...*fuck*...just like that..."

We're rewarded with a hitched gasp. Her first orgasm of the night is quietly violent as she trembles wildly between us. She takes in soft, whimpered gulps of breath and I hear Donovan hum with pleasure.

Our eyes meet, and a grin slices across his mouth. "She's

so tight around my fingers," he narrates for me. "Like a vice. Throbbing so hard for me."

I can't help the groan that leaves me, because now I can't stop imagining how good those orgasmic pulses of hers would feel around my cock.

I shudder. I'm throbbing now, too.

Donovan's eyes sweep over me. He notices things. The same qualities that make him a good doctor also make him a good lover—he notices when your breathing changes, when your dick gets hard, or when your body goes tense because you just can't take anymore.

Kinda like Kenzi's body is doing now in his arms. He removes his hand from her panties and gently kisses the side of her face.

"Want a taste?" Donovan asks me. He lifts his sticky fingers.

Like a dog, I take his hand in my mouth. I lick Kenzi's sweet, sweet arousal from him. I suck each digit. Lick the spaces in between. When he pulls his hand away, I find myself aching for more.

It's intoxicating, and my heart hammers in my chest. I want so badly to bury my head between her thighs.

Kenzi's nuzzles against me. The heat of her breath patters against my cheek. I tilt my head and my mouth finds hers.

It's soft and sweet, kissing like this. In this moment, I decide: *I like being married.* Our lust is a low, burning thing. But our love is strong, comforting, and gentle.

Her forehead rests against mine. "Let's clean up," she says.

DONOVAN

hank God we're the only boat anchored out for the night.

Anyone else would think we've lost our fucking minds.

Kenzi's beautiful wedding dress and our nice, expensive suits sit in messy piles in the cockpit.

Kenzi is wrapped around Jason like a koala bear, her legs strapped to his hips, her arms clinging to around his shoulders. He hangs over the edge of the boat, grasping onto the safety line.

The moonlight spreads like broken yolk through the dark water. It illuminates their naked bodies and kisses their skin.

"Three...two..." Jason counts down.

"Oh my God, no!" Kenzi shouts. But she's laughing.

"Ready?"

"Is it cold? Oooh, I bet it's cold."

"*One*," I finish for them and give Jason a shove.

Kenzi screeches on the way down. They hit the water with a splash and, when they reemerge, they're both cackling.

"Asshole!" Kenzi shouts at me.

I lean over the stanchion. "How's the water? Cold?"

"It f-feels s-so good."

"Really? You're shivering."

"Jump, you coward!" Jason barks up at me. "I double-muskrat-dare you!"

Well. I can't ignore a muskrat dare.

I brace for the impact, swing my legs over the edge, and take in a deep breath.

Then I dive.

The water is so shocking, it nearly knocks the air out of my lungs. I get a mouthful of that Atlantic Ocean salt. When I break back into the air, I gasp and blink, the water stinging my eyes.

"Christ, it's cold."

"Refreshing," Jason corrects.

"It actually *does* feel good once you're in it," Kenzi adds.

I tread water and she's not wrong—after the initial shock, my body slowly grows accustomed to the chill. I needed it, anyway. The three of us were running too hot, my blood boiling with lust.

This gives me a second to reset so I don't cum the second I plunge inside of her.

I dip underneath the water again. Hannsett Island is forever in my blood, and growing up here meant being part-fish. Sometimes, I wonder if Joan will grow gills with all the time she spends on the ocean. I pull the water through my arms, diving deeper. It hurts to open my eyes, but I squint just long enough to find Kenzi's legs in the dark. I catch her foot in my hand and nibble her toes before resurfacing.

"You're lucky I didn't kick you in the face," she informs me.

"I could think of worse way to die."

Kenzi wraps herself around me now. Her body is soft and warm against mine.

"Your vows…they were really special." She nuzzles her nose against mine. She drips on me and I tread water for the both of us.

"So were yours."

Those sea green eyes peer into my own. "Are you happy?" she asks quietly.

Checking in is my love language. My heart gives a double-beat. "Yes. I couldn't be happier."

I mean it. Her lips meet mine and we kiss sweetly.

"Check it out," Jason says, "we're glowing."

I look over at him and, sure enough, we *are* glowing. The phosphorescence lights up in the water, like fireflies dancing around our bodies with every swish.

Even me, the realistic, the cynic, has to admit: *this is fucking magical.*

The three of us splash around in the water. We swim around the boat. We kiss and grope and lick the sea salt from each other until we finally all clamber up the short ladder to get back on board.

There are three towels stacked neatly by the back of the boat. I take one and pass it around so we can all dry off.

Kenzi pulls her towel around her shoulders and bundles herself up in it. Her towel-clad hands move like paws to her mouth.

"Cold?" Jason asks.

She nods. "Brrrs."

He pulls her against him, tucking her into his body. "We'll warm you up."

He tilts her chin up and presses a kiss to her mouth.

I love watching them. I love the way she melts against his lips. I love that she has to get onto her tippy-toes just to reach his mouth.

Normally, I'd be weird about being naked in public. But we're all alone out here. It's nighttime. We're on the water.

I drop the towel and step behind Kenzi, wedging her between us.

I want her. Right here. On the cockpit.

I call it the "Jason King effect."

When you're around him, you feel invincible.

Normally, I measure risk over reward. I consider and reconsider my option. I think about things logically and rationally with my brain, not my heart.

But tonight, I'm under some kind of spell. I find myself following my instincts.

And right now, my carnal nature is telling me to fuck my new wife under the crescent moon.

I part her legs and I know she's thinking the same, because she's practically radiating heat when she hooks her leg around my hip and grinds against me.

We kiss, mapping each other with our tongues, and then I peel her off of me and twist her around. She falls into Jason's arms and he claims her mouth now as I press myself inside of Kenzi. She moans softly, the sound muffled in Jason's lips.

This is a language the three of us know well. We talk without words, communicating with rough fingers and gentle sighs.

I love you with each kiss.

I want you with each touch.

I can't get enough of you with each thrust.

We're caught in the spell of each other, and I bite Kenzi's shoulder just to ground myself.

She reaches back and her fingers slip through my hair, gripping.

I've got you, she says, and I reply by tightening my fingers around the moons of her hips and plunging deep inside of her.

KENZI

'm reeling with pleasure.

My entire body is buzzing as Donovan moves inside of me—deep, hard thrusts. He claims me. He's rough, but loving; his touch simultaneously worships and punishes.

My hips meet his, rolling in tandem. Jason's lips move down my body, touching my breasts and the roundness of my belly. He sinks to his knees and my legs tremble with anticipation when the heat of his breath hits my sex.

I've already come once, and now I'm teetering on the edge again.

I need to hold off. They're not going to stop until they've satisfied themselves in me, and my husbands have a wicked stamina. If I let go now...I'll be weeping through my fifth orgasm before the night is over.

I grip the large steering wheel just to feel hard wood under my fingers. It stabilizes me just as Jason's tongue slowly savors me. He licks me everywhere, lighting up every nerve, and when I hear Donovan swear against the crook of my neck, I know Jason is lavishing him with affection too—his tongue playing on the place where our bodies join.

It's too much.

I'm fluttering with pleasure. I feel my knees give and I start to sink, but they won't let me. Donovan's strong grip on my hips keeps me upright and Jason hooks my knee onto his shoulder so I'm trapped, grinding against his mouth.

I collapse against the steering wheel, gasping on short breaths, as I beg: "Please, Donovan…come in me…I want to feel it…"

He gives a shuddering thrust and groans as my request sends him over the edge. My toes curl when he pulses inside of me, filling me. I cry out as I finally let myself let go, clinging to him, draining him.

I'm still throbbing when he pulls out of me. I whimper, my hips wiggling, feeling so empty without him.

Donovan gently spins me around. I fall against his body. When he kisses me, I swoon against his lips.

Jason's mouth nuzzles back between my legs. But now he presses his tongue inside of me, deep. I gasp into Donovan's mouth, arching back.

He's tasting Donovan on me. The thought makes me shiver.

"Can you give us one more?" Donovan murmurs.

My nipples are tight in the chill.

"I…I don't know…"

Donovan nips my bottom lip. Then he eases me down. "Come here."

The both of us sink to our knees. He lowers me back so I'm in Jason's lap now. Donovan kisses me and I whimper as he reaches between us, guiding Jason inside of me.

Oh God. I'm so sensitive, that this much pleasure *hurts.*

I whine, both wanting more and wanting less. I grip Donovan's strong shoulders, my head falling forward.

He cradles me and his hand slips into my hair. He grips hard, hard enough that I feel it pull on the roots, and the pain-pleasure sensations make me lose my mind.

"Ride him," Donovan coaxes.

I'm lust-dumb and sore. As I move against Jason, I hear him groan, "Fuck, baby, that's good."

I'm tingling. The ache turns into a low, burning fire and suddenly, a switch flips inside of me.

Fuck. I need this.

"Fuck," I whine. I slam my hips back into Jason's lap. I hump him at a quick, hungry pace. He fills me so deliciously and I can't get enough of it.

I'm delirious with need.

The only thing anchoring me is Donovan's strong grip on my hair. I whine as I fuck myself on Jason's cock, over and over again.

"That's a good girl," Donovan encourages. His warm breath hits my lips. "Come for him. Now."

I howl so loudly, they must hear me all the way on the island. My orgasm is so intense, it's blinding, and I ride out each wonderfully painful throb on shaky legs.

I'm mewling, whimpering as Donovan licks the inside of my mouth, licks my lips and my throat.

It's a treat when Jason spills over inside of me.

When he fills me now, releasing his pleasure with a low groan, I no longer feel the thorns of anxiety.

I feel a shot of *love*. Pure and unquestioning devotion.

I grind against him, the two of us riding out the throes. Donovan kisses me and then tilts over my shoulder to claim Jason's lips as well. Jason lets out a noise that's practically a purr, vibrating like a big, sated cat.

He is our King, after all.

"I love you," I tell them. "I love you both so much."

It echoes back at me: "I love you," and "I love you." This circle of affection.

Blissed out, I snuggle in their bodies. Arms and legs are tangled together, a pile of limbs and warm skin and sweet kisses.

"Can we sleep out here tonight?" I murmur against Donovan's shoulder. "Under the stars?"

"Why not?" Jason says. "It's a perfect night."

I stare into the sky. Not a cloud in sight. Nothing but the bright moon and a sprinkling of stars.

"Perfect," Donovan repeats, and I feel that word in my chest, *perfect*, thumping over and over.

My life, my family, this night…

It's *perfect*. I wouldn't have it any other way.

THE END

NOTE FROM ADORA

Still can't get enough of the Three Muskrats?

If you're itching for more, you can sign up to my newsletter to get a FREE bonus short story that takes place in the period that Donovan and Jason just started living together, right before Kenzi re-entered the picture.

Download here: https://adoracrooksbooks.com/two-truths-bonus/

You can also read more about this family in All I Want For Christmas is Them, a spin-off novel that takes place 20 years in the future. Otto is all grown up and has a poly trio of his own. Plus, you get a peek into what an older version of these characters looks like :)

Keep reading for a sneak peek of "All I Want For Christmas is Them"…

XOXO,
    Adora

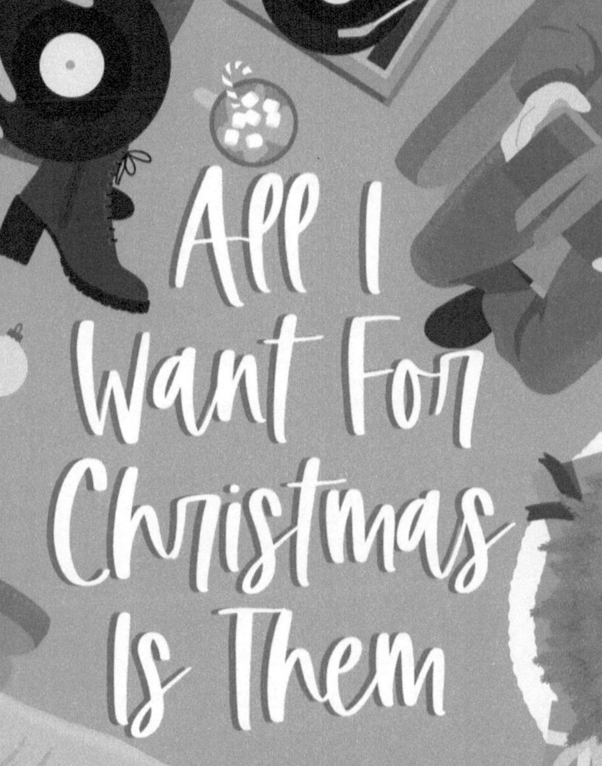

All I
Want For
Christmas
Is Them
A SPICY WHY
CHOOSE
ROMANCE

USA TODAY BESTSELLING AUTHOR
ADORA CROOKS

1

———

OTTO

"Close your eyes."

Naomi's eyes are beautiful. Big. Brown. Doe-like. Perfect eyebrows, which furrow now in excited puzzlement. "What?" she asks.

"Close. Your. Eyes. Love."

At the pet name, she smiles and obeys.

I'm sure we look ridiculous right now—sitting across from each other at a rickety metal table outside of Citarella's. The table legs have snow caked to them like white moss. It's late December in Long Island, and we're crazy people for sitting outside.

But Naomi and I are also creatures of habit, and this is routine. When she spends the night with me, I take her to get coffee while we wait on the Long Island Rail Road to zip her back to the city.

I'm a stay-at-home writer, so I have time to kill. Naomi works two jobs in the city—she's a tattoo artist and a part-time barista. Put her crazy hours with our near long-distance relationship (forty-five minutes one way on the LIRR is no easy feat), we have to carve out time for each other, or else we'll never find it.

We've been dating for almost six months now, but the shine hasn't worn off. I take my time admiring her with her eyes closed. She's a bundle of faux-fur-lined navy and anticipation.

Naomi is objectively beautiful. Thick black hair so long, it falls over her breasts. Golden-brown skin. A small, button nose with a septum piercing. Wide, feminine curves.

But what's really beautiful about her—and I mean, breathtakingly stunning—is her smile. She's spent the latter part of her twenties rebelling against her conservative upbringing from her Iranian-American parents, and it shows with tattoos, piercings, and a *fuck you* swagger. She's a badass, and I can readily admit that I'd probably lose a fight with her.

But when she smiles…every wall and hard edge she'd built up over the years come crashing down. She has this sweet, innocent, Disney-princess smile that makes my heart do a barrel roll every time I see it.

I take a small box out of my coat pocket and pass it across the table to her. "Okay. Open them."

She does. She blinks down at the box. "What is this?"

"Merry Christmas."

"It's not for another two days, psycho."

"Merry *early* Christmas, then."

She squints at me and then promptly tears the top open.

She shouts and immediately closes it.

"Otto!" she says, her voice shaking with laughter. "You can't give this to me…*in public*."

I shrug. "What do you give the woman who has everything? The one thing she asks for."

She bites her plump lip. I can see the excitement dancing in her eyes.

Even in the frosty winter weather, my blood goes hot.

About two months ago, after shagging each other's brains

out, Naomi and I lay side by side in sweat-slicked sheets and pillow-talked.

"Tell me your kinkiest fantasy," I said.

Even in the dark, I could see her blush. "You're going to think it's weird."

"I promise, I won't."

"Okay. Well. I have this fantasy that I'm wearing a sex toy —like one of those remote-controlled vibrators? I'm in public, and my boyfriend keeps turning it on at inconvenient moments."

"Hot."

She'd scrunched her nose. "You think it's weird."

"No, I think it's hot."

"It's…the lack of control, I think, that turns me on." Naomi reached up and tugged her fingers through my hair. "And the thought of doing that with someone I trust."

"Are you saying you trust me?"

"Eighty-nine percent of the time."

"I'll take those odds."

That was then. This is now. Now, Naomi stares at me with the eyes of an uncaged cougar.

I want to give her everything she ever wanted.

If Naomi wants expensive earrings, I'll get them for her.

If she wants matching tattoos, I'll grin and bear it.

And if she wants to orgasm in a room full of people, then I'm damn well going to make it happen. It doesn't hurt that the thought makes my pants tight.

"You know me way too fucking well," she says.

"Wear it," I tell her. "Tonight."

The demand in my voice makes her eyes go wide. She draws her fingertips over the top of the box, teasing it.

"Otto Stratton," she says, her voice low and coy, "you're a fucking bastard."

"I know." I get up to lean over the table and press a kiss to her mouth. Her lips are warm and soft and urging against mine. "Do you love it?"

She smiles into my kiss. "I love it."

I grin. "Wicked."

2

———

DIEGO

$\mathcal{I}$ have no idea how I'm going to tell him.

I stare at the blood panel results in my hands, trying to wrap my head around it.

The results are for Otto Stratton. Otto has been my best friend since we were teenagers. But even after all that time, I don't know how I'm going to tell him.

"Diego."

The sound of my name jerks me to attention, and I lift my eyes from the paper.

Dr. Adam Donovan is the dirty-blond forty-nine-year-old CEO of Lighthouse Medical Center. He wears a button-up, a severe frown, and light crow's-feet around the crinkles of his eyes, but I've never seen him crack a smile, so he must do all his laughing off the clock.

He's also Otto's dad and my boss. The fact that I've known him nearly my entire life doesn't mean I get an easy ride—if anything, he's harder on me than anyone. As a new resident fresh out of med school, I have a lot to prove, so I immediately sit up a little straighter in my seat when he addresses me.

"Yes?"

"What're you doing?"

"Nothing." I quickly fold the paper up and stick it in my back pocket.

He's the *last* person who needs the details scrolled on the page.

His eyes flick to my pocket, but he ignores my obvious deceit.

"We're seeing a patient in the east wing. Walk with me."

I'm taller than Dr. Donovan by only a couple of inches, but he's faster, and I have to pick up my pace to keep up as he speed walks to the elevator and punches the button.

It's not uncommon for Dr. Donovan to have me tag along. Since I graduated med school, I've been something of his shadow, following him around while he mentors me on different cases, coaching me through my residency.

I know it's nepotism. I grew up with his son. Our families were tight. When my mother passed in March, he tucked me even tighter under his wing.

But extra attention doesn't mean he's going to make anything easy for me. Even now, waiting on the elevator, I feel a pop quiz coming on.

"How long have you known Mr. Humphrey?" Dr. Donovan asks.

"Mr. Humphrey's Hardware?"

"That's the one."

"All my life."

Hannsett Island is a small tourist town. In the summer, we're packed, but in the off-season, our population dwindles to a couple hundred.

Everyone knows everyone.

The elevator doors open up, and we step inside. Donovan pounds on the Close Door button.

"And how many times have you seen him smile?"

"Once. When Patterson fell off the ladder wrapping wreaths around the lighthouse."

"Exactly. Keep that in mind."

The elevator dings. Donovan exits, his white coat billowing behind him, and I follow him down the hall.

The rooms on the third floor are nice. State-of-the-art equipment, comfortable beds, and full-wall windows. When the curtains are pulled aside, you can look out past the white-and-red striped lighthouse, over the cliff top, and beyond the sparkling blue waters. Miles and miles of crystal blue between Hannsett Island and the mainland, only interrupted by the red-and-green blinking buoys, the joyriders in their sailboats, and the ferry that carries tourists to our small, Margaritaville-style beach town.

It's a good place to sit out the worst days of your life and a reminder that quality of care comes at a price.

At least it did, until Dr. Donovan was instated as the CEO about a decade ago. Half the floor is still sectioned off for people who need anonymity—which often includes celebrities or the rich and famous. The other half is where people go when they're in hospice care or debilitating recovery, regardless of income.

It's how my mother spent her last days looking out over the flat blue coast of Hannsett Island, even though she was a single mom on a bartender's salary.

The point is I owe Dr. Donovan a lot. Which is why I feel even worse holding the secret in my pocket from him.

I follow his lead into room 304. The patient, Hugo Humphrey, is sitting up in the hospital bed. The seventy-one-year-old man is what I'd call "Doc Brown Lite"—he's got a mess of white hair that explodes from either side of his head. His thick eyebrows are constantly furrowed, his mouth forever pinched in a disapproving scowl.

Except for today. Today, he's wearing a wide smile that stretches across his face.

"Look at who we've got here!" Mr. Humphrey exclaims when he sees us. "Diego, boy, don't you look spiffy in your scrubs. Come a long way from stealing candies from my jar, haven't you?"

Then he laughs. It's a strange sound, like a cat coughing up hairballs. I don't think his lungs are used to it.

"Thank you, sir," I say, because I'm not sure how else to respond to that.

This whole thing feels Twilight-Zone-y.

His wife, Helen Humphrey, is a small, slender woman with a gray bowl cut. She keeps her hands in her lap as she sits beside him. Her mouth is fitted with a nervous, pinched smile.

"Someone's in a good mood," Dr. Donovan says. The edges of his eyes crinkle with a smile.

Dr. Donovan might be a grump with his staff, but he's always had good bedside manner with his patients.

"It's nearly Christmas," Mr. Humphrey responds. "What's not to love?"

"You're right about that," Donovan says. "Do you mind if Diego stands in while we talk?"

"Not at all." Mr. Humphrey swings his smiling face between the two of us.

"Great. You wanna tell me what happened?"

"It was the darnedest thing. Helen and I were having breakfast, I got up to fix myself another cup of coffee, and down I went!"

"He fainted," Helen interjects, her voice thin as she fidgets with her hands. "I got him up and immediately took him here."

"Have you been feeling woozy?" Dr. Donovan asks. "Any dizzy spells prior to this?"

Mr. Humphrey shakes his head. "I've been right as rain."

"Mind if I take a look?"

Dr. Donovan plucks his penlight from his pocket. He leans over Mr. Humphrey, and I watch him test the man's pupils. He has Mr. Humphrey follow his finger, then clicks off the light and pockets it.

Dr. Donovan asks if Mr. Humphrey has had any changes in his medication, any other accidents. It's a "no" on both accounts. I take mental notes as I watch them work.

Donovan straightens up once his exam is complete. "Diego will take a blood sample from you, and we'll run some tests. Find out what's going on. You just hang tight and let us know if you need anything in the meantime, alright?"

"Thank you," Helen says. She keeps looking between all three of us, her eyes batting around anxiously.

Something doesn't feel right.

Before we leave, Mr. Humphrey stops us with "Is…Jason here today?"

I can practically see Dr. Donovan's bones stiffen. But he presses on a smile. "I can check. Why do you ask?"

"Hold on—Helen, get my bag." Helen lifts his satchel from the floor and sets it on the bed. Mr. Humphrey starts rummaging through it. He pulls out a book and hands it over.

"If it's not too much trouble," he says, "do you think he could sign it? My daughter-in-law is a big fan. I thought it'd make a good Christmas present for the girl."

It's Dr. King's book, *Cut Out Negativity: Mindfulness & Life Lessons from a Surgeon.* It's got a picture of the doctor on the cover—tall guy with a winning smile.

Dr. Jason King is our own mini celebrity. His book hit the bestsellers list, and he's done the talk show gamut. Honestly? It's pretty cool.

At least, to everyone except Dr. Donovan. He frowns at the book but then takes it and nods. "I'll see what I can do."

"Thanks," Hugo says, still smiling wide.

Donovan and I break out of the patient's room.

"What do you think is wrong with him?" I ask.

Donovan's blue eyes meet mine. "You tell me."

This is a test—one of many he likes to throw at me.

Being a resident underneath Donovan is like learning to drive on the highway. Scary as hell—but you learn fast, and you learn how to do it right.

"Seems like he's got…a bad case of Christmas spirit?"

"Alright. What else? This is your case now."

I think. "A sudden change in behavior could be the result of a brain injury when he fell."

Donovan just listens and nods. "Mmhm."

If he has any better ideas, he doesn't share them.

"So…we should give him a CT scan to make sure," I continue.

"Put it in the system," Dr. Donovan says. "And pull some blood samples."

"Will do."

I start to head down the hall to get the kit, but Donovan turns and adds, "Oh, Diego?"

"Yeah?"

"While you're there, check in on Otto's results, will you?"

Now, my heart does an Olympic-worthy three-point turn in my chest.

Because I've already checked Otto's results. They're sitting in my back pocket.

They're screaming, *High potassium levels. High sodium levels. Toxicity in his blood.*

But Donovan can't know that. Because if he knew, he'd freak out. Then Otto would freak out. And then Otto would never talk to me again.

I'm a terrible liar.

I can't play poker. I can't organize surprise parties.

Everything I feel is always written in big, looping letters on my face.

You have honest eyes, Otto once told me. *It's a good thing.*

I'd blushed—I'm sure he saw that, too.

Fucking honest eyes.

"Okay," I say, trying my best to be stoic. "Will do."

Dr. Donovan, luckily, is in too much of a rush to over-think my painfully panicked response. He just nods and then exits into the elevator.

I exhale a breath as soon as he's out of sight.

The paper in my pocket is practically *burning*.

Liar, liar. Pants on fire.

My phone buzzes, and I reach into my pocket to pull it out. His nose must be itching, because Otto's contact picture (*Otto, standing behind the wheel of his father's boat with big sunglasses, shirt open, a captain's hat, and a goofy smile*) lights up my screen.

[text: Otto] Don't forget, Savage tonight.

I frown at the text. Then I respond:

[text: me] Wouldn't forget.

[text: me] Hey. Just so you know.

[text: me] I've got your results.

[text: me] We have to talk.

Three bubbles pop up. Then nothing. Then three bubbles again, before:

[text: Otto] Later. Let's just enjoy tonight.

I press my lips together. I want to tell him there might not *be* a later if we don't have this conversation.

But that's not something you can say over text. So I just reply:

[text: me] Okay.

I mean to leave it there, but Otto keeps going.

[text: Otto] What are you wearing?

I snap a selfie of my current state—hospital greens.

He sends back:

[text: Otto] Wear that blue button-up you got from Cole-man's. It looks good on you.

He adds a couple of "fire" emojis for good measure. I can't help the smile that crosses my lips.

Even when Otto frustrates the hell out of me, he still manages to make me smile.

That, in a nutshell, is why Otto is, has always been, and will always be my kryptonite.

I give his text a thumbs-up react and get back to work, trying to steer clear of thoughts about tonight.

* * *

Want to know what happens next? Read "All I Want for Christmas is Them" for rest of the story between Otto, Diego, and Naomi!

ALSO BY ADORA CROOKS

Find All Books + Tropes on My Website:

https://adoracrooksbooks.com/all-books-tropes/

If You Love This Book, You May Also Like...

The Royal's Love (Royal MMF Romance)

My steamy encounter with the Prince of England went viral. Now I belong to the prince and his bodyguard. YOLO, I guess?

His Secret Love (Celebrity MMF Romance)

We live and love behind closed doors. Until she blows our charade to pieces.

Double or Nothing (MMF Romantic Suspense)

I'm on the run with two ripped, possessive Navy SEALs. Their only weakness? Me.

Happy Reading!

XOXO, Adora

ABOUT THE AUTHOR

USA Today bestselling author Adora Crooks writes romance with heart, action, humor, and steam.

She currently resides in the magical city of New Orleans with her beloved and their two nutty mutts. Adora lives off of coffee, cookies, and book reviews and daydreams about dirty romances with happy-ever-afters.

Sign up to Adora's newsletter to get exclusive deals on Adora Crooks stories, including ARCS and upcoming releases. XOXO.

www.adoracrooksbooks.com